B. J. Irons

Meduso is dedicated to those who have lost loved ones. Just look up at the night sky when you are feeling down. Let the patterns of the stars (*katasterismoi*) serve as a constant reminder of the wonderful memories you had with them.

Acknowledgments

First off, I want to say that this is the first book in the Mythologay Series. I have had such anxiety and fear in writing a series, but am so thankful I pressed through all of it. I cannot wait to continue this series and bring these amazing retellings to the world.

Thank you, Matt and Ed, for being my rocks during this writing experience.

Cate, I owe it to you for dealing with my constant text messages and emails back and forth about this work. You did nothing but heighten my creativity and motivation on completing this novel.

Have to give a big shout out to my amazing Bookstagram family and friends. Your support and affirmations mean the world to me!

Thank you to Spectrum Books and its affiliated team members. It was a pleasure to work with each and every single one of you. I look forward to working with you all on future projects as well.

And thank you to my mother Gina, brother Jimmy, and the rest of my family and friends for your love and support.

Most importantly, thank you to the LGBTQIA+ community. I will continue to support my community and give us more fun reads in the near future!

About the author

B.J. Irons works in the field of education. Many of his personal experiences as a gay man have contributed to his books.

Being a part of the LGBTQIA+ community himself, B.J. hopes to continue to bring more colorful and fun fictional works to his LGBTQIA+ readers.

Other titles by B. J. Irons

The Cul-de-Sac

Rippling Waters

Sinfluenced

The Gift That Keeps on Taking

Follow B. J. Irons on Instagram:

@BJIrons

Prologue

Venomous snakes for hair.
A glare that will cast people to stone.
Beheaded by the tragic Greek hero, Perseus.

It's a safe assumption that we all know the basic facts about one of Greek Mythology's most famous monsters, Medusa; the beautiful maiden cursed and turned into a Gorgon. Her tragic story and death at the hands of the hero, Perseus, has been told countless times for thousands of years.

But the thing with Greek Mythology is just that. They are myths. Narrated, fictional legends as old as time that have been passed down from generation to generation. Time has a way of changing the original tale. So, how can we be sure that the myths we think we know are the real story?

What if important aspects of these myths have been altered? What if the monster wasn't really a monster at all? What if Medusa wasn't actually Medusa? What if her name was Meduso? And what if she wasn't a her, but a him? This is the tale of Meduso and his death at the hands of the hero Perseus' sword. It is a tale of innocence, love, betrayal, and tragedy.

Act I

Meduso: The Innocent

Chapter 1

"Come closer, Meduso. He won't bite," my mother, Ceto promised.

I reluctantly stepped forward, slowly reaching my hand out to stroke the head of the serpentine creature that was rising out of the water to greet us. Its eyes were fluorescent yellow, glaring at me. It seemed unsure as to whether or not it could trust me.

I continued to rub his bubbly green scales. It was the thickest of material I have ever felt in my entire life. No garbs, furniture, or any other item in our palace could compare. My touch must have been enough to soothe the creature. The lids of its eyes closed and he slightly purred as I traced my hand from the base of his snout to the pointed edge of his nose. I was hesitant to touch the tip of it, which looked more like a talon of a ferocious eagle. I repeated the motion over and over again.

My timidness melted away, and I instantly felt a kindred spirit with the dragon. Out of the corner of my eye, I could sense the pleasure behind the smirk my mother now showed.

"Meduso, this is your brother, Ladon."

I turned to face my mother as she said this, but didn't stop rubbing Ladon. My mother had informed me that there were two siblings I had yet to meet, including Ladon. The other was named Echidna. It would only be a matter of time before I would have the chance to meet her, too. Throughout my entire life, my mother explained that when I was of a certain age, I would be able to meet them, and that day had finally arrived.

We stood in the grotto connected to our oceanic palace. The ground and walls were made of the finest cerulean gems of apatite and larimar. The brightness of the stones and lit flames around the grotto were our only means of light in the underwater cave. Our palace lied in the deepest depths of the ocean, far from any trace of light reaching it.

The grotto was one of my favorite features of the palace. Every time I visited, I was instantly put under a calming spell with the ripples of the water reflecting off of the glistening blue walls, constantly in motion. I moved about the cave in a fluid-like manner, aware of every breath I was taking. It was as if every worry I had in the world was expelled from my body and into the crystal blue. I found all aspects of water very serene. Whenever I was in the ocean, or here at the grotto listening to the slight trickling of drops from the icicle-stalactites striking the surface of the pool, I was put into a meditative trance. It cleared my mind, my body, my soul.

My attention reverted back to Ladon, who could also sense my tranquility. He moved his head closer to me and pressed his snout against my chest, rubbing me with it. His massive head, alone, was the size of my entire body. I was startled at first, but then smiled and chuckled at his reaction. I was beginning to experience a kindred spirit with my brother, the aquatic serpent-dragon.

"Ahhhhh!" I yelled at the startling sight of another head pop out from Ladon's slithery body, identical to his own. Then the number of heads and faces continued to emerge and multiply from him until there were about one-hundred of them.

My mother placed her hand over her mouth in attempt to hide her laughter from my surprised reaction. "It's alright, Meduso. There is nothing to fear. This is Ladon in his truest form. He only presented himself to you with a single head, knowing it would placate you. Don't let Ladon fool you. He is a very clever creature."

To any other god or mortal, Ladon would be viewed as a hideous sea monster. But not to me. Maybe it was simply because I didn't know any better. My parents had sheltered my sisters and me in this underwater palace for years. It was only last year that I experienced my first steps onto fertile soil. A rush of excitement flowed through me as I experienced it. I had never felt anything like it. The dirt seeping up in between each of my toes as I stepped on it was a unique feeling to me. A feeling I wanted to experience again. I was also finally able to meet other gods and goddesses that I had only ever heard stories about from my father, mother, sisters, and the Graeae, our family servants.

Specifically, it was the Goddess of wisdom, Athena, that I was drawn to in all of her glory, power, and beauty. She was a sight to behold and was held in the highest regards by the patrons of Athens. My parents offered me and my sisters to Athena, striking a deal with her. When we were to become of age, we would be presented to Athena to serve in her temple. Athena accepted this offering and in return, promised my parents that no mortal, nor god, would attempt to reach our oceanic palace in pursuit of hunt or war. She had granted us eternal peace for this.

I remember it like it was yesterday. I shied and hid myself behind my mother's serpentine body upon coming in contact with the goddess for the very first time. She was a fearsome creature to behold.

"Come, Meduso. No need to be afraid of me," Athena declared as she kneeled down to her knees so that she was at eye level with me. Her tone was warm and maternal. "Soon, I will be the one to watch over you when you come to my temple to serve me."

I stepped aside from my mother, fully exposing myself, and came forward towards her. At the time, I had no idea what to make of this. Was she going to be a second mother or guardian to me?

It wasn't until we parted from Athena after that meeting that my mother and father made me sit with them at the dais in the throne room back at the palace to explain my fate.

"Meduso, you must bring pride to our family by serving Athena. There will come a day when you and your sisters will be sent to serve her," my father informed me.

"But why? I like it here! Why do I have to go!?" I

questioned him with an immaturity.

"You must understand, Meduso. Our family is part of the old gods. Zeus and the new gods now hold the power on Mount Olympus. We must be obedient if we don't want them to wreak havoc upon us," he explained.

My mother then interjected. "Athena requested our assistance in a war at sea. We assisted, and she was grateful for our help. We told her about our children and she offered to protect you all from the wrath of the other gods, only if you became her temple servants."

From that day onward, the Graeae were rigorous in their daily lessons with my sisters and me. They worked tirelessly to prepare us for a life on the surface, and that moment when we would be presented to Athena was just a year from now.

"Ladon must go now. Say your goodbyes, Meduso. You will see him again next year," my mother informed me.

"Next year? Why does he only visit us once a year? Where does he go all this time?" I was curious to know.

"Ladon is protector of the Garden of the Hesperides. He cannot be absent for so long. If Hera were to learn of his prolonged absence, we would all face her wrath," she explained.

"But what's in the Garden of Hesperides?"

My mother gave a heavy sigh but smiled. "The orchard is home to her golden apple tree. It was a gift given to Hera and Zeus during their wedding from your grandmother, Gaia. The Hesperide nymphs tend to the grove, but nevertheless Hera demanded the tree be protected from thieves and some of the nymphs that she did not trust. Therefore, Ladon, who never sleeps, was assigned as the tree's guardian."

I still didn't understand why he was the sole protector of the garden. Why weren't there other creatures who took shifts in guarding it? Why was Ladon forced to have to be separated from his family for all but one day of the year? All because the Goddess Hera had distrust in her nymphs and demanded it? It sounded very selfish to me and illogical, but I wouldn't dare express these thoughts to my mother out of fear of her reprimanding me for questioning the thoughts and ways of an Olympian goddess.

"Well, what's so special about a golden apple?" I asked.

My mother raised a brow at me. "Have you ever seen a golden apple, boy?"

I shook my head.

"Well, there you go. That's why it's special. It's a rarity."

Her answers were still not satisfying to me. I closed my eyes and pressed my soft, silky cheek against Ladon's face, the face that I had originally petted, not the other ninety-nine others. It was a dichotomous pairing to have my smooth, supple skin against his tough, hard scute. I could feel Ladon reciprocate with affection by allowing me to hold him in an embrace. I sensed his breathing slow as the air from his exhalation drifted through the golden locks of my hair and hit my scalp with a pleasurable warmth.

I had only just met my brother, but knowing that I would only see him once a year gave me grief. My heart tightened and practically shriveled into nothingness when she informed me of this. It was as if I was handed an entertaining plaything only to have it stripped right from me and told I could only play with it once a year. A piece of my soul was broken off and would go with my brother. Discouraged, I separated from Ladon and allowed him to back away from us in the shallow water of the grotto.

His one-hundred monstrous heads began to diminish and he returned back to his original serpentine, draconic self with one head. With swift speed, and grace, he dove back into the waters, leaving my mother and me to ourselves.

"Dear child, tell me what the matter is?" My mother wiped a single teardrop from my cheek as she asked this.

"I just met my brother for the first time, and now I won't get to see him again for a year!?" I raised my voice, but then realized I may have overstepped my boundaries with my mother. A nervous expression was displayed across my face.

My mother, Ceto, was a goddess herself. Goddess of the deep seas and its creatures and monsters. The whales, sharks, squids, octopi and even the most bizarre of sea monsters were at her beck, call, and command. She was a fearsome sight to behold with her moonlight blue skin and bright apatite eyes that matched the walls of our grotto and palace. Her hair was thick, with navy strands coming from her head that were almost lifelike. Sometimes, I expected the tips of her hair to open their eyes or stick out a slithering tongue. Her upper body was similar to mine, to that of a human, but her lower half was composed of deep purple scales extending into a tail, similar to a dark mermaid.

"Poor boy. There are many things in this world that are unfair. You still have much to learn, Meduso." She rubbed my back in comfort and held her hand on it as we walked from the grotto and back into the palace.

I hated when my mother said things like this. That I had much to learn, or was still too young, or I would understand in due time. She kept coddling me and making statements like these for years. It kept only reminding me of my inferiority to her, my father, and my sisters.

As we walked the halls of our oceanic palace, one of my older sisters, Euryale, came up and strode with us. "You finally met Ladon! What did you think? Did he scare you? I bet he did!" my sister said in a chipper manner.

I shook my head as my mother spoke up for me. "Meduso carried himself fairly well. You could take a lesson from him, Euryale." She gave the two of us a wink and moved down the hall ahead of us, leaving my sister and me to ourselves.

"Hmph!" Euryale grunted. "She's exaggerating. I handled myself just fine when I first met Ladon years ago.

I mean… I was startled at first, but just a bit!"

I tried not to snicker at my sister, but then I heard my mother shout back at us, "Euryale howled and cried so loud that even the creatures from the furthest oceans away could hear her!"

This made me laugh uncontrollably. My sister nudged me in the side. She then began to whisper. "Don't believe her. She's lying!"

Somehow, I doubted Euryale. When my eldest sister Stheno and I would play tricks and pranks on her, Euryale would wail out bellowing cries and screeches that were gut-wrenching. So, it didn't take much imagination for me to think about how she acted when she first met Ladon and his one-hundred heads.

As my mother increased her distance from us, Euryale felt comfortable enough to have a one-on-one conversation with me. "It's sad, isn't it?"

"What's sad?" I asked.

"Ladon and Echidna. They've been kept hidden from us for years and now that we're old enough to be let in on the secret, we're told we can only see them once a year!" Euryale exclaimed.

"It was hard to watch him go. I even cried about it," I revealed.

"Well, I shouldn't be complaining as much as you. After all, you'll only get to see him…" she then paused, realizing the hurtful words she was about to utter.

I knew exactly what my sister was going to say. That I would only get to see him in my limited lifetime, or something along those lines. Euryale wasn't wrong, though. Our parents were gods, and Stheno and Euryale were both immortals. I, on the other hand, was born as a mortal. My life would end, and I would be gone from this world and sent to the Underworld at some point in time. A concept I never quite understood nor could fathom. Everyone around me would go on living for hundreds and thousands of years. I would experience death, as they called it.

My father, Phorcys, God of the sea and dangers of deep, explained it to me rather bluntly when I was little. I can still remember his exact words to me to this very day. "Meduso, fear not, son, but you are what we call in this world a mortal. An unfortunate omen bestowed upon our family. It's not your fault, though. It was a curse struck upon our family from the Olympian gods. A warning to let us know of their power and our place in this world. If we want to remain at peace and in isolation from the rest of the world, we need to abide by their rules."

Euryale meant no harm in what she was saying to me. I knew deep down she cared about me and there was no malevolence behind her abrasive remark. "It's okay Euryale. I understand..." I had no intention of making her feel bad, so I did my best to change the subject. "Tell me of Echidna and what to expect."

My sister's eyes lit up as I made this request. Her face equally brightened. "I'd thought you never ask!" she stated with jubilance. Secretly, Euryale was a gossip. She loved to inform me about everyone's business and the latest scandals and stories occurring up on the surface and on Mount Olympus. She reveled in having the opportunity to tell me things I was not privy to already.

"Echidna is similar to our mother, except her skin is viler and grotesque. Black with dark green scum," Euryale described.

"Does she at least speak?" I asked.

"Of course! She's not like Ladon in that sense."

"Well, why have I never met her yet? Why doesn't she live with us?"

"Meduso, you think things so simply. She married Typhon, an enemy of Zeus. She lives in a very isolated cave in Arima, the mountains of Cilicia."

Euryale expected me to make sense of all of this, but I was still at a loss. I had no idea what any of this meant, besides the fact that Echidna's husband was an enemy of Zeus. And well, being an enemy of Zeus was someone I knew never to associate with.

Euryale must have caught on to my cluelessness. She rolled her eyes and further elaborated on the subject. "Cilicia is on the surface. Echidna lives on the land, which is why we never see her. That and she has to stay in hiding based on the fact that she is married to Typhon, that ugly, stupid monster."

Things were starting to become a little clearer for me.

"So, Echidna is in hiding? In fear of Zeus and his wrath?"

"Precisely. Our parents lied to the Olympian gods claiming that we disowned her. That she was banished from our oceans and was to never to be seen by any of us again."

"Our parents lied to the Mount Olympus gods!?" I exclaimed, shocked as ever.

Euryale covered my mouth with her hand to keep me silent and peeked around the corners to make sure no one was overhearing our conversation.

"Shhh!!! Don't let anyone else hear you say that! But yes, they did, for our own protection. We check in on Echidna once a year. She informs our father when it is safe to visit. We wouldn't dare step foot in that cave knowing Typhon…"

Euryale was caught off-guard, as her statement was interrupted by a deep, loud voice that sounded almost demonic. "That will be enough, Euryale!"

She and I turned around to see that our father, Phorcys, stood behind us. Euryale became immediately apologetic. "I'm sorry, father, I was only…"

"Go!" he screamed at her. Euryale sprinted down the hall and out of sight. I too started to head in her direction, but was immediately halted by my father. "Not you, Meduso! Come with me!"

I stopped dead in my tracks and turned around towards my father, but hung my head low, not daring to look him in the eye. The anger in his voice led me to believe I would be punished. As I heard his footsteps, I then glanced upward to see he had his back to me, and so I followed him, heading into one of his private chambers.

"Son, it's time for you to start learning more about the

surface." His tone was more solemn and less irate. My head lifted to directly meet my father, Phorcys's gaze. My father was a fierce god. He was strong, muscular, and his features were oceanic at its finest. His hair long and silver, swaying back to his scaly, fishlike tail. He had skin, or rather a carapace, similar to that of a crab. His hands were that of humans, like mine, but his legs were the claws of crustaceans.

"But I thought I've learned all about the surface already. You've told me about the gods and goddesses that walk the surface and we met Athena..." as I explained my learned lessons to him, he pounded his fist down on the throne he was now seated in to silence me.

"No, Meduso! Foolish boy. The gods and goddesses only walk the surface to associate with the mortals, when necessary. Most of them remain on Mount Olympus or elsewhere in the clouds, in the depths of the oceans like us, hidden in mountains or somewhere secluded on the surface. It is the mortals who live, breathe, and walk on the surface freely."

There it was again. That word that my father cringed at every time he mentioned it. Mortal. He rarely talked about mortals, yet I was one of them.

Did he despise me too?

I continued to listen to him. "Soon, the time will come when you and your sisters will walk among them yourselves. *It is important for you to know that mortals must be obedient to the gods.* Do you understand?"

I nodded.

"Good. Now I know you and your sisters sometimes speak ill-willingly of them, but such conversations should never take place on the surface. For the gods are always listening. They can see and hear everything you say when you are on their world. Just like your mother and me. Do you, Euryale, and Stheno, really think all of your discussions within our palace walls are private?"

My eyes widened. This was a revelation to me. I had no idea my mother and father possessed the power to hear our conversations from opposite ends of the palace. I knew they were a god and goddess, but I imagined their powers had limitations. Now I found myself attempting to recall all of the talks I had with my sisters, hoping that there was nothing too shameful I had told them that my parents would be discouraged or angered by.

"Father. I'm sorry. I..."

"Save your apologies, boy. Let this be a lesson to you. When you serve Athena, you are to be loyal and faithful to her. Never question her motives, thoughts, or actions. Do you understand, Meduso?"

"Yes, father," I obediently replied.

"Because if you defy her or any other god or goddess for that matter, you will bring shame upon yourself and to our entire family. She will treat your actions as treason and our entire family will suffer retribution," he explained.

"I understand, father. I will be a devout servant to Athena. I promise."

"The last thing your mother or I need is for Zeus or the

other Olympian gods to think we are against them! Those sowed seeds of doubt will lead to our demise!"

I nodded and scratched the back of my head in nervousness. Though Phorcys was my father, even I was intimidated by him.

I will never forget when I was little, Euryale and I both snuck into his prohibited weapon room and play fought with some of his obsidian tridents and swords. When he found out we had crossed him, we were summoned to the throne room. The red flames in the room turned to black and blue. Phorcys' eyes changed to deep red. He grew to be five times his normal size as he hovered over us, shouting. "You will never defy me again! Do you both understand? And you, Meduso! I will send you to the Underworld early if you ever disobey me again!"

After that scolding, I did my best to avoid him as much as possible. Whenever we were together, I kept my head low and said as little as possible. This was the relationship we had throughout my entire life. I was constantly walking on eggshells around him.

"Father... will you please tell me about the mortals? Are they like me?" I inquired.

It was difficult for me to picture what anything on the surface looked like since I was only exposed to it once for a brief amount of time. After all, I had been isolated to the deepest depths of the ocean and this palace for almost seventeen years now. I had no visualization to base my thoughts off of. However, my father and mother claimed that I was a mortal, so I pictured other mortals to have the same physical characteristics as me.

My sisters and I looked far more different than our parents, our Graeae servants, and the other creatures I've encountered in the ocean depths. Our skin was pale, milky and smooth. Our appendages were of the same silky material and consistent throughout our entire bodies. My hair was golden yellow, and I had hazel-green eyes.

My father chuckled at my question. "Yes, Meduso. They look like you. You and your sisters are what some call humans, except your sisters are immortal humans. They will live on for eternity, like your mother and me. You, on the other hand… well, we don't need to repeat this story once again, do we?"

"No, I understand." I did not care to hear my father clarify the difference between a mortal and immortal for what would seem like the thousandth time. I was reminded of it on a daily occurrence. I would age quicker than my sisters and would eventually die. My soul would flow to the Underworld and eventually into non-existence, oblivion, or whatever that meant. I was still unclear of what that outcome looked like.

"Good. Well, why don't you settle down for the evening? Tomorrow your sister, Stheno, will take you to the surface to meet Echidna. I want you to be well rested and to have your wits about you when you do walk the surface," my father stated. "I want you to take more opportunities to roam the land and get used to it. After all, it will only be a matter of time before you are permanently living up there, serving in the temple of Athena."

"Yes, father." And I did as he instructed. I went to bed earlier than usual that evening, although it was difficult for me to sleep with all the new excitement going on around me. I would be experiencing what the surface was like more often now. It would be a whole new world to me. It would also be my first time meeting my sister, Echidna. The uncertainty of what to expect kept me awake, staring at the luminescent aquamarine ceiling in my room.

My thoughts drifted to everything my father had mentioned to me, especially hearing him say: It is important for you to know that mortals... they are obedient to the gods. Just what exactly would I be expected to do on the surface? What would Athena and the other gods demand of me? I tossed and turned, eventually dozing off into a slumber.

Chapter 2

"You foolish brats! Give it back to us!" Deino screamed.

"You will be eternally damned to the Underworld for such cruelty!" Enyo declared.

My sister, Euryale, and I were in the Great Hall of our palace the following morning. Euryale stole the single eyeball of the Graeae and tossed it to me. She and I decided to have a little fun with Deino, Enyo, and Pemphredo, our three servants, and technically our sisters, though we often never referred to them as such.

Together, the three of them were known as the Graeae. Each of them hooded in black cloaks, with traces of their gray, knotty hair able to be seen. They too had similar physical features to my sisters and me, but their skin was more droopy and tougher, like an animal's hide. They were decrepit and much older than us.

Deino, Enyo, and Pemphredo were inseparable. They had no choice, having to share a single eyeball among them as a means of sight. Without one of them in possession of their eye, they were permanently blind. As a result of this, they kept the eye close to them, so as to not lose it. However, whenever Euryale or I saw an opportunity to snatch it from them, as a joke, we did it.

I tossed the eye back across the room to Euryale, over the Graeae's heads. "Catch!"

Enyo reached her hand up, hearing that I had thrown the eye in the air, but she was unable to snatch it back from us.

"You will be punished for this!" Pemphredo yelled, as she kneeled on the ground, feeling around on the floor in a desperate attempt to somehow find the eye.

Euryale then threw the eye back towards me, but a different hand managed to grasp it. It was my oldest sister, Stheno. She held the eyeball out to Deino, who grabbed it, regaining her sight.

"Thank you, Stheno!" Enyo cried. "Your brother and sister could learn a thing or two from you!"

"Yes! Rotten little sea scum!" Pemphredo followed in with.

"There will come a time when you will pay for these little pranks of yours, Euryale and Meduso! And I will make sure we are there to see that day!" Enyo wailed.

The Graeae then scurried out of the hall to attend to their other duties in the palace.

"Aren't we getting a little too old for this?" Stheno asked us. Her arms folded over her chest, seeming to be disappointed at my sister and me for our childish behavior.

Euryale and I just stared at each other for a moment, and then, as if on cue, we both answered our sister in unison. "No!"

Stheno shook her head, vexed at our response. "There will come a time when these little games of yours will not be accepted. You really could get into trouble for this, especially on the surface."

Euryale rolled her eyes. "Well, all the more reason for us to get them in now, while we can get away with it!"

I laughed at my sister's quick wit.

"Anyway, Meduso, get yourself together and meet me in the grotto. We will depart for Arima shortly," Stheno sternly demanded, before walking out of the Great Hall.

"I wouldn't worry too much about Echidna. She can be stubborn and a little full of herself, but just play along with her. Stroke her ego a bit, and you'll be just fine," Euryale explained to me.

"Is she pompous?" I asked.

"You will see when you arrive. She's sort of all over the place. You would be too if you had to be married to that fool, Typhon."

I gulped at the mention of Typhon. Euryale smirked at my reaction, slapping her hand to her forehead before shaking it. "Typhon won't be there, of course, silly. Remember? He's stuck in Tartarus."

I let out a heavy sigh of relief as she revealed this.

Typhon. It was a name I heard of from the tales my father once told me in regards to Zeus. I also heard about him from the Graeae's lessons.

The story goes that Typhon fought Zeus to overtake the cosmos. Typhon was indeed a powerful, uncontrollable, monster. A force to be reckoned with. He had hundreds of snakes that grew from his shoulders and back that released breaths of fire. Typhon himself also had the capability to emit and control flames. However, he was no match for Zeus and his thunderbolts. Once Zeus had defeated Typhon in a battle that shook the sky, the land, and the darkest depths of the oceans and Underworld, he condemned Typhon to rot in Tartarus for eternity. The wickedest of fates and cruelest of punishments for anyone to have to endure.

Yet, I was somehow related to this monster, at least by marriage. It was difficult for me to imagine that any sister of mine could be married to such a vile and despicable creature.

There wasn't much for me to do to have to prepare to leave our oceanic palace for the surface. I acquired my sandals from my room and didn't bother to change my beige tunic that I already had on.

I then met up with Stheno and my mother in the grotto.

"You're late, Meduso," my mother declared.

"I'm sorry. I was talking to Euryale and then needed to grab my sandals," I explained.

"Go to the ledge with Stheno," my mother demanded.

I did as she told me to. I walked to the edge of the cliff, overlooking the bright sapphire water beneath us. As I stood next to Stheno, I felt her grip my hand, holding it tightly.

"Are you ready, Meduso?" Stheno asked me.

I gulped and eventually nodded with hesitance.

My mother reached her arm out so that her palm faced the pool beneath us. The water that was crystal blue began to change into a lackluster pewter gray, as if

Hephaestus himself was blacksmithing and forging metals, liquifying them into weaponry.

"I will return you both when the sun sets," my mother informed us.

"Farewell, mother," Stheno shouted. "On the count of three, Meduso. One... two... and three!"

Still clasping my sister's hand, I jumped into the metallic liquid beneath us along with her. I closed my eyes tightly, expecting to feel the wetness of the water against my skin, the break of the pool to splash as we struck it. Instantly, I opened my eyes, and I was not underwater or in the grotto or the deep ocean.

I glanced upward to see the clear blue sky once again. It was only the second time in my entire life I had witnessed it. I inhaled the fresh air from the surface. There was something about breathing in the air from the land that was more invigorating than beneath the sea. I placed my hands over my chest, to feel the heavy rise and fall of my muscles, as my lungs inhaled the quality of the atmosphere that they were not normally used to.

It took me a second to realize that there wasn't dirt or grass on the ground that I was standing on. It was a frigid white substance that sent chills from my feet up through my spine. I shivered before leaning down to touch it in my hands. It was very wet and cold, but it contained the purest white color I had ever seen. Whiter than even Apollo's garments and the ivory on his lyre.

Stheno snickered at my innocence and obliviousness. "It's called *snow*, Meduso. It's found in the coldest regions of the world and on the highest peaks of mountains, where we are now," she elaborated.

I fixed my gaze out to the lower distance to make out grass, trees, and fields that were miles away, beneath us. We were on the mountain tops of Arima.

"Come! We have to trek down this slope to reach Echidna's cave," Stheno ordered.

I followed behind my sister, not saying much to her. I had a closer relationship with Euryale than Stheno. That was only because Euryale was the younger of my two sisters and I had more in common with her. Plus, it helped that she was outgoing and acted much more youthful than my eldest sister. Stheno was very independent, but also extremely fierce and intimidating. She rarely played games with us and tended to be the voice of reason to keep Euryale and me out of trouble, avoiding harm's way.

Stheno must have also felt the awkward tension between us that was now full of silence. She attempted to strike up a conversation with me. "Did mother and father inform you about Echidna?"

"Yes. I believe so. That she is married to Typhon, who defied the Olympian gods. He is eternally damned while Echidna remains in hiding, here in the mountains."

My sister nodded at my description. "Correct. Except there is a little more to the story. You cannot tell a soul as to her whereabouts. The other gods and goddesses assume she is underground, beneath Arima, in isolation. That's merely a cover up so that other gods or the bravest of warriors and mortals don't seek to hunt and kill her."

I was trying to make sense of all of this, but was too naïve to understand the reasoning behind it.

"Why would mortals want to kill her?"

Stheno sneered at my lack of knowledge. "Because, Meduso, a mortal who bears the strength to be able to kill a god or goddess, let alone an enemy of the ruler of all gods, will be blessed beyond imagination. They will receive countless gifts from other gods and mortals. They become kings and queens of the world, gaining great possessions. Not to mention the fame that comes along with the fortune. Their story of being a mortal who killed a god will be passed down for generations to come."

"So, it's all in the name of selfishness?" I cynically stated.

"Yes. That's one way to perceive it," Stheno added.

From the stories my parents, sisters, and the Graeae had told me about gods and mortals, I was able to recognize that I was extremely judgmental of them. Through the countless tales that I learned about, I saw a pattern in a majority of them. That gods, goddesses, and mortals usually made decisions and took actions for selfish reasons.

Prometheus giving fire to mortals, and Zeus punishing him by tying him to a rock for eagles to feed upon his liver. All because Zeus feared anyone getting even a slight amount of power could threaten him.

Hera assisting Jason to fulfill a prophecy so he could kill King Pelias and become king in his place. But Hera didn't do it from the goodness of her heart. She only did it out of revenge on Pelias, for he honored all the gods but her.

And don't even get me started on Narcissus.

Now, seeing these selfish ways affect my family only made me more skeptical of them. That Ladon was forced to be the guardian of the Garden of Hesprides only because Hera was insecure with the nymphs there. That Echidna was tucked away in a cave at the peak of a mountain, only because of her association with her husband, who challenged Zeus. And based on the advice my father and mother had given me, the gods and goddesses held their power over my family's head, forcing my sisters and me to serve them at one of their temples in the future. Their motives were irrational and illogical. It all stemmed from their desire for power, and they pushed the boundaries with evoking that power, no matter how much harm it may have caused to others.

"How come the gods aren't kind, Stheno? I always hear about their *wrath* or *anger*, but rarely have I been told stories about them performing decent acts, simply out of kindness, receiving nothing in return."

She stopped dead in her tracks, causing me to halt as well. My sister turned around and stepped towards me, placing her hand over my heart. "Meduso, you are so innocent and so kind. But you view the world so simply because you have yet to experience it. I knew mother kept you hidden away for far too long," Stheno revealed.

"What do you mean?"

"Let me try to explain it, so you understand. Suppose the gods and goddesses were always nice to the world and to the mortals. Let's just say they trusted every single mortal walking the surface. Do you think the mortals and the gods would live peacefully together?" she asked.

I shrugged. "I wouldn't see why not."

"That's where you're wrong, Meduso. Mortals long for power, fame, and wealth. Seeing a god who has it allows them to visualize that it's attainable. Humans would take advantage of the kindness of the gods, which would lead to lying, stealing, cheating, and even killing. After all, the gods would be kind, right? The mortals would have nothing to fear. They wouldn't face punishment or have any accountability for their actions."

My sister's hypothetical scenario began to sink into me. After all, I had only ever heard about mortals through stories. I still had yet to ever meet another mortal in my life.

"You will see soon enough, Meduso. Mother and father have both encouraged you to explore the surface after our visit with Echidna. When you meet with mortals, and talk with them, you will come to understand their poor behavior and their true nature," Stheno confidently expressed.

I began to consider her words, and those of my parents and everyone else around me. Perhaps from experience, they did know the true nature of humans. I was in a deep moral dilemma with my thoughts on the actions of the gods. Hopefully, when I would be able to interact on land in the near future, I could then solidify my opinion.

Stheno and I continued to descend the mountain until we passed the precipice. The slope flattened, leading to a narrow trail. We followed this trail until we were able to see a bare hole right in the middle of the mountain. Stheno led the way inside, grabbing a lit torch at the entrance, carrying it with her as we explored deeper into the cave.

It felt like a never-ending tunnel. We continued to walk for several minutes until we finally reached a very large and circular room within the cave. The torch was no longer of use to us since there was a massive oculus overhead, allowing light to enter.

A figure came forth, stepping into the light. My mouth gaped open. For being Typhon's wife, I was expecting to see a monstrous female creature. A repulsive, murky beast with fangs and talons, smelling of putrid, rotting flesh. But this was not what stood before me. She had similar features to my mother. The lower half of her body was composed of forest green scales, coiling into a snake's tail. Her upper body was that of a human, but not just any human. An alluring one. Pleasant to the naked eye. Fair-skinned with shiny hair, the color of emeralds.

"Come forward, brother and sister," the figure commanded.

Stheno and I approached her, now allowing me to get a closer glimpse of her jade eyes that matched the jeweled tiara on her head.

She slithered just inches away from us. Her palm

rubbed along my cheek, with her fingertips tracing my chin. She studied me carefully.

"My. Oh my! And to think Ceto and Phorcys had the capability to produce such a lovely creation," she said to me. Her fingers now spun in a circular motion to feel my hair. "And these beautiful golden locks. You will tempt all of the mortals with this face. Dare I say the goddesses and even the gods too?" Echidna winked at me before stepping back to give us separation.

"Meduso has yet to be introduced to the mortals, Echidna. He will begin to socialize with them soon," Stheno proclaimed.

"Ahhh. Is that so? His gorgeous features and now the added layer of innocence and naivety will do wonders in the mortal world," Echidna declared.

My face began to turn as red as the rose of Aphrodite. I did not know whether to be appreciative or stunned by her flattery. I've never had anyone pay me such compliments in my entire life.

"Tell me, my dear, what is it you desire?" Echidna asked.

"Desire?" I questioned.

"Yes. What is it you seek from this world? Power, riches, a gorgeous woman... or maybe a handsome man?"

Stheno cut her off. "That will be enough, Echidna. There is no need to tarnish the boy's mind."

I was unsure of what Echidna meant by *desiring a handsome man*. I've never even set sight on a mortal to know what aspects of them I was captivated by. Most of the stories I've been told involved a male being in love with a female. However, Euryale did share some rumors she had heard about certain Olympian gods taking some of their male servants as lovers. But I did not know where my attractions lied, based on my lack of experience.

"Oh, don't be so dull, Stheno!" Echidna exclaimed. "At least give the boy some direction! He'll wind up as dull and stupid as Koalemos if you keep him secluded any longer."

Stheno shook her head. "I think you of all people are the last immortal that should be giving me advice. Look at the direction you chose for yourself. And know where it put you!"

"Hmph. I'll never understand you and our parents. Choosing to stay isolated in the oceans while the rest of the world around you is drastically changing." Echidna continued to express her disdain for the traditions and beliefs of our family.

As my sisters continued to banter back and forth, I stood still, just staring ahead at them. Their silhouettes became blurry and then non-existent in my line of vision. Was I having an out-of-body experience? Instead, a new sight was before me. *Some sort of rope. No, it was a net with a gigantic fish caught in it, in the water, except the water was fairly shallow. I could see its translucence and the glimmer of light shining through it. I swam toward the caught fish, trying to free it with my bare hands. The fish was able to escape, but as I tugged away, I realized I was snagged within the confines of the net. I tried my best to yank away, but to no avail. As I glanced upward, I realized I was being pulled towards the surface, until…*

Stheno called out to me, bringing me back to reality. "Meduso! Are you okay!?"

I just glanced at her blankly. "Yes. I'm fine. Why? What is wrong?"

"Your eyes…" Stheno began, with a worried expression on her face. "They turned pure silver, for a moment," she revealed.

"What? Are you sure?" I was extremely bewildered, not even sure if I believed what she had just shared.

"A vision." Echidna slid close to me and raised my chin up with her hand, glaring into my eyes. "Did you have a vision, Meduso?"

"A vision? I mean, I saw a fish being caught in a net just now. I'm not sure where. I've never experienced anything like this. What is happening?" I felt shook up.

"It's nothing to worry about, dear brother. You just had a vision. Call it a *gift*, if you will. A sight into the future or a major phenomenon happening elsewhere in the world. Such things gods usually experience. I'm surprised you, as a mortal, are able to have them," Echidna confessed.

"This truly is your first time experiencing this, Meduso?" Stheno asked.

"Yes," I admitted.

"Hmm. I wonder what it could mean. A fish in a net?" Stheno was puzzled.

"View it as a mark of destiny, Meduso." Echidna advised. "Whatever you do, never run from these visions you have. The Fates are reaching out to you, for a reason. They want you to see this. They want you to be brave and follow through with these visions."

"Do you really think so?" I turned to Stheno to see if she had the same opinion.

"I think you should inform our mother and father about this first," Stheno recommended.

"Oh. Don't listen to her, Meduso! They've held you back long enough from whatever your destiny may be. Press onward, dear brother. If I were you, I would leave the oceans the second you get the chance to, and never look back," Echidna advised.

"Yes. Echidna did the same, Meduso, and look where she ended up. Locked away, alone in a barren cave in the mountains!" Stheno wittily remarked.

Echidna's eyes flared at Stheno as she made this comment. Her once pale skin shifted to a dark green color to match her scales. She was now angered. "I'd watch your tongue, Stheno! Although I am your sister, I am not to be made a fool of! Do not trifle with me!" Echidna threatened.

Stheno stood her ground. "And what are you going to do? Make any tumultuous action and the gods and goddesses will know of your location. An empty threat, if I've ever heard one."

"How dare you! Get out, now!" Echidna vilely screeched.

Stheno grabbed the torch and turned back to face me. "Come, Meduso. We leave!"

I just stood there, equidistant between both of my sisters. Echidna glided to me, caressing my cheek one last time before our departure. "You are more beautiful than I had ever imagined, brother. It will serve you well in their world. Never put that beauty to waste." Those were her parting words as Echidna swiftly skidded out of sight in the blink of an eye, deeper into the dwelling of her cave.

I followed behind Stheno as we left, ascending the mountain once again.

"That Echidna! Curse her!" Stheno grumbled.

"I don't think she was so bad, Stheno. Much more pleasant than I had imagined."

"Meduso, that was only one side of Echidna that you saw. Remember, she is the wife of the most cruel and vicious monster known to existence. Do not forget. It takes a certain someone to be able to commit to that," she explained.

Once we reached the summit, Stheno held out her hands to me for me to take. I clasped onto them and we closed our eyes, summoning our mother for our return. Within a flash, I opened my eyes, and I was once again standing on the ledge of the cliff in our grotto.

"How does Echidna fare?" my mother, Ceto, asked.

Stheno shook her head and dismissed herself. "Troublesome as ever! We have much to talk about, mother!" She headed back into the palace, with my mother following in pursuit.

I chose not to join them, knowing Stheno would have private affairs to discuss with my mother and father. I sat on the edge of the bluff, gleaming into the crystal blue water, reflecting on the vision I had.

A net with a fish? What could it mean?

I found myself coming up with little to no answers or guesses.

I was then reminded of Echidna's counsel and the last words she spoke to me.

Never put that beauty to waste.

Little did I know that I would carry this guidance with me for years to come. Never did I picture that it would end up shaping my future.

Chapter 3

Stheno had informed our parents about our visit with Echidna. She also described the premonition I had with the fish in the net. Both my father and mother met with me on multiple occasions to provide words of wisdom to derail all advice that Echidna had left me with.

They postponed my initial experience to be alone on the surface for a few weeks, until they felt comfortable that I would heed their guidance.

Remember, Meduso, do nothing to upset or displease the gods.

Put everything Echidna had told you out of your mind.

Think nothing about your beauty or love with another mortal.

You must stay pure if you are to serve Athena in the future.

Finally, the day had arrived when it was time for me to begin my own adventure. My own exploration of the world above, without anyone beside me to whisper in my ear. I was elated to be able to have the opportunity to create my own thoughts and views of the world, without influence from anyone else.

It was just my mother and me in the grotto once again. She placed her hands on my shoulders. "Promise me, Meduso, that you will represent our family with pride and be respectful to those around you, especially any god or goddess you may encounter."

"I promise, mother."

She wrapped her arms around me in an embrace. "Remember, son. You have exactly one full year on your own. I will send Euryale or Stheno to check in on you once in a while. After one year, you will return here. We must then prepare for you to serve Athena. Is that understood?"

"Yes. I understand," I replied.

"Okay. Now stand on the ledge," my mother instructed.

I stood, watching the shift in the color of the water that my mother had formed.

"Wait. Where exactly in the world will I be visiting?" I asked.

She simply smiled at me. "Your mind will carry you there, Meduso. Just close your eyes and picture where you want to go. The rest will be in the hands of the Fates."

I did as my mother advised. My lids were firmly shut and I slowly approached the very edge of the cliff before jumping into the pewter gray pool below. The only vivid image I had in my mind was the large fish in the net, in the shallow waters.

Sure enough, I opened my eyes, and there it was, swimming towards a huge fish, trapped in a net. I swam over to it and released the creature from captivity. I became tangled within the net, but noticed that it was now moving, pulling me to the surface. As I emerged from the water, I saw a figure holding the base of the net in his hand, dragging me up with it.

I reached for the end of the rather large boulder nearby to prop myself up. In one fell sweep, the figure reached under my armpit and lifted me up. I was now face to face with the man, or rather, boy. I gazed into his hazel-green eyes, astonished. He looked so similar to me, at least based on his limbs, skin color, and other broad physical features. He stood slightly taller than me, and parts of his body were tighter, with more girth to them than my own. Specifically, I was able to witness the thickness of the muscles in his arms and legs. They were of much greater proportion than my own.

"What were you doing down there!?" the boy asked.

"Helping save that fish that was caught."

"You released that fish!? That was my next meal!" he irately stated.

"Well, I'm sorry. You'll have to find something else to eat," I retorted.

"I guess so. Are you from around here?"

"No. My family and I live in the ocean," I explained.

"Oh! Are you a god?"

"No. I'm a mortal. A human," I answered.

"Ah. Well, that makes two of us. Wait a minute... if you're a mortal, how are you able to live in the ocean?" he inquired.

"Our palace is at the bottom of the ocean. There is no water within it. And I am the son of Phorcys and Ceto, God and Goddess of the deep seas and oceanic creatures or monsters, is what some might describe them as," I revealed.

The boy's mouth dropped once I had shared this information with him. Was I too forthcoming?

"So, your parents are gods, but somehow you are a mortal?"

"Yes. A curse sent down from the Olympian gods, to remind my parents of where their loyalties should lie," I explained.

"Hmmm. That's interesting," he said.

"Yes. This is my first time meeting another human, I'll admit."

"Really? Wait? Is this your first time on land, ever?"

"Sort of. I've only been on land twice, to visit the Goddess Athena and my sister…" I paused, remembering Stheno's words as to not tell anyone about Echidna or her whereabouts. I tried to be as vague as possible when speaking about her. "…my sister who left the ocean long ago."

"And what prompted you to come here to this island?"

This boy had an awful lot of questions. However, I sensed an innocence and compassion from this individual, so I felt comfortable enough to continue to share my background with him. "I had a vision from the Fates about the fish in the net," I confessed. "I was told that any vision I have is a sign of destiny. So, the Fates must have guided me here."

"Well, that's unusual. I'll be the first to tell you, there's not much that goes on here, on this island," he confessed.

"And where exactly am I? What island is this?"

"The Island of Seriphos in the Aegean Sea. It's beautiful here, is it not? White sands, azure waters, lush green grasses and forests and a few mountains here and there."

As he described this place, I spun around to take in the scenery. This island did seem very paradisiacal, unlike where Athena's temple was, settled on dirt and stone at the Acropolis of Athens, where I had once been.

"Yes. It does seem very inviting," I agreed.

The boy then held his hand out to me. "I'm Perseus, by the way. What do they call you?"

"Meduso." I wasn't sure why he held his hand out to me. I had a muddle look expressed on my face, which he must have picked up on, because he reached out to grab my hand with his, and shook them together up and down.

"This is how we greet one another on land," he explained. "We shake hands, like this."

Although I was embarrassed by not knowing this traditional standard to say hello, I simply smiled at his generosity in teaching me. His touch also sent a spark throughout my body. It was a peculiar feeling. I've never experienced this from being touched by my parents, my sisters, or anyone else, for that matter. There was something soothing, soft, and yet, at the same time, wild and eccentric about his touch. It felt warm, and I secretly wished he never let go of my hand, but he did.

"A pleasure to meet you, Meduso."

"You as well, Perseus."

He collected his fishing equipment from off the rock and then turned his back to me. "Come with me," he directed.

"To where?" I asked.

He chuckled. "Well, there aren't many places to go around here, but the least I can do is show you the island and where I live."

I nodded and decided to follow Perseus. I had no other place to go and, at the same time, I was beyond intrigued by him. I wanted to get to know him more. Hopefully, he was willing to want to get to know me as well.

We circled the island and its beaches for the next several hours before he led us more inland to where the stone homes of the island's inhabitants were located. I pointed to a rather large stone structure that stood tall on the peak of the highest mountain on the island.

"What's that?"

"That's King Polydectes's fortress. He is the ruler of Seriphos and lives there. I've only ever seen him once, when I was younger. He doesn't come down to these parts of the island much. Between you and me, I hear he throws long parties often, where the cups are constantly overflowing with wine."

"And what's wine like? I've only ever heard about it in a few tales, especially those of Dionysus," I confessed.

Perseus smiled at me. "I've only ever tried it once. It makes your mind very fuzzy. Can't say I enjoyed it as much as I anticipated."

"Oh. Well, I'd like to try it sometime, especially if it is

considered the gift of a god."

Perseus wrapped his arm around my shoulder. His grip around me was very rough, but I was able to feel the tightness of his muscles against my side. Again, another jolt struck me, feeling his body against mine. I enjoyed his proximity to me.

"I'll make sure you at least have one cup of wine before you leave this island. How long do you plan on staying, if I may ask?"

"Ummm. I think a year, maybe? My mother, Ceto, stated that I will have one full year to explore the surface before I am summoned back to her palace. Then, I need to prepare to be sent to Athens. I was promised to serve Athena at her temple upon my eighteenth year," I explained.

"Well, if you plan on staying here for the entire year, I can offer my home to you for your stay, unless you would prefer to seek a place elsewhere?"

I nodded at the cordiality of his proposition. "That would be wonderful."

"Then it's decided. Here, let me introduce you to my mother, Danaë, and my tutor, Dictys, before we settle in for the night."

"Sure."

We then passed through a steep pebbled trail that broke off, leading to the many stone homes of the island residents. Near the end of the trail, we arrived at the larger of the homes I've seen on the island. Perseus led us into it.

As I stepped into the building, I saw a man seated in the corner, fidgeting with some string, wood, and metal, working on a contraption I had never seen before.

"Dictys, this is my new friend, Meduso. Meduso, this is Dictys. He's a great man and an even better fisherman."

The tan, white-bearded man rose from his chair and let out a deep belly laugh. "Perseus, you really outdid yourself with that introduction there, boy."

The old fellow approached and scrutinized me up and down. "A little scrawny, but young. You'll come into your own soon, son," he stated.

"Ummm. Thank you?" I wasn't sure whether or not to be insulted or take this as a compliment. I was willing to give the elder man the benefit of the doubt and believe the latter.

"Meduso, I forgot to mention that Dictys is the brother of King Polydectes," Perseus mentioned.

I was rather surprised by this comment. "Oh? Well, if you're the brother of the king, why do you live down here and not up on the mountains in the fortress?"

Dictys reached his arm behind my back and then patted me on it. "Brazen little guy, aren't you? Clearly, you've hung around Perseus for a little too long. But yes, I choose to live here. I have a love of the sea. I can't bring myself to ever part ways with it. Its view, its smell, the fish and creatures within it. I feel a kindred spirit to the water. A feeling I never want to be absent of."

I completely understood where Dictys was coming

from. Being near or around water put my mind at ease, as well. I made sure to visit our grotto back home at least once every day. It was a safe haven for me and I could never picture being away from any sort of sea or ocean myself. I was glad that out of all the places I could have wound up at, I ended up here at Seriphos, surrounded by the sapphire Aegean water at all angles.

"So, where is it you come from?" Dictys questioned me.

I then told the fisherman everything there was to tell, about my parents, my sisters, our underwater palace, everything. I was unsure as to whether or not spilling this information so openly to people was in my best interest. However, there had been no reason for me not to, at this point. My trust in Perseus, and now Dictys, was growing unless they did something to make me feel otherwise.

"And a vision of Perseus's fish net is what led you here?" Dictys followed up with.

I nodded. "I would like for you to teach me how to fish, if you don't mind. Again, this is one of my first times on land. There is still so much I want to learn!" I emphatically declared.

"Energetic as ever! I'll tell you what. I will show you a few tricks tomorrow morning. Perseus can then teach you everything else. He is an expert fisherman himself now. The master has now been outdone by his apprentice, eh?" Dictys winked at Perseus as he stated this, causing Perseus to smirk.

"That would be wonderful. I am grateful!" I graciously

stated.

Perseus then chimed in to disrupt my excitement. "Then it's decided. But it's getting a little late, and I still want Meduso to meet my mother. So, we should be off now."

"Of course. I believe my wife, Clymene, is presently in Danaë's company. When you go, please tell her I request her presence at home, if you happen to run into her," Dictys requested.

"Yes. We will be sure to," Perseus affirmed.

We then left Dictys's home and headed back up the trail not far off to a smaller stone abode. As we entered, two women were hanging fabrics on a rope spread across the room.

"Mother, I've returned. Sorry I'm late. I met a new friend by the sea," Perseus explained.

His mother's head peeped out from behind one of the linen fabrics she hung to get a glimpse of Perseus and me. "Oh? You brought a visitor with you?"

She stepped forward to reveal her full self. Danaë was extremely captivating. An exquisite woman, with beautiful bronze hair, the same color as Perseus's.

"Yes. Mother, this is Meduso, the son of Ceto and Phorcys."

"Ceto and Phorcys? The same Ceto and Phorcys of the deep oceans and sea-monsters?" Danaë inquired, with a look of bewilderment on her face.

"The very same ones. This is Meduso's first experience on the surface, mother. He's lived in a palace deep at the bottom of the ocean his entire life," Perseus explained.

Danaë squinted to get a better view of me. "Well, Meduso, it's a pleasure to meet you. If you don't mind me being so bold as to say, I am quite shocked you are the son of those sea-monsters! You are an extremely handsome young man. You must have been a gift from the gods to them!"

This was the first time I had ever heard anyone describe me as a gift from the gods. My father always made it known that I was a curse from the gods, a complete contradiction to what Danaë had viewed me as.

I couldn't help but blush at her compliment. "You are too polite."

"And so well-mannered, too!" she added.

I stood silent, a little embarrassed by all of the laudable remarks Perseus's mother was giving me.

It was Perseus who found a way to interject, seeing how bashful I was behaving. "Oh. I almost forgot! Clymene, Dictys has asked that you return home."

The older, frail woman frowned. "That husband of mine! It's a wonder how he can be out at sea for days, yet can't be at home by himself for even seconds!" Clymene proclaimed. "But very well. I will be off now. Take care Danaë, Perseus, and young man. Welcome to Seriphos!" She placed her fragile hand on my shoulder before heading out.

Perseus then took a seat in one of the spare chairs in the room and motioned for me to sit in the one beside him. "Mother, you have to hear Meduso's story of how he ended up here on this island. It's fascinating!"

Danaë finished hanging the remainder of her fabrics before sitting in the seat across from the two of us. "Well, of course. I am curious to know how the son of the god and goddess of the deep oceans found his way here, of all places. Do tell me, Meduso," she enthusiastically requested.

And so, I filled her in on my history and the details of my childhood up until this very point in time. She stared at me, almost entranced by every word that escaped from my lips.

"So, the Fates led you here to this island. I wonder what their intent is. Perhaps you were meant to meet my son, Perseus. He is a very special boy. The son of…" Before Danaë could even finish her sentence, Perseus had cut her off.

"Let's save that story for another time, mother. It's getting rather late." Perseus stood up out of his seat.

The son of who?

Clearly, Perseus was not proud of his father. Otherwise, he wouldn't have minded his mother sharing this information with me. I was now intrigued to learn about his father, but knew better than to press on about the subject. My attention shifted back to Danaë.

"Well, only if you insist. Do you plan on heading home?" she asked.

Perseus nodded.

"Where is Meduso to stay?" she questioned.

"He can stay with me for a while or at least until he

gets tired of me." Perseus winked in my direction as he said this. "I find myself to be quite tolerable. Don't you agree?"

"Only time will tell…" was my rebuttal. I didn't intend to be as witty as my reply may have come off as. It was meant to be spoken as a matter of fact.

Danaë placed her hand over her mouth in an attempt to conceal her laughter. "Well, have a good night, you two. And welcome to Seriphos, Meduso. The island isn't exactly exciting, but never the less, the people here make it quite charming," she shared.

"Thank you for the warm hospitality," I stated.

Perseus then hugged his mother before we departed. We travelled back down the trail side by side. I had assumed we were heading to Perseus's dwelling, but we were apparently going elsewhere.

"Would you like to set up a fire on the beach? I'm not tired yet, and I figure you aren't either from all the excitement you've had today," he suggested.

"Yes. I would like that very much." Truth be told, it didn't matter to me whether we stayed on the beach or went back to Perseus's place. I was starting to grow fond of his presence and enjoyed his company, no matter where it was.

And so, we descended the trail and walked along the shoreline until we were at a spot on the beach where Perseus knew that no one would disturb us at.

"Hang here for a moment and I'll fetch us some wood," he requested.

Before I could even respond to Perseus, he bursted into a sprint with quick acceleration. In a matter of a few seconds, he returned with an enormous stack of wood that I would imagine that even four strong male humans could not carry in a single trip. His abnormal agility and brute strength were astounding. This did not make any sense to me. No human could attain such a feat. Something was amiss, and I found myself determined to get to the bottom of it.

Perseus neatly arranged the wood in an organized fashion and created the fire. I sat in the sand nearby and could not keep my eyes off of him, admiring his skills. I was drawn to his gracefulness as he ran, and the way his face scrunched when he concentrated with great focus in order to light the flame. It was very charming to me.

Once the blaze was high enough, he sat across from me with the fire between us, keeping us warm from the chill of the night.

"Have you lived here at Seriphos your entire life?" I found myself striking up the conversation.

"Pretty much. My mother and I arrived here for the first time, when I was an infant."

"Oh? And where did you come from before then?" I was curious to know.

"I'm not sure."

"Your mother doesn't know?"

"It's difficult to talk about," Perseus revealed to me.

"I don't mind. I'm a good listener," I shared.

Perseus chuckled at my comment.

"I'm serious. I've spent my whole life listening to tales, stories, and lessons told by the Graeae and my parents. They have lived far longer than I could ever imagine, being immortals."

Perseus's expression changed and he became stern. I feared that he was actually taking pity on me. "I'm sorry. I didn't realize…"

I shook my head and interrupted him. "There's no need to be sorry. You've done nothing to apologize for."

We sat in awkward silence again, both of us just gazing into the mesmerizing fire before us. I found myself sneaking glances beyond the fire, over at him. The complexion on his face was glowing with the embers. His hair was finer than the thread on the spindle of the Fates. I realized that I had been staring at him for far too long once he peered up from the fire and made eye contact with me. I quickly searched elsewhere, ashamed that he had caught me watching him.

He must have sensed my uneasiness, for he made a proposal. "Care to go for a swim?"

"In the middle of the night?" I asked.

"Of course! Why wouldn't we?"

"Is it safe?" I was somewhat worried about the idea.

Perseus laughed. "Under normal circumstances, it may not be, but you're the son of a sea god. What's the worst that could happen?"

I shrugged and had no argument to the accurate point he made.

Perseus stood up, flicking off his sandals and then

stripped his tunic off, throwing it down into the sand by the fire. He was all flesh. I managed to get several glimpses of his perfectly sculpted body before he darted directly into the water. I took off my clothes as well and followed behind him into the sea.

Surprisingly, it was not as dark out here as I had anticipated. The moon was nearly full in the night sky. It cast a decent amount of light down upon us. A blessing from Artemis herself.

We went out as far as the water rose up to our necks.

Perseus then pressed his hands forward, creating a large wave of water striking my face. He began giggling at how caught off-guard I was by this. I realized he was playing a joke on me. The kind of joke Euryale and I would have with one another. It provided me comfort in having this light-hearted moment with him, reminding me of my sister. I retaliated and threw water back at him. He then returned the favor in what then turned into a frenzy of splashing each other. Once we were both fully soaked, we cackled out loud. I eventually was the one to have to give up and surrender. After all, I was no match for the strong waves and quick splashes he sent my way with his formidable vitality.

"Okay! You win! I give up!" I relinquished.

We swam back to the shore and sat in front of the fire with our backs to it, allowing the heat to dry us off. Side by side, we surveyed out beyond the sea and into the glimmers of the night sky. I pointed to a few of the blinking objects above us that seemed like they were thousands of miles away.

"*Katasterismoi,*" I stated.

"What is that?" Perseus inquired.

"In one of my lessons with the Graeae, they informed me that on the surface, in the darkness, you can make out small traces of light in the sky. These lights are organized by Artemis and are shaped to tell heroic stories of the past. The gods refer to these lights as *Katasterismoi,*" I elaborated.

We both sat reticent, just appreciating this natural mosaic above us. I didn't want this moment to end. I had made a new friend. Well, in reality, Perseus was my first and only friend. Everyone else I knew was a member of my family, with the exception of Athena. Nevertheless, I relished this experience right now. I wanted to make my feelings known to Perseus.

"This is the first time I've ever seen the night sky in its full artistry. I know you see it all the time, but I've only ever heard stories about it for the past seventeen years of my life. I'm glad to be able to share this experience with you. You have been nothing but generous since I arrived here this morning. Thank you, Perseus, for your patience and for taking me under your wing."

Perseus's face lit up, dare I say as bright as the current scene above us?

"Remember earlier, when I mentioned that not much goes on, on this island? And when my mother told you that it's not very exciting here?" he asked me.

"Yes. I recall."

"Well, I'll be honest, your arrival has made it exciting for me. Everyone around here is dull, stuck to traditions and their daily duties. You, on the other hand… you have this exhilarating aura about you. You're a breath of fresh air. So, thank you too, Meduso, for bringing life to me."

I wasn't exactly sure what Perseus meant by this, but I was able to comprehend that he was appreciative of me as well. And that, I could accept, and be jubilant over his expressed feelings. "You have my trust, my loyalty, and my friendship," I shared.

"Likewise," he replied.

We remained silent for a bit longer until the fire was starting to die out.

"We have an early itinerary tomorrow. Dictys is usually ready to head out to sea just before the sunrise. We should head back and get some rest," Perseus suggested.

"Yes. Let's head back."

No! I didn't want to leave.

But I knew expressing those true feelings was inappropriate. So, I would agree with Perseus and return to his home to go to sleep.

We both wrapped our tunics back around us, slid into our sandals and headed back up the trail to Perseus's home, which looked identical to his mother's. He led me into a room beyond the main area, which I assumed was his bedroom. There was a bed that he laid in and then one in the opposite corner of the room that I flopped down on.

"Goodnight, Meduso."

"Goodnight, Perseus."

It was difficult for me to even attempt to fall asleep. I stared at the ceiling that was unfamiliar to me, studying the patterns in them. The small cracks, the differences in shades in certain spots, and the shapes of the different stones embedded within it. Being able to familiarize myself in a new setting put me at ease and would eventually allow me to fall asleep effortlessly.

Despite this, it took me another hour or so to eventually reach slumber. I then realized why that was the case. Being so close to Perseus for most of the day, I grew accustomed to his presence and warmth by my side. With him being across the room, there was a distance between us I was not used to. A coldness, or chill of sorts, progressed through all areas of my body. Now, having known the feeling of having Perseus near me and touching me, I didn't want that feeling to subside.

Chapter 4

The rays of the sun creeping into the window disrupted my sleep, causing me to rise out of bed the following morning. My eyes darted directly over to Perseus's bed, only to find that he was no longer there. I rose up, drawing my tunic around my body, and headed to the main room of his home. There he stood, lifting a large boulder up and down. I'd never seen anything like it. I couldn't understand where this strength of his came from.

"Just stretching out for the day," he explained. "Did you sleep well?"

I nodded. "Yes. Thank you for asking."

Wrong. This was a complete lie.

I slept terribly last night. It was the first time I had spent the night anywhere that wasn't my bedroom in the palace. Not only this, but I felt odd about Perseus being across the room from me. I was so used to him being by my side all day yesterday that I became a little displeased when the moment arrived where he was unable to sleep beside me. However, I felt it would be an impertinence to reveal this to him. I feared he would become more stand-offish if I admitted my newfound dependence on him.

"Good. You'll need all the rested energy you have to handle fishing with Dictys and me."

"I'm looking forward to it," I confessed.

Perseus carried the boulder to the far corner of the room and dropped it down there before rubbing his palms together to remove the dust from them.

"You ready to head out?" he asked me.

I nodded.

We hiked down to the beach where we met Dictys, who was placing fishing equipment onto his boat. "Ahhh. Good morning, boys! Perseus, would you mind grabbing those crates for me?"

Perseus lifted the heavy wooden bins full of wire and netting and placed them into the stern of the boat.

"Perfect. That should do it!" Dictys stated.

We all stepped into the boat. Dictys handed me a wooden oar. "Watch Perseus and me, Meduso. Then follow our lead to match our strokes."

The two began moving their paddles in a circular motion in the water, which allowed the boat to propel further into the sea. Their intensity picked up, providing great momentum. I then studied their movements and then copied them with my own oar. Dictys and Perseus looked back at me to see that I was able to keep up with them.

Dictys commended me. "Not too bad for a first-timer!"

It wasn't all that difficult. Despite me not being as muscular and fit as Perseus, I was still fairly strong compared to most other mortals. After all, my parents were both gods, and therefore I had acquired at least some of their physical capabilities.

I finally turned my head around to see how far we rowed out from the island, which was now a small speck in the far distance.

"Alright, we settle here," Dictys declared.

I withdrew my paddle from the water and laid it down in the boat. The sweat was profusely dripping from my head. I used my forearm to wipe it off. Perseus watched me do this and simply smiled. He didn't even break a sweat, which was honestly somewhat irritating to me, but I smirked back at him.

Perseus began wrapping string around some of the large wooden poles, while Dictys lectured me. "The first type of way we fish is what I call *angling*. See this pole Perseus is using?"

"Yes," I confirmed.

"You weave the string through the holes like this. Then the pole now becomes your base, and we lower the tight string into the water. But there's a catch. The fish won't be drawn to the string unless there is something there to attract them." Dictys reached for a small, slippery creature out of the dirt in an aluminum pail. He knotted the insect on a metal hook attached to the string. "The fish will want to bite this as food and then…"

"They get caught on the hook." I finished his sentence for him.

"Precisely!" Dictys exclaimed.

"You have to lie and deceive the fish in order to catch them?" I asked.

Perseus turned around, snickering at my comment.

"Yes, Meduso. It's okay for us to deceive the fish. They are a gift from Poseidon. He has given all of us permission to treat the fish in this way," Perseus explained to me.

At the mention of Poseidon, Perseus became a blur to me. My surroundings were disappearing and my mind was taking me elsewhere. *I was on a beach somewhere. I couldn't quite tell exactly where. The water was a more marine blue on this shore I was now at. Looking out into the ocean, a large man was emerging from the water. He was a well-built, gorgeous, and an attractive human. His chest was exposed and bare. I found myself striding towards the man into the water, placing my hands against the thick, curved muscles of his chest, almost in a passionate stance.*

"Meduso! Are you alright!?" Perseus shouted.

I came out of the trance shaking my head. I was back here in the boat again, far out in the Aegean Sea.

"Yes. I'm fine," I replied.

"Your eyes. They turned completely silver!" Perseus explained.

This must have been another one of my visions that the Fates had given me. What could it mean?

"Yes. It happens once in a while. It's nothing to worry about," I stated, trying to alleviate any worry he may have had.

"Are you sure?" Perseus raised his brow.

"I'm sure. Let's continue with the lesson." I stirred them away from the topic and back to fishing.

As Dictys continued to provide me with details on the

migration patterns of different types of fish and strategies for the optimal ways to catch each of them, I was only half-listening. My mind was still completely distracted by the vision I had just seen.

Where and when did this scene take place?

Who was the man coming forth from the sea?

Why did I place my hands on him in what seemed to be a loving and passionate gesture?

The man wasn't Perseus...

I then frowned at the last thought. I became ashamed at the idea of having my hands pressed against another man in what seemed like an impure way. A flood of emotions and past reminders of my parents overcame me. I recalled what they had informed my sisters and me of on multiple occasions. *You must stay pure if you are to serve Athena.*

There were still so many questions swarming in my head that would have to go unanswered for now. I forced myself to glare over the edge of the boat into the serene, brilliant blue water. I closed my eyes, reminding myself of my surroundings, protected by the Aegean Sea. My mind became cleansed once more and I diverted my attention back to Dictys and Perseus.

"Now that we've gone over the basic concepts of angling, let's discuss netting," Dictys went on. "Perseus, why don't you take over from here?"

"Sure! So, Meduso, netting is a skill we use when we are in need of abundant fish. A net should be arranged in the following way." Perseus held the net high in the air, fully spread. "Make sure there are absolutely no tangles or knots before you toss it overboard."

He then threw it out into the sea, and I watched the net sink beneath the surface of the water. "Now we just sit and wait for several minutes. Then we pull it back up to see what we've captured. If the gods are watching us in the moment, they will bless us with a great deal of fish!"

And so, the three of us sat in the boat, patiently waiting and hoping for Poseidon's deliverance.

"Dictys, I would love to hear about you and your brother, King Polydectes, and how he became the ruler of Seriphos," I expressed with interest.

The old man gave a heavy sigh. "Very well. I will tell you my story. There was once a King of Magnesia in Thessalia, named Magnes. He was a tyrant of sorts and acted as most kings of our time do. Beyond his wife, he was fond of many nymphs, specifically the Naiads who originated in Seriphos. As it turned out, this king became extremely enamored with a particular nymph who became his mistress. She gave birth to two young males, with Magnes serving as their father. A scandal this would truly be, if anyone in the kingdom of Magnesia had learned of Magnes's betrayal and his laying with a common Naiad nymph."

Perseus and I sat intently listening as Dictys continued on.

"Because of this, he separated himself and all emotional ties to the nymph and his two sons. He banished them from Magnesia. The boys' nymph mother was forced to raise her children on her own. As a result, she migrated back to her home on the island of Seriphos. The boys grew up being the only males on the island. The eldest of the brothers was crowned King of Seriphos with the blessings of the nymphs and the gods. His younger brother was offered to serve alongside the king as a member of his counsel. However, he had no desire to serve with the king. The boy grew fond of the beaches of Seriphos and the Aegean Sea. He wanted to live among the townsfolk and so the king allowed this path for his brother and let him grow to become a skilled fisherman and a loyal servant of the sea."

"And...?" I began, expecting a little more to the tale.

"And, that's it. That is my story," Dictys stated. "Some people have long stories and some have short ones. Mine is rather short. But you two... your stories have only just begun. Will they end up being long or short? Only time will tell, but you both have the power to craft it."

Perseus and I glanced at one another as Dictys mentioned this, trying to imagine our own stories and what would unfold in the future to further develop them.

I still had no idea about Perseus's past. Yes, he told me he and his mother arrived at the island of Seriphos when he was a baby, but he failed to tell me where they came from prior to arriving here. Plus, there was the awkward moment last night when Danaë was about to reveal the details of Perseus's father, to which Perseus interrupted her before she could even share that information. What did he have to hide?

I would need to find the right time to inquire about it. But right now, out here on the sea with Dictys was probably not the most ideal of circumstances to ask him.

Perseus shot up from his seat. "Let's take a look to see what we got." He pulled the net up. Low and behold, there were at least twenty fish trapped within the confines of the net.

"Well, what do you know!? And on the first grab of the day!?" Dictys cried out. "This is indeed a blessing from Poseidon! And I have a feeling it has something to do with our new-comer here!"

I grinned at Dictys's remark but doubted this was the case.

"I'm not so sure about that." I stated with cynicism.

"Keep him by your side, Perseus. He's a good luck charm!" Dictys further stated.

Now I was completely blushing. The thought of someone sharing the idea of Perseus being with me at all times was enough to leave me sheepish.

But what stunned me even more was Perseus's response to Dictys.

"I don't plan on letting him go anytime soon."

After our fishing excursion came to an end, we arrived back on the shore. Dictys lined the fish and carried them over his back. "Why don't you boys come over for dinner later? And invite your mother, Perseus. We have plenty of fish to go around."

"I will do that," Perseus confirmed.

"Alright. You boys have fun. Don't get into any trouble!"

"No promises there, Dictys!" Perseus jokingly stated.

The old man roared with laughter, before heading into town, leaving Perseus and me to ourselves.

"Alright. It's your turn," Perseus announced.

"My turn for what?"

"To teach me something. Come on. I know there must be some neat trick or skill you learned deep in the ocean that none of us mortals know of."

I smiled at him, and then came up with an idea.

"Is there a lake or small body of water on the island anywhere?" I asked.

He nodded. "Yes. There is a spring closer to the opposite end of the island from us. The Naiad nymphs were said to have presided over it."

"Perfect! Will you show it to me?"

"Of course. Just follow me."

Perseus and I trekked around the island to the spring. He recommended we take the long way around and walk the sands of the beaches to get there, rather than cut through the forests. Now that we were alone, I felt now was a good a time as ever to press him about his past.

"So, when are you going to fill me in?" I asked him.

"Fill you in on what?"

"You, and everything there is to know about you. Don't think I didn't pick up on the conversation we had with your mother last night when you stopped her from sharing the whereabouts of your father."

"Fine. I don't usually discuss this story with anyone, so do you promise it will remain strictly between us?" he requested.

"Of course, Perseus. I told you this last night. You have my trust and my loyalty. Forever," I stated, to pacify any fear he may have had.

"Okay. Well, only my mother, Dictys, and now, you will know. My mother is the daughter of the King of Argos," he shared.

Argos. I recalled the city on several map scrolls I studied. It was west of Athens. A city with a long line of succession of kings throughout history.

"The King of Argos, Acrisius, was disappointed in having his first-born as a female, who happened to be my mother. He grew impatient with not having a son. So, he sought guidance. Like many kings, my grandfather had the chance to gain counsel from the Oracle at Delphi. He was expecting to hear promising news about getting a male heir to his throne. However, what he instead received was a warning. The Oracle informed him of a prophecy. That he would eventually be killed by his only daughter's son. Me!" he revealed.

I stopped in my steps, very aghast by what he had just told me. "The prophecy states that you will kill your grandfather?"

He nodded. "So I've been told."

I cringed as he confirmed this. I couldn't picture Perseus killing another human being. I shuttered at the thought of it. He was too compassionate of a person to ever murder another mortal. I didn't want to even picture the idea, nor think that he was even capable of such an atrocity. I refused to let this prophecy taint any of my feelings towards him.

Perseus continued with his narration. "Now in fear for his life, King Acrisius became menacingly obsessed with the idea of his daughter giving birth to a son that would be his death-bringer. Therefore, he refused to allow my mother to ever socialize or meet another man to be able to have a child. He locked her up for years, imprisoning her in one of his castle's chambers."

"How cruel!" I asserted.

"Well, unfortunately for my grandfather, even he couldn't disrupt the fulfillment of a prophecy from the Oracle. You see, the King was foolish enough to not fully enclose her room. There was no ceiling, and thus the sky was visible and open to her. While my mother was trapped and isolated, a mysterious rainstorm came in from above. But it wasn't just your typical rain. No. These were showers of golden rain."

"Showers of gold?" I gave Perseus a quizzical look.

"Yes. The drops of rain were of the purest gold, my mother told me. The rain then took shape in the form of a god who kept her company and often visited her when no one was watching. Eventually, she became pregnant from that god. Needless to say, King Acrisius was dumbfounded at how my mother was able to bear a child. She recited the story of the golden rain and admitted a god had frequently spent time with her, but my grandfather could not bring himself to believe her. My mother was petrified that her own father would kill her and the child she was carrying. However, King Acrisius would never be ludicrous enough to murder her."

"And why not?" I asked.

"Because that would only anger the gods by the off chance that my mother was not lying to him. And he did not want to face their wrath. So, he did the only thing he could think of. Hide and send her off, never to be seen or heard from again. He placed us in a wooden chest and tossed it into the sea. We drifted for what my mother said seemed like days until the chest washed up on the shore of Seriphos. Dictys was the one that discovered it. He was shocked when he opened it to find my mother holding me, as a baby, in her arms. She was weak and malnourished, barely holding on to life. Dictys and Clymene took care of us, nursing my mother back to health and raising me."

"I... I don't know what to say, Perseus. I'm sorry that happened to you. King Acrisius should be punished for such an action. Did anything happen to him?"

He shook his head. "Not that I'm aware of. He is still the ruler of Argos."

"Do you ever think of going back and confronting him?"

"I don't think I would be able to. His warriors would most likely kill me on the spot. Plus, I don't think he knows my mother and me are alive and well. It would not surprise me if he still thought we were drifting at sea or that the chest had sunken and we were at the bottom of the ocean. It's best for us to lay low for our own safety and for the safety of the people on this island."

"Well, I'm sorry that happened to you. And your poor mother. To be treated in such a way by her own father. But at some point, you will have to return to Argos, Perseus. You are the rightful heir to the throne, no?"

He let out a deep heavy sigh. "I'm not sure. I can't picture leaving Seriphos now that I'm here," he confessed. "It's my home. The people here, my mother, and Dictys. I don't think I would be able to leave them all behind."

"I understand. But you would make an amazing king, with your compassion, kindness, and amazing strength and skills." As I said this, I was reminded of the portion of the story where Perseus mentioned that it was a god who came into his mother's chamber and eventually became his father.

"I appreciate you thinking so highly of me, my friend," Perseus stated.

We continued to walk along the beach, before I posed the inevitable question to him.

"Perseus, you mentioned that your mother was visited by a god who took the form of the shower of gold. That god was your father. Who was the god?"

He paused and stood silent in the sand, staring at the ground. He seemed disheartened or even ashamed.

"You can tell me, Perseus. You can trust me," I reassured him.

His gaze shifted up to me, yet he still maintained the nervous expression on his face.

"Zeus... my father is Zeus, king of the gods."

Everything was finally starting to make sense to me. Perseus's strength, agility, and skills were above that of any human. No human could even come close to doing the things he did. The reason behind that was because Perseus wasn't actually a human. He was a demi-god.

When Perseus revealed this to me, I was stunned. It led me to believe that the vision of the Fates did specifically lead me to Perseus and not the island of Seriphos itself. I was destined to meet him. And who was I to go against destiny? I couldn't deny it. I was overjoyed by the thought. The more I got to know Perseus, the more I found myself drawn to him, not wanting to separate.

Once we were close to our destination, we moved inward from the beach and into the forest. Perseus pushed through some bushes and several shrubs, eventually leading us to a quaint spring in the middle of the woods. I circled the spring, analyzing the various flowers around it, on the hunt for a specific one.

"What brings us here?" Perseus inquired with mystery.

"There is something my mother, Ceto, taught me on our way back from our visit with Athena. There is a flower known as... Ah, here it is!" I exclaimed. "Come over here, Perseus. Watch!"

He knelt down on the ground beside me.

"See these?" I cupped my hands around the bottom of the vibrant red flowers that were already blossomed. "These are anemone. Do you know how these flowers came to life?"

"No. How did they?" he asked.

"Aphrodite, Goddess of beauty and love, once had a lover named Adonis, who tragically died. She wept for him for days, high up on Mount Olympus. Her tears fell from the sky and spread across all parts of the world. When her tears met the ground, they sprung into this flower, known as anemone. They have ever since been sacred."

"Oh? And what can these flowers do?" he inquired.

"My mother taught my sisters and me a harmless spell." I closed my eyes, still holding the flower in my hand. Suddenly, the crimson flower began to shrink back into a budded state. Feeling the petals wrap together to close around one another, I then opened my eyes and tilted my head up to watch the sky. Soon enough, it began to rain.

Perseus covered his head with his arms and hands, feeling the drops of water strike him. "How!? How did you…!?"

"Wait. I'm not done yet." I stepped over to the spring and dipped my hands into the water, once again closing my eyes. Every drop of rain I had called forth that touched the surface of the spring then transformed into asters. Hundreds of the star-shaped wild flowers of various colors of white, pink, yellow, and purple scattered, covering the entire spring, so that no water was visible. It looked as if it had morphed into a colorful field.

Perseus reached his hand to feel the asters, not being able to believe that they were actually real. "This is beautiful, Meduso! I've never seen anything like this."

I smiled, pleased that he was impressed with the one magical skill my mother had taught me. She was an ocean goddess, so she had many unique powers and skills related to the waters. This was one she was actually able to teach me when we were on the surface for a short time. Even being a mortal, the blood of the sea gods still coursed through my veins, so I did possess some occult abilities, but very few. This was one of them.

I sat on the ground, staring into the lake garden with the peaceful flowers slowly drifting around it, admiring their elegance and delicacy. Perseus proceed to do the same, right next to him.

"Speaking of Aphrodite, I've heard that Aphrodite is the goddess of love. Do you think she is the one who causes people to fall in love?" I asked.

Perseus nodded. "Yes. She and her son, Eros, are said to strike arrows at mortals. These arrows have the power to make two people fall in love."

"So, that must mean they have yet to strike us if the both of us have never been in love yet?"

Perseus could not help but smirk. "It would seem that way."

Thoughts of love continued to permeate through my mind. "Have you ever loved someone?" I asked.

Perseus scratched the back of his head, his face slightly blushing by the question. "No. I haven't really."

"Well then, how would you know if you love someone if you've never experienced it before?"

"I'm not quite sure," Perseus revealed. "Based on stories I've heard and from the experience of others, you get this feeling in your stomach that just won't go away. It's like whenever you're around a person you love, your mind just races with wild thoughts about them, and then when you're not around them, all you can do is think about them."

I took in Perseus's words carefully. Everything that Perseus just described to me was sort of how I was feeling about my relationship with him.

Was I in love with Perseus? No. I couldn't be. Friends can't love friends, can they? I sat back and stared at the asters in the lake once more, cherishing the gorgeous display I created. Perseus proceeded to do the same. His hand brushed against my own. Out of natural reaction, we both flinched and moved them away from one another. However, I longed for his touch in this very moment. To be able to feel his skin against mine, with this miraculous scene before us, would be wondrous.

I slyly placed my hand down on the ground between us, just inches away from him. I sensed his hand was slightly moving closer as well. I didn't dare to make eye contact with him, in fear of trepidation ruining the moment.

He, too, continued to be brave with his movements, and instantly I felt the tip of his finger rest on the top of my hand. I merely let it sit there and remained still, just absorbing the spectacle before us and having the closeness of Perseus. It was all I could ask for.

Chapter 5

There was so much excitement in just a single day. I had learned how to fish for the first time, and I had displayed a raining of flowers for Perseus to see. Eventually, he and I travelled back into town and met Dictys and Clymene at their home for dinner. Danaë had joined us, as well.

"I wanted to share the news with you all, now that everyone is gathered. I received a message from my brother, Polydectes," Dictys stated.

"That's *King* Polydectes, dear. Need I remind you of the respect he still demands?" Clymene corrected.

Dictys rolled his eyes. "I am in my own home. I can refer to him however I so well please!"

"Yes, but it's good practice to..." Clymene began, but her thoughts were put to rest by Dictys.

"Enough!" he shouted, slamming his fist onto the table, which was the most irritated I've seen him since I arrived. "Now, where was I? Oh yes! My brother has announced that in the coming months, Seriphos will host its first set of yearly Island Games!"

"Oh my! Something we can all look forward to," Danaë shared.

"Yes. And if I was a gambling man, I would know exactly who to bet all my riches on in each event." Dictys glanced over at Perseus as he said this.

"What sort of games will be held?" I inquired.

"There will be races, jumping competitions, archery, spear-throwing, discus-throw, wrestling, sparring matches, and more!" Dictys enthusiastically announced. "Perseus, you should start training immediately."

Perseus smirked at the thought and then looked over to me. "What about you, Meduso? Will you participate?"

I shook my head. "I technically don't live on Seriphos, so I don't think that would be fair. But I wouldn't mind helping you train."

"I would welcome your assistance," Perseus affirmed.

Although Perseus was rather calm about this announcement, I knew he was secretly thrilled about the Island Games. Seriphos was too tamed for a demi-god. Perseus needed more exhilaration in his life. These competitions would be just a stepping stone for him. It was only a matter of time before Perseus came to the conclusion that being here on this island was holding him back from the great adventures that awaited him in the surrounding world. I had a hunch it was on the horizon.

"It's only a few months away. You have no time to waste. I suggest you start training first thing tomorrow morning," Dictys advised.

Perseus agreed with him. His training would need to begin as soon as possible. He needed to prepare for as many wins as he could obtain.

"Let's all eat before the fish get cold," Clymene suggested.

And so we feasted on our catches of the day. During

dinner, Dictys offered me some wine. I glanced over at Perseus, who was smirking. I tried it.

"It's not so bad." I began drinking more. By the end of our dinner and visit at Dictys's home, I could start to feel the effects.

Perseus and I returned to his home to retire for the evening. As we laid in our beds, he called out to me from the far corner of the room. "Thank you, Meduso, for agreeing to help me with my training in the coming months."

"Of course, Perseus. It would be my honor."

"I don't think I've felt this way about anything in my life," he explained. "It's as if Hephaestus summoned a fire within me."

"It's a combination of motivation and excitement. You've never had something to really look forward to. Now that you do, you want to be the best at it," I shared.

"You're right. That's exactly what it is. You are so wise."

I laughed. "I would not go that far, but…"

Perseus interrupted me. "I would…"

I tossed and turned for a few hours, still finding it cumbersome to doze off for the night. There was no way I would be able to fall asleep anytime soon, so I quietly got out of bed with the intent of taking a stroll for the night.

However, before I could make it out of the room, I began to hear heavy grunts. I turned back around to see it was coming from Perseus. He must have been having a nightmare. Epiales and Nyx were fully active in their torment over him. Perseus continued to become louder, this time with clear words escaping from him. "It's... okay... hold on... mother... cold... hungry." His body was now convulsing.

I couldn't stand the sight of him distressed, so as an instant reaction, I hopped into his bed and wrapped my arms around him, preventing him from shaking. It was difficult to control him because of his god-like strength, but his rhythm began to slow down. I whispered into his ear. "I'm here, Perseus. You will be fine. Just rest."

He twisted to face me, yet remained sound asleep. His arms wrapped around my side to squeeze me tight. His grip soon relaxed and he held me gently, as I embraced him, too. I ran my fingers through his hair, cherishing this intimacy between us. Perseus rested his head on my chest, and I admired the scene. I couldn't even describe how I felt in this very moment. It was a feeling I had never experienced before. All I knew was that I wanted every night to be like this, with us holding each other as we drifted off into a slumber.

I shut my eyes for a short time to rest, but then was forced to open them upon feeling Perseus's head shift. His bright green eyes were visible, just staring up at me. He didn't flinch nor hesitate, noticing that I was in his bed with him. He accepted it, and from what I suspected, also felt comfortable with me being here. I felt his hands now tracing up and down my body.

"Thank you..." he muttered, when he realized I was awake.

"You're welcome. You were having a nightmare, so I thought..." I trailed off.

"No. It's okay..."

I still sensed somewhat of an awkward tension, so I thought it was in my best interest to return to my bed. However, as I even slightly moved to separate myself from him, he pulled me back down into the bed.

"Wait... Don't go. Can you please stay with me for the night? I feel that I can sleep at ease with you here. Your presence is appeasing," he explained.

I nodded. I hoped he would reach this conclusion. I was delighted by the request. "Yes, Perseus. I won't leave your side."

We laid still for the remainder of the night, in each other's arms. For the first time since being home at the palace, I was able to peacefully fall asleep. And from here on out, it would be tranquil, because I planned on laying with Perseus every night, so long as he would have me.

We both woke up the following morning with smiles on our faces. I knew we would need to rise and start his training right away, yet I had no desire to release myself from our embrace with one another. However, I eventually gave in to the inevitable and got up out of the bed. He, too, followed in pursuit.

"What do you want to start off with first?" I asked.

He rummaged through his belongings in the main room, pulling out a bow and a few arrows. That easily answered my question, but he made the obvious known to me. "Let's practice with archery."

We headed down to the beach with a few other tools at our disposal. Perseus headed into the forest to chop off a stump from one of the already dead trees, making quick work of it. Together, we sat on the ground, carving it into a perfect circle.

As I rolled the handmade target back towards the beach, Perseus sprinted by me, having already chopped another piece of wood, creating a stand for the target to sit on.

Show off!

"Now don't judge me. It's been several years since I last used a bow and arrow," Perseus admitted.

"I'm not here to judge. Just here for the support." It was true. There wasn't much I was able to help with here, besides running toward the target to retrieve his shot arrows once he released them.

I stood further down the beach, able to make out the tiny dot that was Perseus holding his bow, ready to release the arrow. The arrow dashed in the air and struck the target dead on, right in the center.

Unbelievable! Then back to back, two more shots were

fired and again, they were right on the mark. I encouraged Perseus to back up even further, but no matter how far the distance he put between him and the target, it was a flawless shot every single time. Dare I say that he would make a formidable opponent, even for Artemis?

I myself was getting a decent exercise, having to jog back and forth from him to the target and vice versa to return the arrows to him after each firing round. Eventually, I found myself panting, deeply gasping for breath, when I returned to him. "I think you're a sure win for archery. Care to train for a different event?'"

He nodded, much to my relief. I don't think I could go on jogging for much longer without passing out right on the warm sand of the beach.

"Dictys mentioned something about a discus throw last evening, did he not?" Perseus inquired.

"Yes. I recall him mentioning that."

"I'm not sure where we can acquire a discus from," Perseus stated.

"Let's take a break and head back into town. Perhaps Dictys may know of where we can retrieve one at."

Perseus agreed with my recommendation and we hiked up the trail to learn Dictys was not at home. "He went up to the fortress to attend a meeting with his brother. What can I help you boys with?" Clymene asked us.

"Do you know where we can find a discus?" Perseus asked.

"Hmmm. Give me a moment." Clymene left the room. We were able to hear her searching through a few things in the adjacent room. Soon, she returned with a metallic round object. I could not quite tell whether it was made of iron or lead.

"Is this what you're looking for?" she asked.

Perseus took it from her and scrutinized it. "Yes. This is exactly what we need. Thank you, Clymene!"

"Of course. Just watch where you throw that thing! Make sure no one is around you when you do use it," she advised.

"We won't!" Perseus yelled back to her as we were already walking out of the house and making our way back down towards the beach. I've never seen a discus thrown in my entire life, so I was extremely curious to see how the process worked.

"I've only ever seen it done once," he shared. "You stand like this, and hold the discus so it rests against your forearm." Perseus stretched out his arm to illustrate the action he was describing to me. I became distracted with the tightness of his muscles as they contracted while he spun. "Then, you just release it into the air, and off it goes."

This time, Perseus performed the actions all in one sequence, in their full entirety. As he let go of the discus, it traveled far down the beach, except I was expecting him to throw it straight. Instead, the discus curved off and missed the shore of the beach entirely, landing in the nearby woods.

"Clearly, I'll need to practice this event more," he confessed.

I chuckled. It was refreshing to see that Perseus was still part human and made some errors. I would be vexed if he was perfect in everything he did. This gave him something to work on and to improve upon himself with. And with this discus throw, even I was able to offer my insight to help him better his skills at the sport.

Start out with your feet more spread apart.

You released it too soon.

You released it too late.

Try positioning yourself this way when you throw it.

Make sure you're angling it like this.

Follow through with your arm even after you let it go.

Perseus was extremely coachable and adapted to all of my critiques. Yes, there were still times when he completely messed up and the discus went off course, but overall, he was immensely improving at throwing it. I was surprised at how quickly he picked up on the skill.

After a few hundred throws, we decided to call it quits.

"What next?" I asked.

"Let's practice swordsmanship and sparring."

"Do you have swords?"

"Yes. I have two wooden ones at my place I used to play around with when I was a child. We can use those," he replied.

"I'll race you there!" I stated, running ahead of him back into town.

"Really?" Perseus laughed as I suggested this.

It was fairly foolish of me to even think I stood a chance at racing against a demi-god, especially one who was the son of Zeus, but I decided to have fun with him. It wasn't a complete shock when Perseus zoomed right by me. He moved so fast that I felt a gust of wind hit me in the face, blowing my hair back.

When I arrived at his house, he was leaning against the stone wall, holding two wooden sticks in his hand. The way he rested against the wall so confidently was very seductive. I felt my blood rush at the sight of this alluring pose of his.

He tossed me one of the wooden swords, and I caught it mid-air.

"Have you ever used one of these before?" he inquired.

I shook my head. "No. Can't say I have," I fibbed.

"Alright. I will make sure to go easy on you, since it is your first time."

Little did Perseus know that I had stellar swordsmanship skills. Never have I used a wooden sword before, though. I've only ever used real ones, made of the finest iron and copper. So, technically, I was telling him the truth. I just wasn't so forthcoming with the details around it.

Our form of entertainment was very limited in living in an oceanic palace. Stheno, Euryale, and I pleaded with our father and mother to allow us to have swords and take up the trade. It was our father who favored the idea and was the one who took us in as apprentices, teaching us the art. After many years, my sisters and I would practice on one another. There were multiple occasions where we struck through our bodies, inflicting several bloody wounds. During these occurrences, my mother rushed to our sides, pouring sea water over the torn flesh. The lacerations closed and healed in just a matter of seconds. Our inflicted pain was therefore very fleeting whenever we did go too far.

Perseus led us into an open clearing in the forest. We stood across from each other, on opposite sides.

"Are you ready?" Perseus raised his wooden sword high in the air as he asked this.

"I was born ready!" I winked at him.

"Confident! I love it!" He chortled at what he thought was an over-expectation of my skills.

Perseus ran at me, lunging forward with his sword. I pivoted to the side to dodge the strike. He continued to relentlessly come at me from all different angles, but it was all in vain. I managed to avoid every single attack he attempted.

"Maybe I shouldn't go so easy on you, then." Perseus swung high and I raised my sword to block him. I swiped upward, causing him to retreat. As I did this, he aimed low at my legs with a sweep. I jumped in the air, causing him to stumble to the side.

"And I thought you were a demi-god?" I teased.

This time, I decided to go more on the offense. I pressed my sword forward at his side. He too blocked all of my attempts, until I had one final surprise in store for him. With my quick reflexes, I saw he poked his sword, aiming for my torso. I spun to the side, lifting my wooden sword in the air and slammed it on top of his, which was aimed horizontally. The force was enough to disarm him. His weapon fell to the ground. Perseus bent over to retrieve it, but before his hand could even touch the hilt, I pressed my sword forward, so that the pointed end was directly on his throat.

He had nowhere to go. No more moves to make to counteract me. My focus and seriousness on the spar diminished. I sent a bright smile his way. "It's over!" I announced.

Perseus instantly gripped the sharp end of my wooden sword and pulled it with all his might. Still holding on to it, the force was enough to bring me forward and I fell to the ground on top of him. It completely caught me off-guard. "What was that for!?" I shouted, still confused by his reaction.

He didn't say a word. I felt him grab the back of my head. Perseus pulled me down to him, giving me a deep, passionate kiss. Our lips were locked. I widened my eyes, unable to believe what was happening, but feeling the softness of his lips pressed against mine allowed me to close my eyes and take it in. I kissed him back, tracing the palm of my hand along his warm cheek.

I felt as though jolts and sparks of thunderbolts were traveling directly from his body into mine. I was unable to tell if they really were actual charges going through me or if it was just my imagination. After all, he was the son of Zeus. It could potentially be a possibility.

We rolled on the ground not daring to allow our mouths to separate from each other. Urges burst through me, wanting to feel his skin against mine. I opened my tunic, exposing my full body to him. He followed my action so that I was able to get a glimpse of his beautifully crafted frame. I was now able to fully admire it, in all its glory, unlike the other night, when I only got a quick visual of him naked, before we swam in the sea.

He wrapped his thick arms around me so that the palms of his hands rested on my bare, lower back. I moaned feeling his touch. It prompted me to press my body further into his. Our tongues greeted one another. The carnal heat, emitting from him was tangible. We were chest to chest, with our legs and other lower, now hard, parts of us rubbing against each other.

This was the most gratifying feeling I've ever experienced. I've never felt anything more pleasurable in all my life. And seeing Perseus pull me closer to him and refuse to let me go and separate his lips from mine, I knew he must have had similar feelings. Our rhythm was almost melodic. It continued to intensify, and then the *crescendo* hit me. Pure ambrosia. I rolled over off of him, with my back against the ground, just staring up at the colossal trees and sky above me. My heavy panting waning until my breathing stabilized.

Now that I had experienced this performance, I wanted an encore. Plenty more of this in the near future. Sure enough, I didn't have to wait much longer. When Perseus and I laid in bed together that night, we kissed again and felt one another's bodies. This time, I allowed him to reach the *crescendo* first, before me. For many months after that, there wasn't a single night that went by where Perseus and I didn't make passionate love.

The day of the Island Games had finally arrived. I sat up in bed that morning, massaging every single one of Perseus's muscles. There was not a single surface on his body that went unattended. My bare hands traced up and down the length of his legs. As I got closer to his foot, he flinched.

"That tickles!" he shouted.

"Sorry." I slyly smiled at him. "Are you ready for today?"

He nodded. "I think so. We've been training every day for the past several months. I'm as prepared as I'll ever be."

The events for today were being held on the opposite end of the island from us on the beach closest to King Polydectes's fortress. There was a service held in which the king was led down to the beach in a parade-like fashion. Stands and seats were created so that every resident on the island would be able to attend the event. A tall podium and elevated throne were at the center of it all, where the king would be viewing the games from.

The competitors were all waiting nearby. I sat in the

crowd next to Clymene and Danaë as each athlete was announced and introduced during the opening ceremony. Dictys was seated near his brother, along with many other individuals and dignitaries, with important titles.

Once all the participants were called out, they all stood lined up beside one another with pride, their chests sticking out with triumph, including Perseus. I analyzed his competition, honestly unsure of their skill sets. I had no idea what to anticipate, but I imagined Perseus would be a sure winner in many of the competitions today.

First came the events that required great endurance, including running and swimming. The athletes were required to complete one full lap around the entire island. Us viewers were able to witness the runners at start of the race, but then we sat for some time, waiting to see who would make their way around the final bend and toward the finish line. In only five minutes, Perseus was already spotted sprinting to finish the race. We cheered him on along with the rest of the residents of the island that went wild with excitement at the sight of him.

Even the second and third place runners were fifteen minutes behind him. I glanced over in the direction of King Polydectes, who was now seen whispering to Dictys with a stern expression on his face. For being a king of such a charming and yet what seemed like an under-developed island, he was not very inviting. I was expecting a simple-minded man with a permanent smile on his face, who was generous to everyone. I was not getting this vibe from King Polydectes one bit.

Once all of the athletes were finished the race, there was an hour break so that they could recover before the next event. King Polydectes stepped forward to explain the rules for swimming. The athletes were required to go out to a tiny boat that was far off in the distance, swim around it, and then return to the shore. This, too, turned out to be a waiting game for everyone. Perseus was already out and back on the beach finished, before anyone could fully make it out to the boat yet. They weren't even halfway done.

The audience roared with cheers and claps at seeing his great athleticism. This time, while Perseus was alone at the finish line, waiting for the other competitors to complete the race, I noticed the king step forward and approach him. They were wrapped up in conversation. I was curious to know what exactly he was saying to Perseus. Most likely congratulating him, I assumed.

I scanned the rest of the crowd that was overjoyed, but then I locked my line of vision with a familiar individual directly across from me. I squinted and rubbed my eyes a few times to make sure my sight was not deceiving me. It was Stheno.

The second she recognized me, she stepped out of the crowd and headed away from the beach towards the forest. This was a signal for me to follow her.

I placed my hand gently on Danaë's shoulder. "I will be right back," I informed her.

"Make haste! The next event could be starting at any moment!" she shouted with amusement.

I quickly pushed my way through the crowd until I was able to see the back of Stheno ahead of me. I ran after her until we were in the forest, isolated from everyone else.

She hugged me tightly.

"Meduso! It seems like it's been forever!" This was a side of Stheno I was surprised to witness. She was always so rigid and independent that it was rare to see any sort of emotion from her. This made me truly understand the bond my sisters and I had with one another. Our love and loyalty were much stronger than I even realized.

"Yes. Five months feels like several years," I shared. We stepped back from each other. Stheno had not changed one bit since I last saw her. However, she must have thought differently about me.

"Brother! You look... less youthful. More manly!" She reached forward to grab my bicep and analyzed my legs and chest. "You're not as scrawny as you once were. You're coming into your own," she revealed.

I wasn't sure whether to be insulted or pleased with her remarks. I decided to take it as a compliment, giving her the benefit of the doubt.

"Yes. I've been helping my friend, Perseus, train for these Island Games," I explained.

"Is he the one that's blowing everyone out of the water?" Stheno asked.

I nodded. "That would be him."

We both chuckled at her comment.

"How is Euryale? How are mother and father, and the

Graeae? I miss everyone dearly."

Stheno cracked a smile. "I know. They all miss you as well, even the Graeae. They are all fine. I'll admit, the palace walls are a little less lively without you. But I'm glad to see you are doing well here. You're staying out of trouble, I presume?"

I nodded. Although I had no idea if Perseus's and mine relationship would qualify as *trouble*. When my mother and father explained to me about being pure, they only described it to me in a sense of a male and female committing pleasurable acts. Not once did they reference two men together as being impure. So, I naturally assumed, what Perseus and I have been doing was all right. In any case, I would not be sharing our intimate details. I felt a sense of embarrassment if I were to fill anyone in on that. Plus, I found it rewarding to be able to bottle up those feelings inside. It made the memories all the more special.

"Good! Well, seeing as things are okay here with you, I accomplished what I was sent out here to do. Mother and father will be most pleased when I report back to them."

"It was nice seeing you, Stheno." I leaned in to hug her once more.

"You too, Meduso. Do not forget that you have about another half year left here before you are to return to us. If you choose to finish out the remainder of the year here or explore other places, that is entirely up to you. I don't want to sway you in one direction or the other," she confessed.

I couldn't imagine leaving this island, and Perseus, behind. So, my answer was crystal clear. "I plan on staying here."

"Okay. Well, Euryale will likely be the one to come out and check on you again in a few months. Until then, brother!" With that, she walked further into the forest and out of sight.

I rushed back to the beach to Perseus's mother. "Ah, Meduso! You made it back just in time. They are about to start the discus throw."

I intently watched each of the competitor's attempts. Much to my disbelief, Perseus messed up. His discus went out of bounds, not only during the first round of throwing, but during the second one too. As a result, he was disqualified. It would be the only event of the day that he did not win.

After the Island Games, Perseus was showered with medals, weapons, equipment, and other various rich materials for all of his wins. Danaë, Clymene, and I rushed to congratulate him. Dictys and King Polydectes also approached. The women got down on their knees in the sand, bowing to the king. I repeated their action, out of respect.

"You have quite the strength and skill set," the king shared with Perseus. "I'm surprised Dictys failed to mention your capabilities to me until today... and oh?" Polydectes glanced down at Danaë. "And who is this beautiful creature, I have yet to meet?"

"I am Danaë, your highness. Mother of Perseus."

King Polydectes then scowled at Dictys. "It seems you've been keeping a lot from me, brother. We will discuss more about this later. I have a celebration to attend to. Perseus, you are welcome to join us if you desire. There will be plenty of food and wine, I'm sure the likes of which you are not used to." The king's words were insincere and impudent.

Perseus had the bravery to turn him down. "I appreciate the offer King Polydectes, but I am drained from today. I plan on resting for the remainder of the night. I will take you up on that at a different date, perhaps."

"That's if a later date and offer comes along again," the King spoke with solemnity. "It was a pleasure to meet you all. And you Danaë... I look forward to the next time we meet." He then turned away to leave us.

"Perseus, are you sure you should decline the king's invitation in such a way?" Danaë asked.

"Yes, mother. I have no desire to attend such an event. We know what goes on at his parties and celebrations," Perseus explained, before looking at me.

"Besides, I was being honest when I said I was tired. The only thing I am looking forward to is returning home for a nice, extended nap." He subtly winked at me as he shared this, making sure none of the others caught onto him as he did so.

But before Perseus would be able to get that long nap he was determined to get, he would first need to be rewarded by me. When we would get into bed, I would have all intention of letting him know how proud I was of him for his victories.

Chapter 6

The months passed, but every day was a moment of bliss. Perseus and I were completely enamored with one another. Our days together were nothing but peaceful with catching fish, taking long strolls on the beach, and sitting outside, while gazing at the stars, and sharing tales of gods and heroes. We knew it was only a matter of time before we would need to part ways with one another. In the final month leading up to my departure, each day felt like a dagger getting dug deeper and deeper into my heart.

A few nights before I was set to leave, Dictys came up with the idea of hosting a feast in my honor. He, Clymene, and Danaë all prepped for the event, while Perseus kept me company that afternoon. When the two of us entered Dictys' home, we were shocked by the amount of food that was being served at the table. It was more sea bass, grouper, and shelled fish than any other dinner we've had together. There were ceramic bowls filled with a variety of nuts and berries that could be found on all corners of the island and tons of freshly picked fruits and vegetables scattered across the table.

"Dictys, you shouldn't have," I stated, feeling as though all of this was too much of an imposition.

The old man stepped towards me, patting my back. "Nonsense. You've been such a pleasure to have around.

This is the least we could do."

Danaë then came forward, wrapping her arms around me. "I'm going to miss you, dear. You've brought such joy into our homes. I know my son is not going to know what to do with himself when you…"

Perseus's face turned blood red before piping up to interrupt his mother. "Mother! I think Meduso gets the point."

Danaë turned around to face her son, giving him a wink, before Perseus shifted the conversation completely. "Anyway, I'm sure Meduso's starving. At least I am. Why don't we all sit down and get started?"

Everyone nodded and took their seats at the table, passing around each dish of food to plate themselves. I could not help but feel so lucky at this moment. This was a scene I would cherish for the rest of my life. A nice family dinner of sorts, one that I never had the chance to experience before, even with my real family in the palace. It would be one of the many things on Seriphos that I would miss.

"You won't be serving Athena for your entire life, will you?" Perseus asked with a melancholy tone.

"I'm not sure. I imagine it will be for quite a long time. And I have no clue as to whether or not I will have the opportunity to visit home or anywhere else for that matter. If I am given the chance, I would like to come back here to Seriphos to see you," I revealed.

"Promise me that you won't forget me, Meduso. It's going to be so hard to go back to the way things once were. Before you stumbled into my life, I found it difficult to find purpose and much to look forward to."

I lunged forward into his arms, letting him wrap them around me. "Don't say such things. We'll see each other again. The Fates would not have led me here to you, only to pull me apart from you for eternity. They would not do something so cruel without reason. Just remember that. There was a reason that destiny brought us together. We haven't finished *our story* together yet."

"Yes. And we still have one more day together. I don't want to ever leave your side from now until the end," Perseus confessed.

"Good. Because I wouldn't want you to." I lifted my head up to plant a long, lingering kiss on his lips. I couldn't fathom returning back to a life without Perseus's company. Without his touch, his laughs, his kisses. Now that I had experienced this, I never wanted it to end.

We discussed making a bold move in preventing me from returning to my oceanic palace and to Athena's temple. However, we knew that such an action would be a death sentence. Defying the gods in such a way would only end horribly for us. And that was not an option that should even be considered.

"Is there anything special you want to do for your final day here?" he inquired.

"Yes. I want to spend the night on the beach. It's something I've always wanted to do. Fall asleep under the glimmering night sky while listening to the crashing of the tides on the shore. What do you think?"

He nodded. "That can easily be arranged."

And Perseus stuck to his word. We laid in the sand, holding each other's hands, just staring up at the tiny lights.

"Why do you think that Fates led me here?" I asked him. "What is to become of us?"

"They must have known we would fall in *love*," Perseus said as a matter of fact.

Love. It was the first time he ever used that word with me. But it was true. There was no other word I could use to describe these feelings we shared with one another. So, this is what true love felt like.

Knowing I would die for him.

Being apart from him depressed me.

His touch on my skin sending chills up my spine.

Just the mere sight of him putting a smile on my face, for no reason at all.

The passion, the physical attraction, the sex.

All of these feelings were ones of *love*. I could finally admit it to him too, and to myself.

"I love you, Perseus. You have to know that…"

His attention to the sky was now distracted. He tilted his head towards me and gripped the back of my head, pulling me into him to greet my mouth with his. "I do know that, Meduso. I love you too." He then reached his hand under my tunic, rubbing his fingers from my chest down to my thighs.

"Out in the open like this!?" I asked, worriedly.

A smirk lit up on his face. "Why not?"

"What if Artemis or any other god is watching?"

"I doubt they are focused on us right now, Meduso." His hands teased me as he said this. "I want to pleasure you here and now, with this dazzling scene before us."

And now, in this moment, I wanted him. All of him. And he did not disappoint.

"Ahem!"

I woke up on the beach, hearing a loud cough and grunt above me. Upon opening my eyes, I saw Euryale hovering over me. I shot right up, surprised to see my sister here so early. Me being startled was enough to wake Perseus up from his slumber, too.

"Meduso, it's time to go," Euryale shared.

"But I thought I would get until the afternoon to say my goodbyes."

"I'm sorry. We are in a bit of a rush and I would not want to disobey father," she explained. "Say goodbye to your... *friend*, and we will be on our way."

"Could you give us a moment?" I requested.

"Yes. I'll just take a quick walk down this lovely beach. But when I return, we must go," she insisted.

I nodded in agreement and off Euryale went, leaving Perseus and me alone. I grabbed his hands, pressing Perseus's palms against my cheeks before a tear traced down them. "I'm sorry I can't stay longer."

Perseus sighed, trying to hold back tears. "We knew this day would eventually come. I just wish it wasn't this soon."

"I know. I feel the same way. But again, just hold on to that promise we made to each other. Who knows, the Fates may lead us back together sooner than years from now. It could be only months, weeks, maybe even days until I see you again."

Truthfully, this was merely a false hope I held on to. Deep down, I had a sinking feeling it would be many years from now before I would get the chance to see Perseus again. My worst fear was that the Fates led me to the Island of Seriphos for an alternative reason and not for Perseus. In this case, it would likely mean that I would never be able to see him again.

No, that could not be an option. I was foolish to even think such terrible thoughts. I would make sure I visited Perseus somehow, in some way or another.

Perseus lowered his chin so that his forehead pressed against mine. We still caressed each other's cheeks. "Whether it is days, weeks, months, or years, I promise to find my way back to you." Perseus's arms traveled to wrap around my back, squeezing me tightly, as if he never wanted to let go.

I closed my eyes, trying to engrave this moment in my

memory for a lifetime. I never wanted to forget Perseus's closeness, his touch, his warmth. His lips met mine again for one final kiss. "I love you, Meduso." This time, Perseus was incapable of preventing his tears from immersing.

"I love you too, Perseus."

Our embrace was soon interrupted. Euryale returned from her stroll along the beach. "Alright, Meduso. It's time."

I let out the heaviest sigh of my life, slowly forcing myself to release my arms from Perseus, stepping away from him. Euryale held my hand and we moved into the water together, up to our knees. I looked back at Perseus one last time, trying to muster up a smile on my face, when, in reality, I was completely disheartened.

Euryale grabbed my other hand once we were facing each other, shutting our eyes. When we opened them, we were back home again, on the ledge of the crystal, apatite grotto, overseeing the pool below. Ceto slid over to us. "Welcome home, my Meduso! I'm sure you have been dearly home-sick since you left!"

My mother hit the nail on the head. I really was home-sick, but not for our underwater palace. I was already home-sick over the Island of Seriphos, and it had only been seconds since I was just there.

Once again, I found myself cooped up in the palace with limited freedom to access the outside world. Only this time, the next few months were even worse because I was forced to listen to the Graeae for longer than usual in a given day. They taught me of the daily tasks I would need to complete at the temple and the traditions of the high priests and priestesses there. I was informed of all the potential troubles and influences that could fall upon me as a mortal exposed to other mortals in Athens.

"If you should commit any of these atrocities, you will surely be reprimanded by Athena, herself!" Enyo warned.

"Even worse, a mistake you make could jeopardize your sisters and even extend as a punishment to others in your family. Do you understand!?" Deino added.

"Yes… I understand. You've told me countless times," I replied.

"And we will continue to tell you countless times, boy. Until you completely understand the importance…" Pemphredo scolded.

Serving in Athena's temple for the rest of my life was starting to sound like a luxury compared to having to listen to these blown out of proportion lessons from the Graeae that I had to suffer through.

After tolerating them for hours a day, I had very minimal time to relax and do things on my own. It was becoming increasingly difficult to even be able to visit the grotto once a day for me to meditate, but no matter what, I made it a priority to go there even if it was only for just several minutes.

Euryale would sometimes join me. But today, she was a bit of a distraction for my liking, bombarding me with a barrage of questions I was not expecting.

"Tell me about that boy I saw you on the beach with," she demanded.

"There's not much to really say about him. He was just a friend," I lied.

"You're not telling me the truth. I didn't walk the beach and give privacy like I had told you. I hid in the forest nearby and watched you two," Euryale admitted.

My mouth dropped. I could not believe Euryale did that. Sneaking around to spy on me! Well actually, I could believe it... this was Euryale we were talking about. Why would I think otherwise? She was more than capable of doing it. I should have realized this sooner.

"I can't believe you watched us! That was supposed to be a private moment!" I yelled.

"So, do you love him?" she asked. "It's okay if you do, Meduso. It's nothing to be ashamed of. I won't tell anyone if you do."

At first, I hesitated in answering this, but then lightly nodded.

"I'm jealous," my sister confessed. "I've met a few males on the surface that I talked to. Some of them I really liked and I even enjoyed their company. But, every time I would think to kiss or get close to them, all I could hear were the voices of the Graeae and our parents saying, 'you will feel the wrath of the gods!'"

I chuckled at her imitation of Deino. "You met a few

men when you went to the upper world?"

"Yes. Don't forget, I've spent more time up there than you have. "

"I seem to keep forgetting that," I admitted.

"The only thing you have more experience than me with is *love*," Euryale shared.

We then emerged from the water and sat next to each other on the edge of the cliff. The second we let our feet dangle, the grotto around me started to fog up until it was completely blurry. Then, I was taken away to a new place. Was I having another vision?

I was at a beach. I don't remember this beach at all. Wait? Now that I think about it, I have been here before. It was the same one that was in my last vision nearly a year ago. Actually, this whole scene I was experiencing was the same exact one from that previous vision. The large, god-like figure was walking towards me, coming out of the majestic sea. I sprinted towards him. I reached my palms out to feel his burly chest. He was an irresistible and brawny man. His massive hands held me close.

My sister's voice returned me back to my normal self.

"Perseus, was it? Tell me what he's like," she requested.

I shook my head, annoyed that I had this vision again. What were the Fates trying to tell me? That there was another man, besides Perseus, that I could love and be attracted to? I found it hard to believe. No. I actually didn't believe it at all. This must have been some mistake. Surely, the Fates would alter this vision and provide me with a new one. At least this is what I was hoping for. I averted the thought and returned my attention back to Euryale's question about Perseus.

"He is strong. And I don't mean strong in the *human* sense. His strength is that of a god. Well, he is technically a demi-god. A son of Zeus."

Euryale raised her hand to her mouth, shocked by what I had just revealed to her.

"A son of Zeus!? Well, what's he doing on that boring island, then?"

I shook my head. "First off, Seriphos is not boring. It's very calm and quaint. I rather enjoy it. Secondly, Perseus landed on the island when he was a baby. His grandfather..." I filled Euryale in on the story Perseus had shared with me about King Acrisius imprisoning his mother because of the Oracle at Delphi's prophecy. I mentioned the part of Zeus disguised as a shower of gold to enter Danaë's chamber, and the King shipping them off in a chest into the Aegean Sea, hoping the mother and son would never be heard from again.

"Wow! That's fascinating!" Euryale exclaimed.

"What's fascinating!?" a voice called out from behind us. I craned my neck to see Stheno was approaching.

I gave Euryale a stern look, hoping she took the hint in not sharing the information I just told her about Perseus. I knew if Stheno was given any secrets, she would run and tell our parents. She always did. Nothing was ever safe with her.

"Ohhh. Ummm... Meduso was just telling me about the unique flowers on the island he was on. Yes! That's it… they were some of the most unusual colors, right, Meduso?" Euryale lied, intending to deceive Stheno.

Poor Euryale. She was a terrible actress and not the best at being able to fib to anyone. However, it was more unbelievable that Stheno bought her act.

"Yes. Islandic flowers are much different from those on the mainlands," Stheno added. "Anyway, father and mother request an audience with us. They are waiting in the throne chamber."

"What for?" I asked.

"Just come!" Stheno commanded.

Euryale and I rose up and trailed behind Stheno, who led us to our parents. The deep ocean sea god and goddess sat tall on their turquoise thrones. The seats were at least three times the size of them. They seemed smaller in appearance when compared to the gargantuan chairs.

"Welcome back, son!" my father greeted me with in his usual low and intimidating tone. "How did the surface treat you?"

I bowed to him as he addressed me, a customary standard I often performed when he was seated at the throne. "Thank you, father. My visit was pleasant. I learned a great deal."

"Good! That is exactly what I expect to hear." Phorcys rubbed his chin as he stated this. "Do you feel you are truly ready to present yourself to Athena?"

I believed I was ready to return back to the upper world. Although, really, I just wanted a change of pace. Anything was better than being isolated here in the palace, having to listen to the Graeae day in and day out.

However, I could not help but continue to think about the vision I recently had, touching another man the way I used to touch Perseus. I still could not comprehend the meaning behind it. I needed to talk to somebody about this and about my relationship with Perseus. Someone who I knew would understand how I was feeling and who also once had love lost. Then it hit me like a fury with a quick whip to the back.

I nodded, shifting my attention back to my father. "Yes. I feel as though I am ready, sir. But there is someone I would like to visit before we depart."

My father gave me a perturbed look. "Who do you need to meet with?"

"Echidna. I would like to see my sister one last time, before we leave. And I would prefer to see her alone."

I assumed my mother and father would put up some resistance at my request to see Echidna, but they obliged without any concern. "I will verify that she is safe to see. You can visit her tomorrow morning before your departure to Athens, if all is well," the sea god stated.

"Thank you, father. I truly appreciate this."

I then bowed to him and my mother one last time.

"Meduso, are you certain you don't want Stheno or Euryale to accompany you?" my mother asked.

"I'm sure. This is something I need to do on my own."

"Very well, son. If you do change your mind, just let one of us know. Euryale and Stheno will be available to travel with you, if you so desire." My mother raised her brow to my sisters, expecting some sort of response out of them.

Both of them nodded. "Yes. Just let us know, Meduso." Euryale smirked at me as she said this.

My father then went on to reiterate the expectations he had set for us when we would head to the temple. It was rather difficult to prevent myself from yawning and dozing off, but I knew any of those actions would anger him, and I feared any sort of punishment he might invoke. If anything, he could change his mind about me visiting Echidna, and that was not something I wanted to toy around with.

I needed a fresh perspective and someone who would understand my dilemma. Echidna had experienced love with Typhon. At least it was some form of love, right? I still had a hard time understanding how she could love that vicious monstrosity, but I need not judge her unfairly. She had lost the love of her life, a situation I had recently been put through as well. Not only did I want to discuss my affair with Perseus, but I had all intention of sharing my new vision with her, too. And that vision led me to believe that I would love another man in the future, something I could not fully wrap my head around.

The following morning, I met my mother in the grotto and she teleported me back to the peak of the Arima mountains. It was the same location I had arrived at with Stheno just a year ago. I smiled, remembering how marvelous the white snow was. I bent down to pick it up in my hands. *The sand of the mountains*, I thought to myself. The diverse features of all the places I've been to have allowed me to grow to appreciate the uniqueness of so many different locations. A beautiful gift the gods bestowed, giving us a variety of scenes across the world.

I was able to remember the various shapes and forms of the ridges in the mountains which allowed me to navigate down the correct slopes to Echidna's cave. Nothing had changed here in the past year. The lit torch at the entrance was still bright and ever scorching. I picked it up and allowed it to light my way. In trekking through the narrow cave, I eventually arrived at the spacious, central room where I had met Echidna previously. This time, however, I didn't have to wait on her for very long, for she was already seated in her violet, suede chair. Her luxurious furniture and decorations did seem out of place for being in this damp cavern.

She sipped on a goblet of wine, before addressing me. "Well, well, well, if it isn't my dear, sweet brother. Finally, out on his own. A canary released from its cage for the first time. Or am I also to expect another one of our family members to arrive shortly behind you?"

I shook my head. "I've come alone, Echidna. I demanded I be by myself."

She had a quizzical expression on her face and rose from her chair, slowly slithering over to me. "Oh? Is that so? I am curious to know what prompted you to go against our parents' judgment and feel the need to see me alone." She traced her long fingernail through my tunic, undoing it, so that my torso was now exposed to her. Echidna then stroked her nail from my belly button, up my chest and to my chin. "There is only one reason why a man would want to visit a goddess on his own…"

Her seduction knew no bounds. Even though I was her brother, I had a suspicion if I tempted her sexually, she would not refuse me.

However, she sorely misread the situation and I was about to enlighten her. "I wanted to talk to you privately. I was at the Island of Seriphos for the past year and I met a man…"

The second I confessed this, a sly smirk appeared on her face. "Ah! I see. Was he strong and muscular, with a face carved by the gods themselves?"

I nodded. "Yes! He is a demi-god. A son of Zeus, himself."

"Oh my. Well, do tell me more, dear brother," she requested. Her fingers were now twirling the golden locks in my hair.

"We fell in love. I laid with him every night during my stay. But now…"

I could tell she sensed the sudden sorrow behind me, for she gripped my shoulder in an endearing manner. "You had to part ways, and are now heartbroken, in fear of never having the chance to see this man again."

I nodded.

"Poor, Meduso. This is one thing the Graeae could never teach you about. Something you had to experience on your own. I know the feeling all too well. Not only will I never get to see my husband again, but I was also forced to give my children up as well. Hydra hides in the marshes of Lerna, Chimera inhabits Lycia, and Cerberus watches over the Underworld, serving Hades."

It slipped my mind that Echidna gave birth to these monsters. All of which I have heard about from tales recited by Deino, Enyo, and Pemphredo.

The Hydra is an enormous serpent of the seas, with nearly ten heads, one of which is immortal. Many Greek warriors fell to the monster. It was believed that once you cut off one head of the draconic snake, two grew in its place.

As for the Chimera, I recalled it had body parts of a goat, lion, and a dragon. She was able to breathe fire, a trait undoubtedly passed down from her father.

Of all Echidna's children, I distinctly remember the story of her lastborn, Cerberus. A gigantic hound with three heads. The watchdog kept surveillance over the Underworld, making sure no one escaped the dark kingdom.

But I never even considered her feelings about this. Echidna was truly all alone. Her monstrous children were no longer by her side and she lost her husband, Typhon, to the realm of Tartarus. She's experienced so much hardship. I couldn't imagine being put through that.

"I'm sorry for your losses, Echidna," I said with

sincerity.

"Do not be sorry, brother. I've learned to cope with the anger and the anguish over the years. I knew what I was getting myself into when I married Typhon. I valued all of the wrong things. Power and greed being the worst sins of all that would undo me. I made my bed, and now I must lie in it," she explained. "But enough about my suffering. You've come here to seek out my advice."

"Yes. I head for Athens after I leave here. I am unsure of how long I am expected to serve Athena and if I will ever be able to see Perseus again," I shared.

"That bitch, Athena, will keep you for life if she had her way!" Echidna replied with rage. "She appears righteous and wise to her patrons, fearless with the greatest of bravery during times of war. But mortals are so blind! They do not see her true sanctimony and arrogance."

Now I was becoming frightened at hearing Echidna's opinion of Pallas Athena. Was she really as selfish and pompous as my sister believed? I've now heard mixed information about her, so I would just have to find out for myself when I met her in person.

"So, you think I will never be able to see Perseus again?" I asked, afraid of her answer.

She shook her head. "I'm honestly not sure, Meduso. But if the Fates provided you with a vision to meet him, then I doubt you've reached the end of your rope with him."

"Well, there's something else I've failed to mention to

you. I've recently had a new vision, twice actually, but it involved a new man," I revealed.

"Oh? Well, do tell!"

"I was on a beach somewhere, where the waters are dark blue, not like at Seriphos. Then I saw a bulky, muscular man emerging from the water. He was huge! I ran out to meet him and placed my hands on his thick chest."

"And...?" she trailed off.

"And that's it, I'm afraid. Nothing more."

"Well, I think that's enough to know that you will love again, Meduso."

"Love again? I don't think I could possibly..."

"Dear brother, take it from me. You are... what? Eighteen years of age?"

I nodded.

"You are still in your youth, Meduso. Your wound is still fresh. Once you're absent from Perseus for a much longer period of time, your wound will heal and close. And soon enough, you will learn to love again. But right now, you are heartbroken. Time is the only ailment to a broken heart," she explained.

She wasn't far off with how I was feeling. I did love Perseus and I couldn't imagine ever falling out of love with him, nor finding love in another person, for that matter. "I'm still not so sure about that, Echidna."

My sister let out a heavy sigh. "Do you really trust this Perseus?"

What a thing to say! "Of course, I trust him. Why

wouldn't I?"

"Because he is a demi-god. If Zeus's blood runs through his veins…"

I understood exactly where Echidna was going with this, and I needed to clarify her ignorance. "Perseus is not like that. He loves me and said that he would love no other," I shared.

She shook her head, waving her hands in the air. "I give up. There is no getting through to you at this point. Young love is foolery's misguidance. Well, if you are not in the right frame of mind to understand what I am telling you now, at least heed my words and remember them in the future."

"Yes. I will listen…" I stated.

She went on to tell me tales of all the famous Greek loves and tragedies and compared them to my current situation. Most of which I had already heard before.

"Meduso, do you remember what I told you a year ago, before you and that stubborn Stheno left?"

"Something about *never putting beauty to waste*?" I recalled.

"Precisely. Let me share something important with you about mortals and gods that live in this world. And listen to my words carefully, brother."

"Go on…" I requested.

"Gods and mortals value beauty. If you have beauty, you will go far in their world. Kings only marry the most beautiful of women. Gods take the form of mortals in the world and mate only with those that are the most alluring. Even gods only marry goddesses that are pleasing to the eye and vice versa. Being beautiful and knowing you possess beauty will allow you to understand the power you truly hold. You can captivate, charm, and get your way with anyone. Manipulate others to fulfill your desires. Coax them into doing things to your own advantage."

She seductively pressed her hands against my body once again. "You, brother, have that beauty. Your looks will tempt gods and make mortals jealous. Any male or female would flock to you in a heartbeat. They would sacrifice much in order to bed you. The fact that you charmed a son of Zeus speaks volumes."

My face began to turn red, slightly embarrassed at her flattery.

"Never forget this, Meduso. For if there is something you truly desire in life, you need to use your beauty to your benefit. Use it to get whatever you want out of others."

I couldn't picture myself deceiving others for my own selfish gains. It was not like me at all. But I would do as Echidna had instructed and listen to her advice and remember it forever.

Who knows? It could help me in a desperate time of need.

Chapter 7

I departed Echidna's cave and reached the Arima mountain top. When I closed my eyes, I was transported to a new land. Euryale and Stheno were now in front of me.

"Did you get what you needed out of our sister?" Stheno asked.

"Yes," I replied.

"Good. Now come. Athena's temple is just yonder," she stated.

We pressed onward, and I was able to make out the temple on the Acropolis, in the distance. Its columns were massive, made of the purest limestone. The structure stood tall, rising above the fields of grass below. As we got closer, I noticed that it wasn't just one temple I was staring at. There were four buildings fortified by high walls.

"Which one is the temple of Athena?" I whispered into Euryale's ear.

She chuckled at my ignorance as we ascended the marble stairs.

"They all are, silly. The smaller building to the right of us is the temple of Athena Nike. Straight ahead is Propylaea, the gateway into Acropolis." We passed under the archway and stood in the atrium of Acropolis. Here, we saw many priestesses and priests strolling by in their white tunics. Their clothes were so clean you could practically eat off of them. Three of the young ladies that passed by us huddled together and giggled. They were no doubt making insulting comments about our lesser quality beige garments, I imagined.

However, I would never know that they were actually smitten with me. Their snickering was not to make fun of us, but was because of their attraction towards me.

Who is he? Look at that golden hair!

Those arms and legs! Good gods!

He's mine! Back off!

Those were some of the comments they exchanged with one another in secrecy.

Euryale then tapped me on the shoulder and nodded her head in the direction of the largest of the temples that were north of us. "That's the Parthenon, which you've heard all about from the Graeae, and the structure next to that is our sleeping quarters."

The Parthenon was even larger than I had imagined. It was described to me as being the main temple on the Acropolis, but I had not anticipated just how enormous it truly was. Hard to believe that all of these buildings were devoted to one goddess. I scanned the area and then to my left I saw a statue of Athena, holding a spear in her left hand and a shield in her right one.

What a sight she was. I could sense the pride and wisdom the monument itself invoked. Of all the gods and goddesses I was selected to serve, I was pleased that it was Athena, rather than an intimidating god like Ares or even a dull one like Hephaestus. Of all Zeus's children, Athena was no doubt the most popular one and well-liked by mortals. Being a goddess of wisdom, courage, inspiration, and victory and strategy in war was easy for humans to find so appealing. These were values that mortals held to the highest regard. With this goddess possessing and perfecting all of them, patrons were more eager to serve the deity.

"And who might you all be?" a strange, cracking voice called from behind.

My sisters and I turned around abruptly to see the old woman who questioned us. Her skin was sagging and wrinkly. Her clothing was a bit different from the other priestesses, in that it was saffron yellow. The golden, bejeweled circlet that rested on her head also caught my admiring eye.

Stheno spoke up for us. "We are the daughters and son of Phorcys and Ceto. I am Stheno. This is my younger sister, Euryale and our younger brother, Meduso. We have come to serve Athena."

"Ahhh! We have been expecting you three. I am Eschara, the high priestess of Athena. Come! Follow me." The hunched woman slowly paced ahead of us. Euryale and I shrugged to one another, but once we saw Stheno was already trailing behind her, we decided to follow.

She led us into the Parthenon. There were countless rooms in this temple. I was beginning to seem unsure of myself, wondering how I could possibly get used to navigating this labyrinth. I would need to study and pay attention very carefully if I wanted to please Athena.

Eschara led us to the far back of the temple and we entered a chamber. There were golden shrines and carved images of various famous Greek heroes, heroines, and creatures from the tales I've learned about. A giant altar was at the front of the room. My sisters and I were led there and told to kneel on it. We followed her instructions.

"Now, close your eyes and stay put."

I did as she stated. It was a good thirty seconds that passed by and still, nothing happened.

"Okay. You may open them now," the frail woman informed us.

My sisters and I gasped. Athena stood before us. I wanted to rise to greet her, but remained kneeling. The Graeae informed me that I should always bow before the goddess on my knees and only stand when she commanded us to.

"Children of Phorcys and Ceto. Rise to your feet," Athena said in a demanding tone.

We stood up, still shocked that she was present in our company.

"Eschara here will show you around and your daily duties. Remember, you are here representing me, Pallas Athena. Your actions, behavior, and anything you do now reflect on my deity. Do not disappoint me. For if I'm disappointed in one of my servants, there will be consequences. Understood?"

We nodded. "Yes, Goddess. We understand," Stheno stated.

Eschara proceeded out of the room. My sisters turned to follow behind her.

"Wait. You, boy. Stay for a moment," Athena said to me.

My sisters continued on without me, leaving me alone with the mighty Athena. I would be lying if I said I wasn't petrified of being on my own right now. What if I said or did the wrong thing?

"Come closer. I remember when we first met years ago. I did not expect you to grow into this kind of man. What is your name again?" Athena inquired.

I stepped towards her, only an arm's length away from the goddess.

"Meduso."

"Meduso, I am sure you are aware of your attractiveness. Young men such as yourself get attention for it on a regular basis."

I remember Echidna informing me of my handsomeness, and now Athena corroborated that idea.

"I was told by a few individuals about my looks. Never have I gotten attention for it, though," I explained.

"Good. I must warn you, Meduso. No servant of mine shall ever be *impure*. Do you understand what I am referring to?"

I nodded. "Yes. My parents and tutors taught me of this."

"I know for a fact you will be tempted by young women. They will try and seduce you. Needy little wretches, they are. But under no circumstances are you to give in to them. For if you do, you will fear my wrath! All servants of mine must be pure!" Her voice became deeper and louder, showcasing her power and to remind me of her goddess qualities.

"I will serve you well, Athena. I will not stray and shame you," I promised her.

"That is what I want to hear. Now run along and listen to Eschara."

In a split second, she shape-shifted. Her form was no longer that of a human. She turned into a white dove and flew out of the chamber ahead of me and went completely out of sight.

I caught up with Stheno and Euryale.

"What did she have to say to you?" Euryale asked.

"She just reminded me of the importance of staying pure," I replied.

"Why would she speak to you privately about that, and not all three of us?" Euryale further questioned.

I shrugged. "I'm not sure. But shush. Eschara is speaking. I'm trying to listen."

Truth be told, I knew why Athena pulled me aside without my sisters. It was just as Echidna confirmed. With my beauty, I too possessed powers. Not magical powers as the gods had, but powers of the mind that I could use to get my way with certain things. And Athena feared that I had that power.

The next several months were dull, to say the least. The chores were consistent with scrubbing the marble statues and columns, and washing any trace of dirt off of limestone day in and day out. The meals were the same too. So bland and lacking in flavor.

Athena hadn't shown up again since her appearance, during the day of our arrival. I became increasingly bored. I only had about two to three hours of free time to myself in the evening before bed. I used that time to travel down to the beach, dipping my toes in the sand. It served as a constant reminder of Seriphos and missing Perseus. However, there was something oddly familiar about this place and its water that I couldn't quite wrap my finger around. It's as if I had been to these shores on Athens before, but that's physically impossible. I shrugged it off, concluding that it must have been my imagination playing tricks on me.

I walked this beach every night, staring out into the endless sea, hoping for something exciting to come my way. Any type of change would be welcoming.

Months then turned into years. I was now twenty-three. I had suffered at this temple for a whole five years almost. I was dying on the inside. I honestly had no idea how much longer I could go on like this for. It was dreadful.

Euryale and Stheno coaxed me into appreciating what we had.

"You have to understand, Meduso, we should be grateful to Athena and the other Olympian gods. Our family is associated with the *old gods* and related to the Titans. We could have been potentially killed just for our lineage alone, yet it was Athena who was good-natured and spared our family from any curses and allowed us to live peacefully," Stheno explained.

"I know. I get it. But I didn't realize we would be forced to serve like this for years straight. Don't you ever get... tired of it all?" I asked.

She nodded. "Of course. It can be uneventful at times, but I always set my sights on the future. There will come a time when we will no longer have to serve here, and when that time comes..."

"I'll be dead!" I cut her off. "You forget that you and Euryale are immortals. The amount of years you spend here in this temple is a small fraction in your life. For me, I have an expiration. I am mortal. The years I spend here doing nothing are cutting into the hopes and dreams of my life... my *limited* life," I shared.

Stheno sighed. "You are still young, Med..."

"No!" I shouted, finding myself getting angrier with her. "You cannot keep using that excuse. That my feelings should be shunned because it is based on my youth or lack of experience. I am twenty-three years of age, Stheno. I am a full-fledged man now. I am no longer the young, naïve boy that was secluded in an oceanic palace from the outside world. Those days are gone!"

I started to run away from her.

"Wait, Meduso. Where are you going!?" she called out to me.

But I was out of sight, sprinting down the marble stairs and into the woods, descending the hills until I was on the beach, by the water, once again. I let my tears flow. I hadn't cried in years, but I was so overcome with emotions right now. I began to doubt I would ever see Perseus again. It had been five years since we parted ways and even his face that I swore would be permanently engraved in my mind was starting to become a blur. Being a servant to Athena was terrible. This was not what I had signed up for.

I stepped into the chilly water, allowing my feet to absorb the coolness; a desperate attempt to numb the conundrum of sadness, anger, and the pain I was experiencing. I wanted something different for my life. I needed to escape from here but knew that me fleeing from Acropolis would be deliberately disobeying Athena. I would, for sure, be caught in less than a day and killed, or even worse, sent to the Underworld to be damned for eternity. And from the tales I've been told, the Underworld is full of endless tragedy and boredom. I would be jumping out of the pan and into the fire, and I couldn't commit myself to that.

Realizing all of this, I began to sob even more, now uncontrollably. I felt weak, with no power, no fortitude, and close to giving up all hope, being trapped here in this prison with no escape, just suffocating, knowing that I would have no air of freedom to breathe.

I began thinking of Perseus. The thought of returning to him had kept me going all these years, but now I couldn't help but feel I had been fooling myself. I would never be able to return to Perseus. I would never be seeing him again. I began to worry that Perseus may have already found another person to love. After all, he is a son of Zeus. He attracts the eyes of everyone. No demi-god would wait out their entire life for a lost love to find them again. Why would they?

My frustration led me to now yelling out loud at the sea. "I hate it here! I hate my family for putting me through this! I hate the gods for forcing me into this life! I hate it all!"

More tears fell, and I closed my eyes, wiping them. The darkness I was seeing behind my lids began to brighten. It caused me to open them to witness a sudden glimmering light in the sea that appeared. Was something emerging from the light? A monster? A sea creature? No, it was a human. A man. A strong, well-built man. I blinked several times. Could it be? Was it Perseus?

"He must have come to save me!" I softly mumbled to myself. "To take me away from this horrific place!" I sprinted into the sea, soaking my tunic. The man's round chest was captivating. It made my insides pulsate. I gazed into his glowing cerulean eyes. His hair was wet, but its auburn color shined through the dampness; his face shaved neatly, with a light scruff around his jawline.

Meduso

Upon seeing the man closer, my heart sank. This wasn't Perseus. It was the stranger from my vision! I had no idea who this man was though, but I couldn't deny his beauty.

Guilt soon struck me as my heart raced over the appearance of this man. Was finding him attractive a betrayal towards Perseus? What would Perseus think of me having these thoughts of physical attraction towards another human? The shame tore at me and I did my best to avoid these thoughts about this god-like man emerging from the sea, but to no avail.

I attempted to find rationale for the reasoning behind these lustful thoughts if there were any. The fact that this man was in my vision also meant he was a part of my destiny. The Fates had brought us together. They must have known I would be bitter about being in Athena's servitude, and they sent this vision to tell me that this man would be the one to take me away from here.

Yes! That had to be it!

Lost in my thoughts, I realized I had stopped moving forward towards the man. Before I could think of what to say, the man spoke. "I've been watching you from afar, Meduso. I see that you are in pain and I cannot bear to witness it."

"I'm sorry. How have you been watching me from afar? I don't recall seeing you in Athena's temple."

The man let out a powerful laugh. "I have my own temples, my boy. Do you not know who I am? I am Poseidon, God of the sea."

Chapter 8

Poseidon and I laid on the shore, the moon serving as our only light to get a glimpse of each other's faces. My elbow rested in the sand, propping my head up with it. "So, you are really Poseidon?"

He, too, sprawled out next to me, gazing into my eyes. I refrained from staring back into those entrancing blue eyes of the sea god. "I am. Do you not believe me?"

I could not help but chuckle out of deliriousness. "I cannot lie to you. It is rather hard to believe."

He shook his head. "I am not lying to you, Meduso. This is who I truly am."

My snickering was replaced by a stern expression on my face. This was now the second time the man called me by my name, but I realized I never gave it to him. "Wait? How do you know my name?"

It was he who was now smirking, but seductively. "As I have stated, I am the god of the sea. I have been watching you and your family for years. Every step you have taken into my waters throughout your entire life, I have known about."

I then traced my memory back to all the times I had been in the water, which was here in Athens, when I was younger in the underwater palace, and even at the Island of Seriphos with Perseus. Panic began to strike as I recalled the times Perseus and me dipped into the glistening Aegean Sea in the middle of the night in the bare nude, with the lit-up night sky hovering above us.

Did this man see me… naked? I asked myself.

"You have known about me since I was younger?" I inquired.

He nodded. "Yes, Meduso. I've been keeping an eye on your family, making sure they were being loyal and obedient to the new gods. Having watched over you, I became more intrigued as you got older. You have grown into such a captivating man. And as I watched your encounters with the young demi-god in Seriphos, I became somewhat bitter at seeing him touch you the way he did," Poseidon confessed.

I could not believe he knew of intimate exchanges between Perseus me. So, it was true. This robust man really was Poseidon. It took me a moment to fully digest this situation and the fact that Poseidon had watched me in the seas throughout my entire life. This meant that the god must have also known of my *impurity* with Perseus. Fear instantly took over me, wondering if Poseidon would share this information with his niece, Athena.

But what also astonished me most was Poseidon admitting that he did not like the way Perseus touched me. "Why were you bitter over Perseus?" I bravely asked, hoping I was not overstepping my boundaries with this god.

Poseidon's thick hand then caressed my cheek, causing me to shutter. "Because, Meduso, I find you mesmerizing. You are a beautiful young man. When I saw that demi-god kissing you, grabbing you with longing passion, I realized I wanted that. I needed to feel that with you. I continued to watch you in my seas for years thereafter, constantly imagining what it would be like to have you in my arms. It was torment. But I knew I had to wait for the right moment to take form and introduce myself to you."

I could not believe what I was hearing. Were my ears deceiving me? Did Poseidon just say that he desires me? That he has admired me from afar for many years? I was unsure whether or not to be pleased with myself or feel ashamed. It was difficult to fathom that I could have this effect on an Olympian god.

And here this god was, intimately touching me. I stirred with confusion; my heart being tugged to every corner of my body. Only Perseus should be touching me like this. But Perseus wasn't here and he hadn't been around for more than five years. Would I ever see him again?

Still, I became quite uncomfortable with Poseidon touching me. I turned my head so that Poseidon's hand brushed my cheek and fell off me.

"You know I serve Pallas Athena, correct?"

"Yes," he affirmed.

"So, you must know what she requires of me and her expectations of me being *pure*," I elaborated.

Poseidon rolled his eyes. "I do question my niece's beliefs at times. But if you are concerned that I will tell her about your past, then I should inform you that you have nothing to fret about. She will never know about your affairs with that demi-god. However, I do ask one small favor in return."

I raised a brow, wondering what Poseidon could possibly want from me, but I knew I had no choice but to accept any terms that were thrown my way. After all, if Athena knew I was not *pure*, I would surely be doomed for lying to her. "And what is this favor?"

"I would like to spend time with you. Get to know you more. I am aware that you come out here to this sea almost every evening. I would hope I could meet you here at night."

I was torn. I loved Perseus. But as the years went on, with Perseus being absent, a reality continued to pry at me. The fear of being stuck at Athena's temple for life and never getting to see Perseus again continued to fester like a wound. My patience was wearing thin. I needed an escape, a change of pace from my current turmoil, and Poseidon was exactly that. "Of course. I honestly would like to get to know you more, as well."

As soon as I confirmed this with him, Poseidon leaned in to grace his lips with mine. His hand moved to the back of my neck, pulling me closer. I was startled and quickly pulled away. "I can't do this."

"And why not?"

"Because… I love another," I revealed to him.

"Tell me. Is it that demi-god?"

I nodded.

"Well, let me tell you something Meduso. I, too, have a keen sense of the future. And I can tell you that you will never see that demi-god again."

I rose to my feet in alarm, shaking my head. "But that cannot be. Surely he will come and find me."

Poseidon stood with me, cupping his hands on my shoulders. "The Fates have spoken to me. I am a god, after all. They have told me of two paths for you. Either you will stay with Athena, forever in her servitude, or you can be with me, escaping from her."

I was perplexed. My heart lied with Perseus, but now that this god informed me that I would never see Perseus again, I felt despondent. More tears began to swell up in my eyes.

Seeing how vulnerable I now was in this very moment, Poseidon pulled me closer into an embrace. "Fear not, Meduso. There is nothing to cry about. You have me now. Let that island boy remain in the past. You have so much to look forward to now."

It took another month for me to fully come to terms with knowing that I would never see Perseus again. The more time I spent with Poseidon, the more powerful a spell he seemed to cast on me.

Our relationship was blossoming and I could no longer deny my attraction to the god. Despite this, I could not fully give myself to him.

Poseidon remained respectful with me, but he was a god after all. How long could I expect him to linger for?

"We need to talk, Meduso."

"Talk about what?"

"It has now been a month since I revealed to you my intentions for my presence with you, yet you still have not been fully open with me. I cannot continue to proceed like this if your heart is not set on me."

I was still timid and confused about what to do. "I'm sorry. I just need more time..."

Poseidon interrupted me. "But is that not what I've given you? Have you not had weeks to think things through? I must look so foolish right now."

I felt terrible for making Poseidon feel this way. I extended my hand to reach his shoulder, but Poseidon yanked his arm away.

"I must go," he announced, disgruntled.

"Go? But you just got here. Will you be back?" Paranoia struck me, afraid that Poseidon may never return.

"I cannot say for sure." The sea god sprinted into the water and dove in, disappearing from my sight.

I fell to the sand. The idea of losing not only Perseus, but now Poseidon too, began to sink in. Tears gravitated to the surface of my lids. I did my absolute best to keep my promise to Perseus. I was loyal to a fault, but was my loyalty worth living alone, stuck as a servant for the rest of my life?

No. This couldn't be how my life would pan out. Seeing Perseus again was an unsure thing, but having Poseidon in my life was a guarantee. I now fully understood this and could finally come to terms with it. I rose to my feet and jogged towards the edge of the shore, the end of the tide barely grazing my toes.

Desperation loomed within me, wanting Poseidon to return. "Please, Poseidon! Come back! I'm so sorry for everything! I do want to be with you!"

No response.

My shouting persisted. "I beg of you! I need you, Poseidon! I don't want to go on without you!"

I was about to give up hope when suddenly, a glimmer of light shone through the water. Poseidon's head slowly came up, out of the sea.

I ran into the sea towards him, placing my palms on his chest to feel him. To claim him. The vision I once had of passionately feeling the man emerging from the sea was now really happening, a prophecy fulfilled.

Poseidon leaned forward to kiss me. This time, I was unable to turn him away. A switch turned on; an impulse overtook me, allowing me to release myself to the god by passionately kissing him back.

I was so caught up in this moment, all thoughts of Perseus were cast aside. I let the god claim me. My body tingled, wanting to feel Poseidon inside of me. I was losing complete control of myself, giving in to Poseidon. We continued to get lost in one another and made love on the beach that night. Soon, thoughts of Perseus were drifting further and further away, like a cloud disappearing on a warm, sunny day.

There wasn't a single night that went by where I didn't meet Poseidon out on the beach. We continued to make passionate love there every time. Poseidon serving as my escape from this temple prison. My daily chores and duties became all the more tolerable, knowing I would be greeted by the warm, thick arms of the sea god at the end of the day once all was done. Sometimes, I found myself sneaking off earlier than I should, knowing no one would come searching for me if I left my work just an hour or two earlier than I was supposed to.

Euryale and Stheno also took notice of my sudden change in attitude. Euryale was neatly folding temple cloths beside me as she struck up a conversation about it.

"You seem more chipper than usual," Euryale shared.

"I do?" I pretended to not take notice of my change of heart.

"Yes. You've been so overcome with grief for the past few years. What has happened now, all of a sudden?"

"Just a fresh perspective, I suppose." I had to lie to my sisters. Telling them about my passionate rendezvous with Poseidon was completely out of the question. Not only would they not understand the need for me to take that risk in meeting with the god every night, but I knew my sisters would forbid me from doing so at any point in the future, once this became known to them. Therefore, I had no choice but to keep them in the dark on this.

"Hmmm. Well, I'm very relieved to see you're out of that slump, at least," Euryale replied. "I've been worried about you."

I warmly smiled, hearing her caring sincerity. "I appreciate that. But I think I'm okay now. I was just not in the right headspace for a while there."

"Good. Glad that you came to your senses." Euryale then left me to attend to another chore, now that the white cloths of her pile were all intricately folded. I still had a while to go with my pile in the meantime. Little did Euryale know that I purposefully went slow with my folding, making sure it would be my last task of the day, knowing that no other priestesses nor servants would come into this room for the remainder of the evening. Once the coast was clear, I bolted out of the room and down the empty hallway, out of the temple, proceeding towards the secluded beach.

Upon my arrival, I was stunned to see a different scene besides Poseidon laid out in the sand, naked, showing off his irresistible body. There was a lit fire, with a table full of a variety of foods including, apples, grapes, cooked fish, and various assorted meats. Poseidon approached me with a goblet of wine. "Here, I thought we could do something different tonight."

I accepted the wine and took a sip of it. The taste was unlike anything I had ever experienced. The only other time I ever drank wine was at Dictys's home with Perseus years ago. But this wine was on a whole different level. It was much smoother to swallow and I found myself imbibing it rather quickly.

Poseidon refilled my now empty cup. "Slow down there. You are going to lose your appetite if you drink too much too soon," he explained.

I smiled at him and took a seat in a chair at the table, while Poseidon collected the fruits and smoked fish, putting them onto my plate. "This is wonderful. I cannot believe you went out of your way to do this."

He shrugged. "It really isn't much. You forget I am a god. Setting this up would take hours for a mortal, but for me, it takes only seconds."

This was true. I could just imagine Poseidon snapping his fingers, and all of these platters, chairs, and tables would magically appear. Then, to contradict that, I could envision a few servants laying everything out so perfectly, but taking much longer to do so.

I then tasted the fish, marveling at its flawless taste. I closed my eyes and let out a moan, showing Poseidon how satisfied I was with the feast. It was too late by the time I realized that my moaning sounded a little more sexual than I had intended. I glanced up from my plate to see the flicker in Poseidon's eyes from across the table, allowing me to know how deeply enticed he was by my whimpering in delight.

Over the past several weeks, I had taken notice of the change in Poseidon's mood. Initially, I knew the god was attracted to me and assumed his feelings were purely physical. However, lately, Poseidon was much more eager to please me in a variety of ways.

I would be lying if I said I didn't enjoy the attention and the gifts that I was being showered with. The wheels in my head were turning as I was starting to visualize a potential future with Poseidon, away from this life in Athena's temple. Poseidon would whisk me away to his extravagant sea palace or even a castle on Mount Olympus. I was unsure of where his abode was, but it was no matter to me. Wherever it may be, it would be much better than where I currently was, here on the stoned Acropolis.

Poseidon would be able to claim me, and Athena would be unable to punish me for disobeying her. After all, she would not want to start a war with her uncle, right? I was jumping for joy on the inside at the thought of finally having hope and a means of escaping this wretched place.

I wondered if Poseidon would be willing to take in my sisters as well if they did want to leave here, too. It would take some convincing on my end, but I would be steadfast in making that happen.

After we ate dinner, Poseidon rose from his seat and moved around the table towards me. He lifted me right out of the chair, in his bulging arms, and carried me to a small alcove on the side of the cliffs overlooking the sea. The sea god leaned me against their rocky edges, making love to me from all angles. After releasing himself, he panted, gasping for air, resting his head against my body to regain his strength. "You will be the impossible death of me," he managed to get out before his heavy breathing continued.

My arms wrapped around his head, pulling him into my chest. "I would have no other. I want more of you! And I want you to have all of me. But as of now, you do not fully possess me. That ownership belongs to your niece." I glanced down at him as I stated this, to see the focus written in the expression on his face.

My words were soaking into Poseidon. "Give me some time, and I promise you will be all mine and I will be all yours. I want to make sure we tread carefully with this, and we make all the right moves. I want no harm to come to you or your family," he explained.

"How much time?" I needed to know that this would not persist for years on end. That he had every intention of carrying me away very soon.

"A month perhaps? Maybe less? All I know is that now that I have you, I cannot imagine myself without you. Nor could I picture you being with anyone else. I want you for myself, and would rather be damned to serve my brother, Hades, than to have you love another man."

I kissed him on his forehead. "That's all I want for us. To live in peace and forever enjoy each other's company, far away from here. I need that, Poseidon. I need you," I revealed.

"You have me, Meduso. And you will forever have

me."

He lifted his face to meet mine for another long kiss.

"You know…" I interrupted our moment of passion. "I've been meaning to tell you that I had a vision that I would be meeting you. It's been going on for years now."

"A vision?" He seemed confused.

"Yes. I had a vision, almost like a prophecy or a premonition, that I saw you coming out of the water and I sprinted towards you, placing my hands on your chest, holding you in a loving embrace." I shared this vision which now happened in real life at least sixty times over the past two months we spent together.

"Oh? I am surprised. I did not know mortals possessed the power to have visions, as such."

I shrugged. "Maybe it is because my parents are gods? Nevertheless, the Fates were telling me I would meet you. Perhaps it is a sign that we belong together."

Poseidon gave a wink. "Well, who are we to defy the intentions of the Fates?"

I grinned and then traced my hands up and down Poseidon's massive torso, before leaning back in to meet his lips once more.

Late into the night, we decided to end our bliss, realizing it was only a few hours away from dawn. I needed to return to the sleeping quarters and sneak into bed before anyone grew suspicious of my prolonged absence. And I did just that.

I laid in my bed, staring up at the glossy marble ceiling above me, paying close attention to the intricate patterns and lines etched out within it. I smiled to myself, knowing I was on the correct path, inching closer and closer to my freedom. Did I love Poseidon? I wasn't quite sure. At least I thought that spending additional time with Poseidon would lead me to love him more. If I had to draw a comparison between my relationships with Poseidon and with Perseus, I undoubtedly loved Perseus more. The passion, moments of innocence, and that feeling of emptiness whenever I was not close to Perseus were experiences I did not have with Poseidon yet.

However, Poseidon could provide me with things that Perseus was unable to, including freedom, an established and extravagant shelter, and any wishes and wealthy desires I wanted. Poseidon's godly persona was something that could not be ignored. And the fact that he was a god, willing to spend the rest of his life with me, a mere mortal, spoke volumes. And I loved Poseidon for that.

Deep down, I knew I could have a future with Poseidon, and I needed to find a way to disband all emotions, thoughts, and feelings I had about Perseus if I planned on remaining with the sea god. Holding on to them would be unfair to Poseidon. He was giving me all of him, and therefore, it was important for me to reciprocate and give all of myself to Poseidon as well.

And that meant having to give myself to him without Perseus always on my mind.

I realized I was ready to do this. After all, Perseus would not be saving me from my services to Athena. Now that I thought about it, Poseidon was not as forthcoming about rescuing me from this temple, either. It was something that I continuously brought up to the god. Really, it was a matter that I took into my own hands. I was actually saving myself, and Poseidon was the leverage to help me in the process.

I then recalled my last meeting with Athena. I recited her words over again in my head, carefully:

Meduso, I am sure you are aware of your attractiveness. Young men such as yourself receive attention for it regularly... I know for a fact you will be tempted... They will try and seduce you.

The goddess warned me not to allow my beauty to get the best of me. But she was mistaken. My beauty was not getting the best of me at all. It was getting the best of others.

Chapter 9

"Meduso, I want to take you somewhere special." Poseidon faced me, holding my hands, our fingers interlocked together.

"To where exactly?" I was more so excited about visiting a new part of the world I had yet to experience, although a small fraction of me was partly worried about disappearing from Athena's temple for a long period of time.

However, Poseidon quickly averted any form of hesitance from my thoughts. "It's a surprise. But I will make sure you are back at a reasonable hour. Come…" he assuaged.

I nodded and allowed him to take the reins in our departure to this *somewhere special* he had in mind. I closed my eyes following Poseidon's lead. Upon opening them, I found myself on lush, green grass. I spun around to notice many exotic flowers in the fields to the right of me. To the left, were ruins, some fully sturdy ivory pillars, and structures, while others were demolished into a complete pile of rubble. Upon closer examination, these ruins were of bizarre stones and building materials I had never seen before. But that wasn't the most alarming feature about this place. There was no sky above; just a spherical bubble of aquatic blue that surrounded us. I turned to Poseidon, beyond perplexed with where we were. Was it another world?

"Where are we? I never knew a place like this existed."

"This is the former island of Atlantis," Poseidon revealed. "A sunken kingdom, doomed because of the threat they posed to the gods."

"It's beautiful!" I continued to marvel at the wonders of this place. "Where exactly is Atlantis, Poseidon?"

He sighed. "We are underwater. This island sunk to the bottom of the ocean many years ago. I summoned a permanent dome to serve as armor around it for its preservation."

"But why is it underwater? What happened?" I was quite perturbed that I did not already know the answer to this, assuming that the Graeae had taught me everything there was to know about events of the past.

"This former island was once of our world. I watched over it as protector of the kingdom. My son, Atlas, was king of the land and its surrounding ocean," he revealed.

It stung me, hearing him say that he had a son. Of course, I knew Poseidon had many children. He was a god, after all. He had lovers long before me. However, I could not fault him. As much as I wanted to be Poseidon's only lover, I knew that was inconceivable. Poseidon was a god, and I was a mortal. Poseidon had hundreds, if not thousands, of years on me. How could I expect a god who lived over a thousand years to be committed to a single mortal lover, who would likely live to only be less than one hundred years old? However, I would be remiss if I didn't admit that I felt uncomfortable thinking about Poseidon in the arms of another.

So, this is what it must feel like to be jealous, I thought. It was a stomach-churning feeling. I then remembered Poseidon explaining how jealous he was, seeing Perseus intimately touch me. I now felt guilty over causing Poseidon to also experience this troublesome feeling.

I shook my head to dispel these concerns. "And what happened to Atlas?"

"My son, Atlas, was a demi-god. A former lover of mine, Cleito, gave birth to him. I declared him King of Atlantis. My son was a powerful ruler. He was intellectual, brave, and had many personable qualities that his people were drawn to him for. However, these traits did not bode well for him, for other gods feared his growth and power from them. Atlantis grew to be an unstoppable force. Its armies increased and expanded to conquer and rule over the massive lands of Africa."

I sensed a sorrow in Poseidon. A rarity that I did not expect the god of the sea to burden himself with. I reached to hold his hand and rubbed the back of it with my thumb, hoping it had a soothing effect on him as Poseidon continued with his story.

"Many of my family members on Mount Olympus feared my son's power. I warned him of that fear and recommended that he take caution and accept his current victories and conquests and go no further. However, just like all mortals who first experience the thrill of power, they thirst for more until greed consumes them. Atlas did not listen to my advice. He led his armies onward and closer to Athens. The other Olympian gods and goddesses soon learned that my words had no impact on my son, and therefore, they needed to take matters into their own hands. The Athenian armies and the armies of all of their lands joined forces to take down the Atlantean Empire and my son. As a result of this, and as further punishment, the gods invoked earthquakes, floods, and the worst of disasters to befall the Island of Atlantis. It sank to the bottom of the ocean. My son had no escape and died with his kingdom."

"I'm so sorry for your loss, Poseidon," I expressed with sincerity.

"There is no need for that, Meduso. He should have known of the consequences he faced for defying the gods. I, too, could have done better to persuade him otherwise. I decided to create a protective bubble around this island to preserve his legacy. It would serve as a reminder for me to realize that even I, as a god, have rules and obligations to abide by. That I am not above other gods. This island is a cruel, constant burden that will forever be engraved in my mind."

It was odd to hear this side of Poseidon. Yet, the fact that he was being vulnerable and opening himself up to me confirmed that his love for me was real. *Why else would he feel the need to reveal this tragic tale and the loss of his son to me? To share something so important to him with another mortal was special. It's only meant for the ears of a lover, and I am that lover to him*, I thought.

"So, you must understand why I am somewhat apprehensive about taking you away from Athena. Even a god defying another god can have its consequences. That is why I have been so cautious in dragging you from her. Soon, it will happen, but I want you to fully understand the position I am in and the reasoning behind it. Believe me, Meduso, if I had it my way, I would have snatched you up the second I grabbed you on the beach in the water that first day we met."

I felt the need to reward Poseidon for sharing these dark details of his life with me. So, I grabbed Poseidon and led him into the colorful flower fields, falling into them, on the ground. I pulled the god down so that he laid on top of me.

"I want you here and now," I whispered with temptation.

Poseidon's hands firmly gripped my back so that I arched into him. "And I will take you here and now." His lips trickled against my neck as he unstrapped my tunic to reveal my bare body. He then took his off as well, illustrating his godly figure.

Poseidon pressed down into me. Our bodies collided, eventually becoming one. The ecstasy was unbearable. I could not contain myself. Poseidon was aggressive with me, but at the same time, held me delicately. It was beyond any dichotomy I had ever experienced. But I loved every second of the sea god holding me, controlling me, owning me, and being inside me.

I knew that every moment from here on out was one

that we experienced as a couple. Poseidon was fully devoted to me and I to him. In due time, we would have to come clean to Athena about our relationship, and at this point, I was prepared to do so, knowing that I had nothing to fear with this powerful god at my side. But all thoughts of the future were cast aside for now. I cared only about the feeling of my lover inside of me.

After our session of lovemaking in the field of ornate flowers, Poseidon must have comprehended all that had just transpired, as well. That he brought me here, to confess his burdens and reveal his vulnerability. It must have made him realize that he desperately wanted me in his life permanently, for his next suggestion was indicative of that.

"Let's go to my niece's temple together tomorrow evening."

"Really? You're ready to inform her about us?" I was in disbelief.

He nodded. "Yes. I think it's about time. I cannot stand the thought of being without you for another full day from this moment forward."

I lunged into him for a hug as he stated this. "Thank you. I feel the same way. "But…"

"But what?"

"My sisters… I cannot just leave them at the temple alone, without me for the rest of their days. And what of my parents? Will Athena retaliate and take my actions out on them?"

"Well, your sisters can join us," Poseidon clarified.

"And your parents will be under my protection. Just allow me to negotiate with my niece and I will make sure that happens."

It was such a relief to hear him say that. Now I had absolutely no worries about this plan on the horizon. I shut my eyes, resting my head against Poseidon's chest. When I re-opened them, we were back at the beach near the Acropolis.

It was bittersweet being back here. On one hand, I wished we could have stayed in our own little world in Atlantis, isolated from everyone else. On the other hand, I knew that this would be my last night here in Athens if Poseidon was planning on confessing our affair to Athena tomorrow evening. After that discussion would take place, I would be carried off, out of Athens and to a majestic palace fit for the god of the sea and his lover.

I slept peacefully in my bed that night, knowing tomorrow would be my last day at this confinement. These years of monotonous labor were over, and I knew that my adventures were only beginning.

The following day, I pulled Stheno and Euryale away from the group of other priestesses and servants and into a private chamber to reveal everything to them.

"Now, I do not want either of you to be mad or think you can persuade me otherwise with what I am about to tell you," I began with. "For the past several months, you know how I have been heading off to the beach every night to relax?"

"Yes. What about it?" Stheno sternly asked.

"Well... I've been meeting someone there every night. And it's not just anyone... it's Poseidon himself. We are in love," I admitted, finally getting this secret off my chest.

"Poseidon!? God of the sea!?" Euryale gasped. "Meduso? Are you sure it's him?"

"Yes, Euryale. I've witnessed his powers firsthand. The man is truly Poseidon. We've been seeing each other for the past two months. Poseidon was the man in my vision that I told you about. It all makes so much sense now. He plans to tell Athena about our relationship tonight. Then he will take me away from here to live in his palace with him. And more importantly, he offered to bring you both along as well."

"So, we will be leaving this temple tonight? I better start packing my belongings, although there's not much to pack. Wait. Do our parents know?" Euryale thought out loud.

"No. I will not be partaking in this charade," Stheno grunted. "Meduso, you are being foolish! You just met this god a few months ago! Have you thought this through!? What about the repercussions we could potentially face for this, and our entire family? Surely, Athena will punish *everyone* for your irrational and disloyal behavior. I'm sorry, Meduso, but I cannot join you. And I think you are sorely mistaken in the relationship you *think* you have with Poseidon."

I slammed my foot in the ground. "No Stheno! *You* are the one that is mistaken. Poseidon loves me and he has offered protection for all of us! Surely he would not allow anything to happen to our family either for that matter."

Stheno shook her head and was not having any of it. "Meduso, I know that you hate me saying this, but once again, I have no choice... you are young and innocent still. Poseidon is an Olympian god. He has many children and has had many lovers throughout his immortal life. You will not be his only lover, brother. And once he is bored with you, he will dispose of you and find a new playmate that can entertain him. Come on, Meduso! Do you honestly think he will be faithful to you? Use your brain!"

"You don't get it, Stheno! You'll never understand! Being with Poseidon is better than being locked away here in servitude for the rest of my life. I can no longer put up with this lifestyle any longer. Poseidon has offered me a new life, a chance to fully experience the world around us and the adventures that it holds for me. That is something that will never happen if I waste my years away here." I could sense that my eyes were watering and soon enough, the tears started falling down my face.

Witnessing how upset and hurt I was, Stheno let out a heavy sigh and approached, wrapping her arms around me. "Meduso, I want you to be happy. But more importantly, I also want you to be safe. Now understand,

I do not think we will remain here at Athena's temple for the rest of our lives. Eventually, there will come a time in the future where she will reward us for our loyalty and benevolence, and we will be free to live and do as we please. But we must do our part in fulfilling the promise our parents made to her. We cannot abandon her in this way."

"But you lack empathy for me, Stheno. You must realize that I am aging faster than you both. By the time Athena grants us freedom and rewards us, I will be at death's door. What then? You mean to tell me I've worked my entire life only to enjoy a minuscule amount of it?"

Stheno separated from our embrace and remained silent, unsure of how to respond to my feelings. She turned to Euryale, putting her on the spot. "And what will you do, Euryale? Will you go with Meduso and Poseidon, disobeying Athena and our parents, or will you remain here?"

Euryale turned her head left and right, tossing glances back and forth between Stheno and me. She deeply exhaled before providing us with her answer. "Meduso, I'm sorry. I can't go with you either." Euryale placed her hands on my shoulders. "But I do think you should go with Poseidon. I understand how you feel, brother. You should have the opportunity to enjoy the limited life that you have and not in the confines of this temple. Just promise me you will visit us every now and then. I cannot bear the thought of never seeing you again."

I then leaned forward to hug Euryale, appreciating her support in my decision. "Very well. I promise to return to you all in the future, but I must go to the beach to meet Poseidon now. It is only a matter of time before we make our announcement to Athena."

I stood in the sand, staring out into the sea like a young maiden waiting for any sign of a ship, hoping her husband would return safely from war. But my lover did return. I caught sight of Poseidon's beautiful, lush, full auburn hair rising out of the water. As he moved towards the surface, the wet hairs on his chest clung to his thick, curved muscles. When he came to shore, he opened his arms wide, expecting me to move into them.

I obliged, and he tightly squeezed my much smaller frame into him. "Are you ready to do this?" he asked.

"More than ever," I revealed.

"Well, let's not waste any more time then. Shall we get to it?"

I nodded. Poseidon grabbed my hand as we ascended the hills and towards the Parthenon. When we approached the arched Propylaea gateway, we released our grip from one another, not wanting to draw any attention to ourselves from any of the priests, priestesses, or servants that passed us by.

I led him into the room with the gold shrines and

altars. The very same room where I had met Athena during my first day here in Athens five years ago.

Poseidon paced around the chamber, admiring the gold statues and carvings. "This is astonishing! The purity of this gold is beyond rare," he shared.

I concurred. "Yes, it's all so breath-taking."

Poseidon turned to me with a sexy, sly smirk expressed on his face. "I'll summon my niece shortly, but what do you say we pass the time with some fun?"

That look he gave made me melt. He was so irresistible with the reflection of the gold shimmering on his face. "What do you mean by *fun*?"

Poseidon stepped closer to me, lowering his forehead to place it against mine. "The luxury of all this gold... these riches all around us. Does it not arouse you?"

I smiled at this admission of excitement. I knew exactly where Poseidon was going with this. "It does. But don't you think we could get in trouble if we made love here, right in front of Athena's shrines? Would that not be an act of desecration?" I asked.

The sea god shook his head. "Of course not. No one is watching us, not even Athena herself. It's not going to harm anyone." Poseidon grabbed the side of my head and began nibbling on my neck.

The soft touch of his lips and the tip of his tongue against my skin sent chills down my spine, causing me to whimper with pleasure. "Are you sure? We won't be disturbed, will we?" Part of me was petrified over getting caught and facing serious consequences, while the other half longed to feel Poseidon inside me, among this lustrous, extravagant sight before us.

"Shhhh. Just go with it. Let me make love to you, Meduso. I will make love to you here and I will make love to you in the treasure room of my palace a thousand times after this." Poseidon's hands began unraveling the drawstring on my tunic. He paused to gauge my reaction. Seeing as I was not forbidding him from doing so, he stripped me down before taking his own clothing off.

Poseidon lifted me in the air effortlessly in his arms, kissing me wildly, before softly laying me down against Athena's golden altar. This was really happening, and I could not get enough of it. The thrill of the unknowing and the potential risk we were taking by doing this elicited an intense passion within me. I desperately wanted Poseidon to make love to me. I needed him inside me now, and wished he would never come out.

I held onto Poseidon hard, as he pushed his manhood into me. My fingers tightened their grip on Poseidon's back, leaving red streaks on his skin as I retracted them down to his rear. Poseidon's pace hastened as he thrust into me with all his godly might, while I pulled him in with all of the strength I could muster, a desperate attempt to allow Poseidon to have deeper access inside me.

My moaning was growing louder, and to hush me, Poseidon jammed his tongue right into my mouth, while continuing to pump himself in me. Our ecstasy was heightened to its maximum peak. Neither one of us could hold on any longer. We hit our climax and exploded. With one final grunt, Poseidon reached his breaking point. I too let go of myself, all across my toned chest.

We sat still, unable to move from our current position. I could feel the god's heavy breaths tickle my neck as he rested, trying to regain his composure. Then, the unthinkable happened. I felt Poseidon's thickness return to its hardened state. His pulsating picked up again. Poseidon was not through with me yet. As tired and weak-legged as I now was, I did not have the strength to move. And so I sat there, allowing Poseidon to continue to have his way with me for a second time. How could I forget that Poseidon was a god? His endurance was beyond that of a mortal. I had no idea what had gotten into Poseidon, but our sexual encounters were never like this before.

His explosions into me continued for hours on end, to the point where I eventually lost count of the number of times he let himself go. Poseidon was turning into a wild mad man, never wanting to give up my body. I was insatiable to him. It was as if his cravings and thirst for me were never-ending, and as a result, he never stopped making passionate love to me for the night. I had no idea how long Poseidon intended to go on for, but I never questioned it, nor put a halt to it.

The sun must surely be rising by now, and it was not until his godly senses kicked in that Poseidon realized someone was approaching the chamber. In the blink of an eye, his form disappeared, leaving me alone to myself. I stood and quickly threw my tunic over myself, turning to face the alter so that my back was towards the entrance door. Sure enough, someone had entered as I was adjusting the strings on my tunic.

I subtly turned around towards the priestess who had presented herself, but deep down my nerves were running amok in every corner of my body. My legs almost gave out as I passed by her, on my way out of the chamber.

"Are you okay?" she asked.

I simply nodded. "I'm fine. Just slept the wrong way, last night. Nothing to worry about."

I picked up my pace out of the temple. I was limber, drained, and so weak from Poseidon's ravaging of me. I managed to return to the sleeping quarters and stumbled right into my bed, passing out the second my head hit the pillow.

Chapter 10

I felt emaciated as I woke up from my temporary coma. My sisters came to my side asking why I was so weak and looked so pale. The only excuse I could make was that I had become ill. They believed me and reported my sickness to our superiors.

Eschara arrived to check on me, witnessing the slight change in my skin color and how drained I seemed. "Just get some rest for the day, Meduso. We will check on you tomorrow," The high priestess suggested, kneeling by the bedside.

"Thank you," I softly stated. "I am hoping to be back on my feet by then."

The brittle woman smiled. "To be so young and resilient. I remember those days..." she reminisced, before rising to her feet to leave me some privacy.

Despite how physically and mentally drained I was, I quickly gathered my wits, wondering where Poseidon had gone. Did he already visit Athena without me and share the news of our love for one another? Or perhaps he planned to wait for me to recover. Maybe he expected me to return down to the beach this evening and then he would call upon his niece then.

Still, I could not believe what Poseidon had put me through last night. That's not to say that I did not enjoy the experience. It was just that I was permanently stimulated for so many hours, that he failed to realize the strain it had put my entire body through. I hoped Poseidon did not feel guilty. After all, how could he know that my endurance was no match for his own?

I remained in the sleeping quarters for most of the day, allowing my thoughts of escaping from here with Poseidon to permeate my mind, being unable to sleep. I managed to rise out of bed later in the evening and was relieved that my first few steps were not excruciatingly painful as I had anticipated. I was somewhat sore still, but would not let that deter me from making my way down to the beach to meet Poseidon. My trek took longer than usual, as I moved slowly down the hills, not wanting to accidentally stumble and cause myself any further injury.

As the cobalt sea came into view, I became more eager to dip my toes into the sand. It exhilarated me and elevated all of my nerves, knowing it was only a matter of seconds before my lover would rise out of the water. I waited for that moment, but nothing came.

That was peculiar. Usually, Poseidon was able to sense my presence and came to the surface the second I stared out into the sea, longing for him. I waited at the beach for over an hour, but still nothing. Just the occasional driftwood flowing by.

I became instantly worried by Poseidon's absence. My mind began to run wild with the worst of thoughts.

What if he was hurt?

Was he with Athena right now, without me?

Was he having second thoughts about us, and decided to abandon me?

Did he confide in another god about our relationship and they forbade him from visiting me?

I continued to agonize as the hours passed by, until I eventually realized I needed to return to my sleeping quarters, knowing someone could potentially be checking in on me at any point during the night.

So, I returned to my bed, finding it even harder to sleep with this panic that now stirred within me.

A few days had passed and still no sign of Poseidon. I returned to the beach every night, praying and wishing for his return, but I continued to be disappointed.

By the fourth night, I returned to the temple grounds from my lonesome visit to the shore only to catch Euryale and Stheno jogging towards me.

"There you are!" Euryale exclaimed.

"We've been searching everywhere for you. Eschara has summoned all three of us to the golden shrine room," Stheno explained.

The last time the three of us were summoned to that chamber was years ago when we first came to the Acropolis. Instantly, I knew exactly why we were being called there. Athena must know about the relationship between Poseidon and me. Who knows, maybe Poseidon would turn up there as well, ready to take me away from this dreadful place. That was my biggest hope that could come from this urgent meeting.

I followed behind my sisters into the chamber, seeing Eschara standing at the front of the room, waving for us to come to her. "Kneel before the altar," was all she commanded.

I fell to my knees right between both Euryale and Stheno. Now that we were positioned as demanded, Eschara moved to exit the room, shutting the door tightly behind her.

It didn't take very long for Athena to reveal herself, taking the same human form she did when we last met with her. "Rise, young servants," she ordered.

We listened and did as she instructed. Athena's voice seemed more severe than I last remembered. "Surely, you all know why you have been called upon at such a late hour. Do you not?"

We all shrugged, but each of us truly knew the reasoning behind this sudden gathering. Well, not to the full extent.

"Meduso, would you like to inform everyone of your transgression? Or did you not tell your sisters what happened in this very room just several nights ago?" Apparently, the goddess knew more about my affair with Poseidon than I had imagined. I was horrified and embarrassed to have to retell the incident to my sisters, but I knew there was no other option before me.

"Poseidon and I... we made love here at the altar a

few nights ago."

Stheno gasped. "Meduso!? How could you!?"

"We came here to confess our love for one another to her goddess, Athena," I explained. "But we just got caught up in our bliss. Poseidon then seduced me here, and I gave myself to him."

Athena roared when I made this confession. "*Love*!? Ha! Young man, do you honestly believe my dear uncle *loves* you!?"

"Yes. He does love me. We've been meeting every single night for the past several months. He wants to take me away from here, to live in his palace with him, as his lover," I brazenly shared.

"Foolish boy! Just listen to yourself. And where is Poseidon now? Why is he not here to take you away as you presumed?" Athena inquired.

"I... I am not sure," I admitted.

"I will tell you exactly where he is. He is already on to the next mortal. That's what my uncle does. He locks on to the most beautiful females, and evidently males, and he sets his sights on bedding and making love to them. And that's precisely what he has done with you. It's a game to him. And whether you knew you were playing or not, you have lost."

"No. That can't be true. But he told me..." I began with.

Athena immediately cut me off. "...That he loved you? Let me guess, did he promise to shower you with gifts, and feed you some pathetic line about how you are the only person he could imagine his life with? That he could picture being with no other lover, but you?"

Athena was accurate in all of her statements.

I affirmed they were correct. "Yes…"

"Imbecile! And you believed him!? Well, let me fill you in on what has since transpired. I met with Poseidon today on Mount Olympus. He explained to me how he met the most beautiful man in Athens, one of my very own servants. He then gave himself a mission to not only make this servant of mine *impure*, against all laws I have set forth in my temple, but to add insult to injury, he wanted to personally make love to this man in the holiest of places known to me. It was nothing more than an act of revenge he sought after, to get back at me for other issues he and I have had over the years."

I was completely dumbfounded. It was still hard to believe. *Did Poseidon really use me as a… sexual conquest? Was I just a puppet in some sort of game, as Athena suggested? A family quarrel that I now find myself in the middle of?* I asked myself. I didn't want to believe it but Poseidon's absence for the past several days, and even now, made me fear Athena was telling the truth. He used me and plucked at my heart with his extravagant dinners and love-making. Poseidon even allowed me to think he was showcasing his vulnerability by sharing traumatic experiences from his past. All of it was an act of manipulation in order to bed me.

How could I have been so stupid? I completely fell for the god. I had thought I was the one that was using my beauty to take advantage of the opportunity to better my current situation, when in fact, it was Poseidon using his godly qualities to take advantage of me, instead. I was played like a lyre. And now, no one would come to rescue me from here. I had no other choice but to seek Athena's forgiveness.

"Goddess Athena, I am truly sorry for what I have done. I have completely disobeyed you. I have brought shame to you and my sisters," I expressed with sorrow.

"And I even gave you fair caution," Athena added. "I warned you that your handsomeness would be a temptation to others, and even yourself. I told you that others would attempt to seduce you but under no circumstances were you to give into them. You have now deliberately defied me, and this will be the last time you ever do!" Athena's tone drastically changed, becoming irate.

My sisters finally stepped in to defend me.

"Goddess Athena," Stheno addressed her, "Please do not fully blame Meduso for what you think as him being rebellious. He is still young, and we have sheltered him for far too long from the outside world. He has still to fully grow out of his innocence."

"So, are you saying you and your family are equally to blame for his poor choices?" Athena asked.

Both Euryale and Stheno nodded in agreement. "Yes. We are to blame as well."

I felt the need to interject. Euryale and Stheno should not have to suffer for my decisions. This was all on me, and no one else should be associated with it. "No! This is all my fault. This all happened because of me. Please do not find fault with my sisters, dear goddess. I am strictly the one that should be reprimanded and punished. They were not involved in any of this…"

"Enough!" Athena screamed. Her screech was enough to send a painful chill into everyone's ears. "You have proven yourself to be disloyal, untrustworthy, and worst of all, *impure*. You are no servant of mine! Nor will you ever represent me in any fashion! For committing such a crime, you will be heavily punished! All of you!"

Athena's white wings spread from her back, and she levitated into the air. The candles and lanterns in the chamber faded and went to darkness. Her eyes turned blood red, lighting up the entire room with a crimson brightness.

I shuddered at the terrifying scene and huddled with my sisters, who were now shivering with fear. Athena's voice now deepened into a demonic tone. "You say you are partly to blame for your brother's actions? All of your family members are sea monsters and creatures, are they not!? I'm sure they view all of your beauty as a blessing. Well, no longer will they be blessed!"

The powerful goddess held out her hands with each of her palms facing both Euryale and Stheno. A blinding light reflected from them and was aimed at each of my sisters. We were all forced to close our eyes at its intensity.

"You all slithered your way into my temple only to

betray me! Your beauty will be no longer! Now you will take on the forms of the snakes you truly are!" Athena screeched.

I opened my eyes and stepped back from the altar, horrified by what I was witnessing. Stheno and Euryale were no longer human. The lower half of their body was made of scales. It was the tail of a snake, just as Athena had referred to them as. Black, dark green, and mucky looking. But worst of all, their hair was replaced by live snakes! At least ten of them growing from each of their scalps, each angrily hissing and snapping at unseen enemies.

Euryale cried in horror at her grotesque transformation. The venomous snakes on her head shook with each wailing noise she made. Stheno made circles to get a better glimpse of her new appendages. She placed her hands over her face to cover her eyes, not even wanting to continue to bear witness to her new ugliness.

"Now, heed my warning, monsters. For anyone that gazes into your eyes, they will be turned to stone indefinitely! A justifiable punishment for you all turning a blind eye on your brother!"

Athena pointed at me. The white light immersed from her palm once again, heading straight at me. My legs closed in and felt as if they were mending together. I watched in horror as they transformed, the milky white skin on them turning to dark scales. The upper half of my body remained human, but my lower half was that of a serpent. The color of my scales was of a different shade compared to my sisters. It had a golden hue to it, but with black stripes throughout its entire length.

I yelled at the monstrosity of myself. I then patted my head to notice that I did not have any snakes attached to me as my sisters had. My golden hair was still intact.

Athena's eyes returned to normal and she floated back down to the ground. Her white feathers disappeared, while the candles and lanterns in the chamber relit themselves.

"And you, Meduso. I have different plans for you. No, you will not have serpents on your head. I still need you to be handsome. I will issue a decree across the lands. I will make it known that you monsters have defied me, and anyone who brings your head to me shall be greatly rewarded. However, any mortal who gazes into your eyes will be turned to stone. You can either allow yourself to be killed or be responsible for the deaths of countless noble warriors. A fitting punishment based on your actions, is it not!?"

I was rendered speechless from the shock of it all. But I heard every single one of her words. They clung to me and pinned themselves down to my very inner core.

"Now go! You are forever banished from Athens! I suggest you find a great hiding place, far, far away from here. My loving followers will soon be after you. Let the hunt begin!" Athena laughed almost diabolically.

My sisters and I fled from her sight, slithering away. We now became enemies of the Olympian gods and all mortals. *Was this what the Fates intended? They led me to*

Poseidon and this heinous punishment. Was it my destiny to be this... monster!? I questioned.

My once great love story was now one of tragedy. I would forever be known as a beautiful young man who used his vanity to his benefit. People would think that I used my beauty to defy the gods, and as punishment, half of my body was turned into an ugly, monstrous snake, while the other half remained handsome. Men would learn of my incredible allure and when they hunted me, they would need to fight against the temptation of falling for me, this beautiful serpentine creature I had now become, or else be damned themselves.

Act II

Meduso: The Gorgon

Chapter 11

I would be forever changed after that last day in Athens. There were only two sets of feelings I was able to hold on to in my heart.

The first was guilt. I had led my sisters down the path of ruin with me. They were now forever transformed and punished as these heinous monsters all because of my actions. Nothing I could ever do would be enough to amend for this. No apology would ever suffice. I had to eventually learn to just accept this and bear the guilt for the rest of my life.

The second was distrust. The only two people I could ever trust were Euryale and Stheno. My view of the world was now tainted. I have been deceived and harmed by far too many individuals. I now adopted the idea of *burn or be burned*. I could only look out for myself and my sisters. Everyone else in my path would need to die. I had no other choice but to live by this mantra, for fear that we could be murdered by anyone.

During our departure from Athens, Euryale, Stheno, and I would only travel in the middle of the night, realizing it was the safest time for us to move about in the open. In the mornings and daytime, we camped in any nearby, uninhabited forest or area that we could find along the way. Where were we going? We hadn't the slightest idea. We just continued to move west, as far away as we could from any form of civilization.

We spent nearly four months just hiking through lands, hills, and mountains. We had to pause every time we needed to cross a body of water. I made a small sturdy boat each time that would allow us to safely cross rivers and seas. I still had a vivid memory of the boat Dictys, the fisherman, used on the island of Seriphos. I structurally modeled them after his, and sure enough, they were able to hold all three of us gorgons to safely cross.

We were very fortunate that no one attacked us during our days spent camping in the woods. Each of us rotated as being a guardian of the grounds, watching over the other two who slept. We repeated this process for several months until we finally reached a secluded island. There was no sign of any humans here. It was just us and plenty of wildlife. Surely, we were far enough away where no one would be able to track us down so easily.

"I think we have found our permanent residence. What do you both think?" Stheno asked.

Euryale and I both agreed with her.

"Okay. I guess we should explore this island and get used to our surroundings," she suggested.

This island would eventually become known as Sarpedon. For now, my sisters and I felt no need to give it a name. It was simply our home, isolated from the rest of the world. The layout of this place reminded me so much of Seriphos. The surrounding cerulean water was just as transparent. A majority of the mainland was composed of forests with a few streams, springs, and even a large lake on the eastern side. To the west were mountains with many caves scattered throughout.

Since we were the only monsters here, we each claimed our own cave and then discussed what we would use the others for, including food storage, a gathering place for plants and herbs, among other things.

It was getting late after our first day of exploring the island. For this evening, we agreed that all three of us would stick together and sleep in the same cave. Stheno and I went out to gather wood to start a fire while Euryale collected some berries and other edible plants we could sustain our appetites with. I distinctly remember the many times Perseus showed me how to start a fire and I was pleased at myself for remembering his technique. It must have been almost innate to me now.

Stheno gave me a quizzical expression. "Where did you learn to do that?"

"Seriphos. A friend there showed me how to properly strike these glassy cave stones to ignite the timber," I explained. I still had never discussed about my true relationship that existed with Perseus to Stheno. She still assumed we were just friends. Only Euryale was the one I confided in and knew of my real feelings for him. I caught Euryale slyly grin at me as I made reference to him.

"Anyway, this should be able to keep the fire going for

the entire night," I stated as I analyzed the bulk amount of wood we had gathered.

We all sat facing the flames. Our tails spread to form a circle around the fire, wanting to also keep them warm as well. It was such a unique feeling to now only have one elongated appendage as my lower body. But I now had months to get used to it. However, I could not even imagine what it would feel like to have living snakes in my hair. My sisters' serpents were silent and had their eyes closed. I knew they would sleep through the night.

Those snakes were a never-ending reminder of my culpability. The worst part about our curse was that Euryale and Stheno received the short-end of the stick. We all were transformed into gorgons, but my sisters had the additional repercussion of having to suffer with their hair loss. I should have been the one solely punished, yet Euryale and Stheno were the ones that had to endure more agony than me. It was unfair, and not a day had gone by since the incident where I did not think about my actions and this end result.

"So, this is our new home..." Euryale broke our silence with.

"It would seem so. We will need to hideout here for years," Stheno shared. "If we find that too many mortals discover our whereabouts, then we will need to conceal ourselves elsewhere."

I remained still, just gazing into the fire. I barely said much to my sisters these days. I preferred to bottle up my feelings and emotions. Sharing them aloud would just be painful, and I felt it was best to just avoid them altogether.

"Now that we can finally rest, I think we should have *the talk*," Stheno stated as she made eye contact with Euryale, who nodded at her.

"Yes. It has now been months. We really should clear the air," Euryale added.

I was bewildered at what they were referring to. "What talk?"

"Brother, we forgive you. We know you are burdening yourself with how this panned out," Stheno replied.

"It's not your fault, Meduso," Euryale chimed in with.

"Yes, it is," I clarified. "If it weren't for me, you would still be the way you once were."

"But who says we wanted to be that way?" Stheno sighed. "Look, after that conversation you initially had with us about Poseidon, it really had me thinking. You were right, brother. We had lost our freedom. Forever in servitude to Athena. Now, we are free to live our lives how we would like to. So what if I have a tail and a few reptiles on my head? It's better than scrubbing floors and washing clothes for the rest of our lives."

"Plus, that Athena... she's a nasty goddess!" Euryale shouted.

Stheno and I gasped at our sister's response. It was so out of character for her. I've never heard her say something like that in my entire life.

"She is!" Euryale reiterated. "Think about it. What kind of goddess forces her servants to be pure, preventing them from having children and from loving another? That's just plain cruel!"

I lightly smiled at the reaction of my sisters. "I appreciate the both of you saying that to me. But I will still always feel guilty over how all of this turned out. I'm so sorry."

"Apology accepted, brother. Do not dwell on the past. We must all look forward to the future. Now we have our whole lives ahead of us. Our adventures can finally begin!" Stheno enthusiastically declared.

"Yeah! Now no one controls us. Our parents hold no power over our heads and Athena can no longer intimidate us. It's such an amazing feeling!" Euryale expressed.

This was something I never even considered, but Euryale had an extremely valid point. I no longer had a fear of every decision I would make. Even if I did make a mistake or error, there would be no form of punishment. It was a weight I was finally able to realize that was lifted from my shoulders. Never again would I have to fear someone else's disappointment and reprimand.

After just a few months, I knew Sarpedon like the back of my hand. The shortcuts between the mountains and the beaches were easy for me to navigate. I knew where every species of plant grew on the island. This was beyond valuable in order to help with any illnesses or injuries any of us had. I was able to concoct a medicinal remedy with specific herbs and plants. The island was slowly, but surely, becoming a *home* for me.

Now that I had more free time throughout the day and no longer tolerated the long hours of labor at a worthless temple, I was able to learn new skills and hone my previous ones to perfection. My agility and speed had surprisingly improved with my lack of legs. I was able to glide effortlessly between locations at such great velocities.

My combat skills were also now refined. I was thankful that Stheno also had interest in sparring and fighting with weaponry. Although our natural resources on the island were very limited compared to what we had been used to, we were able to be innovative and carve wood and use shards of glass and stone from the different caves on the island to make various forms of weapons. Stheno and I practiced fighting one another on a daily basis. We were even able to convince Euryale to join in periodically, advising her that there could come a time when she would need to defend herself if we ever faced intruders on the island who were determined to hunt us down.

Over the next year, I became a fierce fighter. Any Athenian army would be lucky to have me as their leader and commander. The muscles in my arms and torso also drastically increased in size. Those were the only muscles in my body that I could now bother to build. My boyish features were dwindling, and I was becoming more and more of a man.

After a long day of exerting our energy on one another, Stheno and I became physically tired from our friendly skirmishes.

Euryale rushed over to us. "I've done it!"

"Done what?" I inquired.

"I can't say just yet, but come back to the dining cave. I've prepared dinner and have a special surprise for us all."

Now I was intrigued. There was not much that Euryale could do to shock me since we all lived on this island together, so I wondered what sort of trick she had up her sleeve and how she was able to stealthily keep this surprise from my sister and me.

We slithered back to the cave and saw a few fish dangling from a drawstring over the fire. A few bird eggs were also cooking on a nearby stone. This couldn't have been the surprise. So, I was curious to learn when Euryale would reveal this to us, but I did not have to wait very long.

She went behind a massive boulder in the cave and returned to us with a large pitcher she somehow made. I dipped my head to get a better look at the contents in the pitcher. It was a scarlet liquid.

"Blood?" Stheno shouted in confusion.

"No! It's wine!" Euryale clarified. "I've made a small grove behind my garden I've been maintaining. I found some grapes on the vines on the east side of the island

and managed to grow them here in the grove. After several months of experimenting and praying to Dionysus, I was finally able to make wine out of them."

"Wait... how do you know it's wine that you actually made?" I asked, curiously.

"Well, I will admit I had to spend several days taste-testing my concoctions and after feeling a bit woozy during my final trial, I realized I mastered the recipe," she confessed.

Stheno and I chuckled at the thought of Euryale inebriated.

"Well, let us try it out. Do not hold back!" Stheno declared.

Euryale grabbed the crafted cups she created and gave us a generous pour of the wine. After taking the first sip, I moaned with pleasure at the smooth taste. It was not bad at all. Euryale had done well. I was quite impressed. We must have all enjoyed the wine more than we anticipated, for Euryale had to make multiple trips back and forth between her grove and the cave in order to restock the pitcher. My mind was fuzzy, and I found myself laughing more carelessly than I normally would.

Stheno had the greatest change in personality. I had never seen this side of her before. She was very touchy and handsy with us, wrapping her hand around my shoulder for a majority of the night.

We continued to imbibe on the wine over the brightly lit fire. We retold many of the memorable stories of our past. "Remember that time you two hid the Graeae's eye in our father's throne room?" Stheno asked.

Euryale and I cracked up, visualizing how angry Deino, Enyo, and Pemphredo were with us.

"Yes. I remember. Father punished me and never let me visit the grotto for a whole month after that incident," I shared.

"Well, I secretly thought it was funny too. I could never admit it, but I had to rush out of the room while father scolded you, brother, because I could no longer contain myself from laughing," Stheno conceded.

We recited more stories and shared in laughter at the memories of them. In recollecting the many times my sisters and I gathered, this had to have been the greatest amount of fun we ever had together. There was never a time I could recall where the three of us were all present and as amused as we were now. It made me hopeful of the future, that there would be many nights like this to look forward to.

"Well, well, well. Aren't we all in pleasant spirits?" an all too familiar voice called from the entrance of the cave.

In an instant reflex, we all rose up into a defensive stance, ready to strike. But as the figure approached, we began to let our guard down. The creature was identical to us, half human, half serpent. It was Echidna.

"Echidna!? How did you find us!?" I asked with vexation. It led me to believe that others must know of our whereabouts, too.

"It wasn't all that difficult. I've studied your paths to the west. I doubt anyone else stalked you as much as I have. Do not forget, although I do try to remain hidden from the rest of the world, I am a goddess. I have the capabilities of transformation and teleportation. I've been watching Meduso here for quite some time. I know exactly of everything that has transpired between him and Poseidon, that dirty god! I am also aware of what has happened to you all because of Athena," she confessed.

"Just what exactly are you up to, Echidna?" Stheno questioned her with skepticism.

"Oh Stheno! You've always held animosity towards me, and for whatever reason, I'll never know. But I did not come here to gloat, nor make any of you feel bad. I came to talk to my dear brother," Echidna explained.

It may have been the wine doing the talking for me, but I felt much braver than I ever have before when I spoke to Echidna. "Whatever you would like to say to me, Echidna, I will allow Euryale and Stheno to also hear it. They have now become involved with every aspect of my life and my actions. So, I no longer wish to withhold any secrets or information from them."

"Very well. I came to tell you what I've always told you. Your beauty…"

Echidna tried to give me further advice, but I instantly prevented her from doing so.

"No! Enough about how I should use my attractiveness to my own advantage. You have ill-advised me, dear sister. This…" I glanced over at both of my gorgon sisters. "This is what your counsel has led to. Embracing vanity has led me down the path of destruction. This is living proof."

"Meduso, now, more than ever, is when you should listen to my words. Do not think that your beauty and charm are what ultimately led to this curse. Your seductive ways allowed you to attract one of the most powerful gods this world has ever seen. If Athena was not in the picture and you were not under her watchful eye, you would still have Poseidon wrapped around your fingers. There were other conflicting factors involved that derailed your plans," Echidna explained. "But enough about that. You should consider your current situation. It's only a matter of time before you are found here. Men will eventually come and hunt you down. Athena has made that abundantly clear. But for your own protection and safety, it's imperative that you do everything in your power to prevent them from killing you. And in order to do that, it's not your skills in fighting or any form of strength that will be your greatest asset. It will be your looks that will entice them and lead them to their demise. You must seduce these men, Meduso. Make them stare into your eyes and it will be the last thing they ever glare upon."

I could not argue with her. Athena made these same sentiments known to me and my physical features were what I would need to utilize in order to survive. This was something I was prepared for.

Echidna moved toward me rubbing her hands against my jawline. "Even now, in this monstrous state, you are an impeccable creature. If you weren't my brother…"

Stheno had enough with where this conversation was going. "Okay, Echidna. I think you have made your point very clear."

Echidna sneered, realizing she had made our sister uncomfortable with the conversation. "Anyway, just understand that you using your beauty is what will now dictate life or death for you." She clenched her hand into a fist. "Make all of those weak, mortal, warriors pay! Force them to bow and serve you! Oh… and if you're unsure of what to do with their stone bodies when you get bored with them, I could always use a few more decorations around my cave."

Chapter 12

I had now reached the age of twenty-five, not that anyone cared, nor should I. Age was just a number that only reminded you of the time you had left in this world, if you were a mortal. It had been months now since my gorgon sisters and I first arrived at Sarpedon.

Echidna had been our only visitor since our arrival on this island. Otherwise, we only had each other's company. No one else. I was actually glad that this was the case. The fewer people that knew of our whereabouts then the less risk there was in having hunters and warriors from all corners of the world find us and try to kill me in the name of their deity.

Stheno and I decided to practice sword-fighting on the beach today. As we navigated there, we noticed a small wooden raft sitting on the sandbar. This immediately alarmed the both of us.

"Go check on Euryale," I quickly advised.

"But, Meduso…" she attempted to persuade me otherwise, but I wasn't having any of it.

"Just go. Now!" I shouted.

Stheno nodded and returned to the eastern side of the island to find Euryale. It was now just me and my sword. I cautiously searched along the beach, finding no sign of life. Then, fear struck me. There they were; recent footprints in the sand leading to the nearby forest.

I followed the footprints, making sure to check behind every shrub and tree I passed along the way. I knew this day would eventually come, but somewhere in my heart, I had hoped it never would. As I proceeded further into the forest, a slight chill grazed across the small hairs on my neck. Sensing the danger, I whirled around to see a sword flying vertically down at me. I was able to use my own sword to block the blow, but as soon as I did, the man swung again, completely missing me. The man's sword swings were erratic, lacking any sense of precision. Surely Athena's hunters were better trained than this? But then I realized the reason behind his poor accuracy. The man's eyes were shut.

He continued to swing aimlessly, refusing to open his eyes. I stepped back quietly, watching this pitiful performance of his, placing my hand over my mouth to hide the noise of my laughter so he wouldn't be able to pinpoint where I was.

"Come out! Damn you!" The man yelled in anger.

I studied him carefully. He was a little rugged, but fairly handsome, with his olive complexion. His brown hair was long, with a matching beard. However, what drew me to him were those exposed, massive legs of his. They were tight and thick, prompting me to imagine what they connected to. But I would only be able to speculate.

"So, you've come to kill me…" I quickly moved to the side and glided to a new location, realizing the man was attempting to move closer to wherever my voice came from.

"You're a monster! An enemy of the Goddess Athena. There is a bounty on your head and I will make sure to claim it," the warrior proclaimed.

"I am no monster. I was once a human too, but Athena turned me into this. Surely, you must see that this is a mistake," I explained.

"The only one mistaken here is you, gorgon! Athena herself said you are a harm to mankind. You expect me to believe you over a goddess?"

I continued to dodge his attempted strikes. "Please, stop this! I don't want to hurt you!"

"Never! You're trying to trick me with your sorcery!" he stated.

"I am not trying to trick anyone. I swear!"

"Lies! You want me to believe you and then when I open my eyes, you will turn me to stone!"

"The only reason I can turn people to stone is because of Athena. She placed the curse on me."

"Liar! The goddess has spoken. She has warned many of your cursed spell with your gaze." He continued to relentlessly swing at the air.

"I'm telling you, I mean no harm! You must believe me!"

"Lies! Your deceit knows no bounds, gorgon. I do not believe you," he replied.

I was now becoming agitated by him. I saw no way of reasoning with this man. Trying to convince him to leave peacefully wasn't going to work.

I knew that only one of us would walk away from this fight. As I watched the man slash wildly with his sword, I silently asked the gods to forgive me for what I was about to do.

I used my inhuman speed to dart around the hunter and deliver a swift elbow to his side. Caught by surprise, the man released his sword. He dropped to his knees and felt around the ground, looking for the fallen weapon. It reminded me of the Graeae, blindly searching the floor for their missing eyeball that Euryale and I would toss around to each other. But this time, I wasn't laughing.

I flicked my tail, wrapping it around the warrior's arms and chest. Trapped, the man struggled furiously as I pulled him in close. I placed my hands on the man's cheeks and, with a heavy heart, told him, "You fought well. I commend you for your bravery. I didn't want it to come to this."

I lifted the man's eyelids with my thumbs. Despite the tears forming, I forced myself to look the man in his terror-filled eyes. It took mere seconds for the man's body to turn to cold stone. I released my tail's grip and backed up. I stared at the face of the man, now frozen forever in horror.

When I finally allowed myself to turn around, I saw my sisters standing several yards away. I slowly began to move past them.

Quietly, Euryale addressed me, "Meduso, dear brother, are you okay?"

I was too upset to respond. I feared that if I even

attempted to open my mouth, I would begin sobbing, and I wasn't sure I'd be able to stop. So, I moved away from my sisters without saying a word.

Later that day, I reconvened with meeting my sisters. We sat in the dining cave together.

"Meduso, I'm sorry you had to go through that," Euryale sincerely said.

"It's hard to believe that we have the ability to turn people to stone, but Athena was absolutely serious about it," Stheno added.

I shook my head. "It was bound to happen at some point or another. At least we got that out of our systems. I'm sure the first one will always be the worst. I know there will be more to come in the future. I just hope the lake is big enough to hold all of them."

Stheno and Euryale both laughed at my twisted comment. "Well, I'm glad to see you are in higher spirits," Stheno shared.

"Yes. I cannot even imagine what must have been going through your mind," Euryale empathized with me.

"I will get used to it. Now, I have my wits about me. But I have to thank you both for being so willing to protect me. I am so lucky to have sisters like you who care for me the way you do," I mentioned.

"Come. Let us not get all sappy on one another,"

Stheno declared. "We should return to the beach and that forest where we saw that man at. We should keep his sword and retrieve any other materials he may have brought with him. Then we need to dispose of the raft."

"Surely, there should be something of use to us," Euryale hoped.

It was agreed. We all swiftly moved across the island, picking up our pace the further we went, knowing it was only a matter of time before the sun would set. I collected the finely forged sword the warrior had used against me. "Not bad at all," I said to myself as I cleanly felt the blade with my palm.

Euryale and Stheno glided ahead of me towards the shore. I trailed behind them to see that they were already emptying the containments of the bag the man had brought. There was a clay pot we could use for cooking. We also found fishing lines which I could easily make into a pole to bait the fish as Dictys and Perseus had once shown me.

There were other materials and equipment we figured we could make use out of as cooking utensils and tools for Euryale's garden. This was not a bad find at all. Each of us was pleased.

"Would it be terrible for me to admit that I hope more men come here to bring us goods like this?" Euryale giggled as she suggested this.

"I would rather not risk the chance of being killed, but yes, I would not mind getting more supplies," I answered.

"We must get rid of the raft now. We have no use for

it, and I would not want to draw attention to this island for those that are merely passing by it," Stheno commanded.

"Well, how do you suppose we get rid of it?" Euryale asked.

"The wood seems usable. It would be a shame to waste it. Are we able to all carry it back with us to use for the fire?" I inquired.

"I think we can handle it," Stheno replied.

"Okay. I guess I don't really have a say in this, do I?" Euryale questioned.

Stheno and I shook our heads.

Euryale sighed, knowing she would have to put in the work and tedious labor to drag this raft with us across the island. "Well then, I plan on having an extra cup of wine after this. I deserve it!"

Chapter 13

Oh, the number of men that have come and gone… to the bottom of the lake. Given how upset I was after each time I killed a warrior, Stheno and Euryale immediately dumped the stoned bodies in the lake, so that they would never be seen again, a way to not have me constantly reminded of these dreadful experiences. I was beginning to lose count of the hunters whose lives I was forced to end. It had been another year spent on the island and no warrior, no matter how strong or skilled, was a match for the gorgons. One right after the other, they all turned to stone.

However, there came a day where I found myself in an unusual predicament that I hadn't anticipated. Word must have gotten out across the world of my beauty. I hid in the forest behind a tree, noticing two men step forward. They had both of their arms spread out, eyes closed, calling to me.

"Gorgon! We come in peace. We have no weapons, just ourselves. Please show yourself to us. Allow us to look into our shields to see your alluring features," the taller of the two men shouted. He was slightly leaner than the other human next to him, but still had an attractive figure. The smaller man was very muscular, to the point where I was able to make out his coursing veins that bulged from his wide arms and legs. Both men stripped down to reveal their full, solid, tight bodies. Nothing was left to the imagination.

At first, I automatically presumed this was a trick they were trying to pull but was impressed with their ingenuity and intellect in using their shields as a way to not have to look directly into my eyes. However, I could see that they were unarmed besides their shields which were placed upright against a nearby tree, that they gazed into. If they were to try and deceive me, I knew I would easily be able to handle them head-on. I felt confident, with nothing to fear.

I came out of hiding and approached them from behind. I was able to see them glancing at me through their silver shields. The shorter, but stockier man was awestruck. "My gods! Even the tales of your handsomeness do not do you justice. Please, come to me. Allow us to service you."

I moved closer to them, raising my brow. "You've come to service me?"

"Yes. I am Plythonakis of Athens and this is Belthos of Athens as well. We want to offer ourselves to you. Allow us to show you a passion you've never experienced in your entire life," the taller man explained.

"You want to… make love to me?" I was quite confused by this whole thing. How could these men be so willing to fulfill their carnal pleasures when they had no feelings for me? I assumed people only made love to one another if they were, in fact, actually in love.

These men now had me curious. It had been over a year since a man last touched me. I would be lying to myself if I said I did not miss being the admiration of another man and having a warm body against my own. Now, I not only had one man who was willing to make love to me but two.

I could not help but give into my longing desires to be touched once again. I stretched my hands to cup Belthos' broad shoulders. The man moaned with pleasure and closed his eyes, spinning around to face me. His hands gently caressed my scales before moving higher to my torso. Plythonakis came from behind, softly kissing my neck.

It was hard to believe that these men had traveled to the end of the world just to gain the experience of making love with me. Because of my lack of appendages, my lovemaking abilities were limited. However, I watched as the men penetrated one another in front of me, using my hands and mouth to join them whenever the opportunity arose. After a wild day of passion, it was time for these men to leave and part ways with me.

These male mortals kept their word, and therefore, I had no reason to believe that they would turn against me. I returned to the beach with Plythonakis and Belthos. They looked into their shields to make eye contact with me as they spoke without any harm being done.

"We would love to return here in the future," Plythonakis suggested. "I wish we could stay and live our lives here with you, but we must return to Athens. We have other duties we cannot ignore."

"Of course. I would thoroughly enjoy your company again," I confessed as the two boarded their boat.

"You are truly out of this world, Meduso. I cannot wait to get my hands on you again," Belthos eagerly expressed.

I chuckled at the two of them. Soon, they departed, while I waited on the shore, watching them and their boat get smaller in my vision as it sailed into the distance. But now, something else caught my eye. It was the dark clouds and atmosphere moving in on them so quickly.

I had never seen the weather change so drastically on the island. But it wasn't just the weather that worsened; the waters did too. There was no way a single boat could survive this type of storm now coming in. Surely, they would capsize. I shouted out to Plythonakis and Belthos as loudly as I could, fruitlessly attempting to warn them of the incoming nefarious climate, but to no avail.

My eyes widened in horror when I saw the incoming tidal wave crash on top of them. As soon as the wave departed, the sea quickly settled and there was still no sign of them.

Were my eyes deceiving me? I could not comprehend what I had just witnessed. No storm and wave could just appear like that without an influence. Something like this doesn't just happen out of the blue. It had to have been from... no, it couldn't be!

"I am glad to see you are doing well, Meduso." The deep voice from behind startled me.

I spun around, surprised to see that the figure was able to sneak up on me so stealthily. But it wasn't just any figure. It was Poseidon.

His form did not change one bit since the last time I saw him. His cerulean eyes matched the sea and his auburn hair glistened in the sun.

"Why did you kill those men!?" I yelled angrily.

"Those men committed a crime in my eyes. They made love to a lover of mine and wanted to live to tell the day. That cannot be allowed."

"And you have some nerve showing your face here!" I exclaimed.

"Do not be so vile towards me. I did nothing wrong to you," Poseidon stated.

"Are you serious right now!? Just look at me, Poseidon. All of this is because of you. This is all your fault!" I shouted.

"Meduso, you had an equal part you played in your demise. Do not be so foolish. Ever should you be so lucky you had the opportunity to bed me, God of the sea," he explained. "You should be honored I chose you out of the countless mortals that would kill for the chance to have me."

I became sickened, my stomach turning in a thousand different directions. I already knew that Poseidon had fooled me, but hearing the god confirm it himself, from his own mouth, was another thing. This was all just some game to Poseidon. He never really loved me at all.

He stepped closer to me, placing his hands on my face,

slightly squeezing my cheeks. "Look into my eyes. Besides your sisters', I am sure mine are the only ones you have been able to gaze fully into, without any damage being done."

Poseidon was right. He was the only man whose eyes I was able to look into since my serpentine transformation.

"You are mine, Meduso. My property and mine alone."

He attempted to pull me into him, but I pushed the god away. "I was seduced once by you. I won't make that same mistake again."

Poseidon's face shifted into displeasure. "Fine! Have it your way, but know that I will be damned to the Underworld before I let another man touch you again. You are mine, Meduso, and only mine! No other man will ever have you. I possess you. I own you!"

I stepped further back from the angered god. As much as I wanted to yell and hit Poseidon, I knew that would be a mistake. Defying a god in such a way would be a death sentence. Thus, I kept my composure but still stood my ground. "Be that as it may, I cannot promise you I will never love again."

Poseidon crossed his arms over his chiseled chest. "You don't have a choice in the matter. No man will ever step foot on this island again for you to love. I will curse the waters surrounding this island. Even the bravest of warriors will never be able to withstand my turbulent sea."

I could not believe that this territorial side of Poseidon

was coming forth. The jealousy was oozing out of him. I simply stood stunned, unsure of what to even say to the god that would not get me into trouble.

"I must go now," Poseidon stated, much to my relief. "Remaining here for a long period of time will surely draw the attention of the other gods," he explained.

Poseidon turned his back to me and stepped into the water, but then paused before leaving. "Oh, I do have something I would like you to have before I depart."

The sea god lowered his hands into the water and began chanting something in a language I was not accustomed to. His hands then rose towards the sky. I looked to the clouds. A beam of light protruded through them, aimed directly at the island. A figure emerged, making its way towards us. As it came closer, I realized it was a horse with the most divine, angelic feathered wings I had ever seen in my life; a beautiful creature.

As the horse landed on the ground, it stood still, lowering its head. I came forward and began petting it. He was magnificent. His hair was the softest thing I had ever felt. I was startled when the horse pressed his snout into my face, causing me to chuckle at its endearing gesture.

"His name is Pegasus, and he is yours now, Meduso," Poseidon stated. "There may come a time where you need to make a desperate escape from this island. Pegasus will be your best means for that," he advised.

I raised a brow at his response. "If you're preventing anyone from coming to this island, why would I ever need to escape it?"

"There could be a number of reasons why you would need to beyond that. Do you not want the horse's company?"

"I do. But how would I use him? I don't have legs to ride him. I would be unable to leave this island on him," I replied.

Poseidon shrugged. "That's not my problem. You can figure it out. It shouldn't be that hard."

I was becoming irritated with Poseidon's vague responses, but that didn't stop me from wanting answers about this glorious creature. "Where did Pegasus come from? How did you obtain him?"

"Do not concern yourself with that. There are just some things that are best left unsaid."

"Wait a second, you're not leaving him here to hide him from someone, are you? Is that your true intention?" I asked with skepticism.

"Rationalize it however you will. This is a safe place for Pegasus, and I am sure you could use the company and you may even come to rely on him in a time of peril," Poseidon said very nonchalantly.

"Fine. I will take care of him," I declared.

"Good. I was hoping you would accept him. Then it is settled." The sea god dove into the water, disappearing.

My attention shifted back to Pegasus as I continued to caress him. "Are you hungry?" I was not sure what to expect. Of course, the horse could not speak, but who knows, if he had wings, he could be capable of other things, right?

Pegasus did not respond to me, but I led the ivory horse into the forest and back towards our caves. "We'll stop and pluck some apples for you along the way. I'm not sure where you came from, but I'm certain you could use something to eat from your journey."

I began to grow fond of the obedient horse. When I returned him to the caves for Euryale and Stheno to see, I shared everything with them that had transpired. I promised to hide no more secrets from them, so I gave every detail of my encounter with Poseidon.

"I think you are right to assume Poseidon has a few extra tricks up his sleeve," Stheno agreed. "I wonder if he stole the horse from someone or perhaps the horse is his son, given birth by another."

Euryale was distracted, not even bothering to listen to Stheno and me. She stood admiring the glorious horse. "Let me show Pegasus the garden. There is plenty of food he may enjoy from there," Euryale suggested.

I nodded. "That sounds like a wonderful idea."

Euryale then took the horse away, leaving Stheno and me alone.

"Meduso, please tell me you have not fallen back in love with Poseidon."

I let out a heavy grunt, annoyed that Stheno would even think such a thing. "Of course not! How could I love a man who betrayed me in every possible way? The only feeling I have for him is disgust!"

"Well, as long as it is not love, then I suppose that is

good. Just remember, Meduso, he could still be lying to you. I have a hunch that there is a great deal that he is keeping from you. You should not trust him so easily."

"I don't trust him at all, Stheno. I will continue to keep my guard up."

I turned my head from my sister, deep in thought. I knew Poseidon would likely keep the curse on the island for as long as I lived. On one hand, I was relieved to know that no warrior would be able to withstand Poseidon's waters to come to the island to hunt me down. On the other hand, this meant that I would remain lonely here with my sisters. No other man would be able to touch and love me the way I needed to be loved.

Chapter 14

It had been a couple months since I last saw Poseidon. However, I knew he watched over me. There were no warriors that managed to make it to the shore of Sarpedon from here on out. And that was Poseidon's doing. Whenever a boat was traveling directly towards the island, Poseidon continued to summon the most severe of storms and rough waters to capsize their ships. Driftwood from their boats and even some of their limp and unresponsive bodies washed up on the shore. It forced my sisters and me to have to dump their remains into the lake, so we would never have to look at the ghastly sight of their dead, decayed limbs ever again.

Although Poseidon's curse may have been protecting me by ridding me of these hunters before they could ever make it to our beaches, it was actually doing more mental harm to me. I wanted to see to these strong men up close. Some of which I was desperate to feel and come in contact with. Now, I would never be able to experience that again.

Poseidon was not joking when he said that he did not want anyone else getting sexually involved with his lover. I felt practically claimed by him, but that was not my desire. I became disheartened, realizing my body and its urges would be unfulfilled, an empty vessel never having the opportunity to have its sexual appetite sustained for the rest of my life.

I kept my mind busy, trying not to think about this island prison I was trapped on. Euryale taught me new techniques in her garden, so I often tended it with her during the day. Stheno and I rarely practiced our combat skills with one another, now that no man was likely to ever step foot on Sarpedon again. My constant desire and anticipation for sexual thrills was no more. Now being on Sarpedon was truly the punishment it was originally intended to be.

One evening, I felt the need to be on my own. I made my way to the beach and set up a fire for myself. A pastime I cherished. I recalled the days when Perseus and I would venture out to the shores of Seriphos and count the stars in the open night sky. I stared up at them, admiring their ephemeral beauty, knowing they would retire at dawn.

"*Katasterismoi*," an unknown voice called from behind me.

I sharply turned around, backing up to prep my stance, ready for combat. The figure held a bronze shield up to cover his face. He continued to speak. "A young, handsome lover once told me that the small traces of light in the sky were created by Artemis. They tell famous stories of the past. The gods called them *Katasterismoi*."

The softness yet bravado in his tone was faintly recognizable to me. The warrior lowered his shield, but then kept his eyes closed, revealing his chiseled face and athletic body. "Meduso, it's me…" he called out.

"Perseus!? It cannot be!?" I exclaimed. But I had no doubt that it was him. It had now been about eight years since I last laid eyes on him. Although this man had similar features to the Perseus I remember, there was something a little different about him. This fellow seemed more stout and his hair was grown out a few extra inches.

"It's me, Meduso. In the living flesh. I promised we would meet again. And I am a man of my word." Although his eyelids still remained shut, he was able to smile in my direction, allowing me to view those gleaming ivories of his. That smile still made me melt, even to this very day.

I slowly approached him, somewhat cautiously, still unsure if this was, in fact, reality. I needed to touch him right now. It would be instant proof that this was not some cruel trick the gods were playing on me. I caressed his soft, smooth cheeks with my palms. "Perseus! It really is you! But how?"

"I want to explain everything to you. But first, I want to be able to look at you, Meduso. I cannot bear to go on for another moment without getting the chance to gaze into your eyes," he confessed.

Although the flames were high and the moon graced us with its luminescence, it still was not enough. Plus, there was no form of reflection he would be able to glance into to prevent me from turning him to stone. However, there was one place that was ideal.

"Let's return to my cave. We can set your shield up

there and then we can cut some of the glass stone from the cavern walls. You can view me through them," I explained. "Come. Hold my hand and I will guide us there."

My fingers intertwined with his. I could not help but simper. The instant our hands were locked, I felt a charge rush right from him and into me. It was as if Zeus's own lightning bolts were passing through us. I slowly escorted him through the forest, making sure he found his footing and did not trip on any of the tree roots nor stumble on any of the debris that we walked on to return to my personal lair.

I had him remain standing in the cave as I set up his shield against a boulder. I had to start another fire, and quickly did so, as if my life depended on it. Without a fire, it would be too dark to see each other. Every second that passed by where I didn't get the chance to fully see his face felt like an extra dagger plunging into my heart.

Finally, everything was situated as best as I could make it for the moment. I placed my hand on his broad shoulders and guided him over to his bronze shield. "You can open your eyes now, Perseus."

And he did. Those were his hazel-green eyes I was able to make out through the reflection of his shield. This was Perseus. My Perseus. However, my sapphire eyes were no more, since my change in appearance. So, these honey-colored eyes of mine would be new to him.

"I cannot believe it's really you. I had heard rumors of a male gorgon that was formerly Athena's servant, living on this island. I had my suspicions that it was you, and sure enough, they were accurate. Meduso, you still look so beautiful. So magnificent."

As flattered as I was, with my face now flushed, I still felt slightly ashamed that he did not get to experience me as he once had. I fretted over the idea that he would no longer be attracted to me with my added serpentine features.

I placed my chin into the cup of his shoulder, still not daring to take my eyes off of him through our reflection. "You have grown into a full-fledged man. A robust and handsome one," I added.

His emotional urges must have been heightened as much as mine were, because he turned around to face me, but had his eyes closed once again. His lips locked with my lips, and we held each other in a passionate embrace as we kissed. I felt trapped in a dream world as our mouths would not dare to separate from one another. This was a dream that I never wanted to wake up from.

Oh, how I missed the feeling of those soft, luscious lips pressed against my own. The taste of his tongue and mouth were just as I remembered them. It was as if our eight-year absence from one another was a minor blip on the timeline and we were back at Seriphos, still as youthful and innocent as we once were.

Perseus tore his clothes off, revealing to me his perfectly round chest and the many curves that formed his abs. Even when we were younger, I always thought Perseus to be extremely muscular, so the fact that their girth had increased only added to my physical attraction towards him.

I was able to fully feel and appreciate his manhood in every possible way. I serviced him with my mouth, pleased that I was able to allow him to release himself. This caused me to become less insecure about my own appearance. Perseus was still drawn to me and wanted to make love to me. It elated me to know that this had not changed.

After an hour of passion, we rested on the floor of the cave, staring up at the stalactites extending from the ceiling. "Perseus, I have so many questions for you. I don't know where to begin."

"Likewise. I have many for you as well. But, let's save all of that for tomorrow. I've had a long journey here to find you, and now that I have, I just want to rest and enjoy our slumber together."

I smirked at his suggestion, but did not dare to look over at him. I had to be very cautious about it, no matter how tempted I was, wanting to stare into those hungry eyes of his. "Yes. Let us sleep now. I want to lie in your arms as we once did in your bed in Seriphos."

I turned so that my back was pressed into his torso, and he wrapped his arms around me in a warm cuddle. "You can rest now, Meduso. I am not going anywhere. There will be many more nights like this to come."

We both woke up the following morning, never wanting to let go of each other. Eventually, we got ourselves together.

"I'm starving," Perseus exclaimed.

"Well, let me run out and get you something to eat. But you have to wait here in this cave."

"Why can't I go with you? I can easily climb trees to collect eggs in the nests. I can also fish for us," he offered.

"Because my sisters do not know of your presence. The last thing I would want to happen would be for them to accidentally look you directly in your eyes," I shared.

"Okay. You make a strong point."

"Yes. Plus, they will never come into my *bed cave*. It's a rule my sisters and I established with one another. So, you will be safe here. Just give me a few minutes and I will be back."

I scurried to Euryale's garden and began gathering some of the easily accessible fruits and vegetables she was growing. For now, this would have to do until I informed my sisters about Perseus's stay with us. Then, he would be able to help us hunt for more variety of foods across the island.

"Here." I laid out the basket of food I collected for him.

"This should hold me over until later. Thank you, Meduso."

He began to chow down on everything with great speed. I nearly forgot about his demi-god nature and appetite. He devoured the entire contents of the basket with ease.

"We need to come up with an innovation," he recommended.

"What do you mean?" I asked.

"There has to be an easier way for me to look at you. It's going to be rather difficult to keep this up, where I am constantly having to make sure I'm closing my eyes around you or trying to glance at you through the shield and other things that give off a reflection."

"Well, there was this unique idea one warrior had when he visited the island. He held a squared piece of glass in front of him at all times. Much to my amazement, he was able to look me directly in the eyes through it, and he did not change to limestone. However, sadly for him, having to hold that glass did no advantage for his swordsmanship skills. He was no match for me."

"Hmmm. Do you have any sort of transparent glass on this island? All of the stones in this cave won't suffice. I can only see my reflection through them," he said.

"Yes, actually. I kept that piece of glass that warrior had. I figured it could come in handy someday." I then rummaged through my pile of supplies and retrieved it. I slowly handed it over to Perseus with care, cautioning him. "Be careful. Some of the edges are sharp."

He examined the material with great focus. I could practically see the wheels in his head turning. "What if we melted this so that it could at least cover my eyes?" he asked, waiting for my opinion.

"That seems manageable, but how will you hold it over your eyes without it falling off?" As I made this remark, I came up with an idea. "Wait, I actually have a solution to that."

I returned to the pile of loose items and then grabbed the fishing line I had. "What if we melt the ends of the glass and place the fishing line in them? Once the glass hardens, the string will be stuck to it and you can tie or wrap it around your head."

"Do you think we could do that?"

"I don't see why not," I optimistically replied.

After several trials and hours of waiting for the glass to melt over the fire and then harden with the fishing line in it, we came up with the final product. We had invented a prototype of what would be known as *goggles* in the future. Not that we would get credit for this invention.

Perseus tied the fishing line around his head and the glass rested on the arch of his nose and bones of his cheeks. He opened his eyes and stared directly at me. Nothing happened, which was the best result possible. They worked!

I now was able to kiss him on the lips and able to look at him as I did so. I held no reservation with the opportunity to do so. I pulled him into me and our mouths collided.

"Now, let's talk," he said. "I want to know everything that happened. As I mentioned yesterday, I heard the rumors about everything that happened to you, but I needed to fully see it to believe it."

It was a torment to have to retell this dreadful tale once again, but I would do it for Perseus. "When I left Seriphos, I spent a little more time at our underwater palace, getting prepared to serve Athena at her temple. Soon enough, when I was ready, my sisters and I traveled to the Acropolis. We became Athena's servants and worked in her temple for five years straight. It was the same routine every single day. Scrubbing floors, washing the limestone columns, cleaning and folding the temple cloths. Can you imagine? This same intensive labor for five years straight? I felt trapped and was losing all hope. My life was passing me by and here I was, realizing I would continue to age while practically being a slave to this goddess. I had no freedom, and I longed for some change and to experience some adventure in the world. And that's when he came..."

I paused before proceeding into this next part of the story. I knew it would pain me to see Perseus's reaction when I would have to tell him about my affair with Poseidon. That I broke the promise Perseus and I made to each other. However, I completely forgot that Perseus already knew this part of the story as did a majority of the world at this point.

"Poseidon?" He filled in the blanks that I did not finish.

"Yes. Perseus, I am so sorry. It had been five years and I had no clue if I would ever see you again. The Fates provided me a vision that I would run into the sea and Poseidon would passionately hold me in his arms. They foretold my affair with Poseidon and led me to predict it. With five years of not being able to see you and having to endure the daily servant tasks, I fell into a deep depression. I walked the beaches of Athens at night to calm my nerves and stress. That's when Poseidon showed up for the first time, at the most opportunistic moment. I was weak and vulnerable and he came out of the water as if he were my savior. He promised to love me and said he would take me away from Athena's clutches," I admitted.

Perseus remained silent for a moment, which caused me anguish. I just watched him, trying to get a read on his face and what he was thinking, but he gave me nothing. Eventually, he let me know his thoughts on the subject.

"Meduso, I cannot lie and tell you that it does not make my stomach turn at the thought of you naked with another man. But I do forgive you. Now, I ask that you forgive me too. I had the same feelings as you when I was on Seriphos. I was lonely when you left. A village girl, named Johakis, comforted and supported me when I was down. She informed me that she would do anything for me. With my sexual thirst still lingering, I did make love to her. But, in the back of my mind, I knew this was just a physical attraction. We had no emotional connection like you and I do. So, I hope you can forgive me as well."

I smiled at Perseus. The thought of him making love to another mortal was unsettling, but I had to get over it. After all, I did the same exact thing as he did. Not being able to forgive him and holding a grudge would only make me hypocritical.

"Of course. I forgive you, Perseus. Let us not remember those minor affairs. We have each other now. That's all I want to focus on," I shared.

"I agree. But I do want to learn a little more about Poseidon. What was he like?"

I exhaled deeply before I described him to Perseus. "He is a god who takes on many shapes. The human form he took for me was that of a large, brawny man. Similar in size to you, but slightly bigger. We did make love, and he took me on as his lover. As I mentioned, he offered to take me into his care and rescue me, giving me the freedom I've always wanted. However, we made love in Athena's temple one night."

I could see the startled expression on Perseus's face when I revealed this, but decided to continue with my story. "I know. Now that I look back, it was a foolish thing to do. Anyway, after that moment, I'm not exactly sure of the facts as to what happened next. Athena summoned my sisters and me to her shrine room. She informed me Poseidon had told her about our affair and that he used me to seek revenge on her. She also shared that he had multiple lovers across the world and was already moving on to his next target."

I let out a deep sigh before continuing. "Athena couldn't just let me solely take the blame for all that I had done. She also faulted my sisters for my lone actions. Thus, she then transformed my sisters and I into this…" I waved my hands across my scales. "Athena informed us that, to add to our punishment, she would cast a curse so that no other mortal would ever be able to look us in the eyes again, for if they did, they would turn to stone. The goddess then declared that she would have hunters and warriors track me down to see which of them was most worthy of killing me. My sisters and I had no choice but to move about in the night and travel as far away as we could from any human life. Eventually, we landed here on this island. And so, there have been many men who have come to this land, all of which were no match for my sisters and me. We were forced to kill every single one of them."

I found myself saying this so matter-of-factly, that I did not even empathize that the thought of me being able to kill so many men could make Perseus feel uncomfortable. However, he showed no signs of it as I informed him of this. "It was a life or death situation I faced, Perseus. There was no reasoning with them as hard as I tried to. I had a mission, and if I wanted to survive and not be murdered by them, I needed to best them or be bested. Yes, I feel shameful about having to do it, but what other choice did I have?"

"I understand, Meduso. You do not need to feel bad on my behalf. I do not fault you. Please, continue," he requested.

I smirked in his direction before going on. "So, after what seemed like countless visitors, my sisters and I have accumulated quite the collection of stone bodies at the bottom of the lake on this island." My dark humor managed to get a chuckle out of Perseus.

"But lately, it's rare that we have any men come to this island now…" I trailed off.

"And why is that?"

"Poseidon made another appearance not long ago. He was displeased of my affairs with some of the men on this island. So, he placed a curse on the surrounding sea. For any ships or boats that now approach this island, he assembles tidal waves and the most dangerous of storms their way, so that they are unable to make it to our shores," I confessed. "Which leads me to the biggest mystery of all that I have to ask about. How did you manage to get here, Perseus? I saw no boat, nor ship arrive. And yet, you were somehow able to avoid Poseidon's wrath and curse. How is that possible?"

"Well, there is much that has happened to lead up to this point and I want to share every detail of it with you. Would you like to hear it?"

"Of course!" I exclaimed.

"Well then, brace yourself. Because some of the events that have happened up until this very moment in time you may not believe, even when I tell you."

Chapter 15

I studied Perseus closely as he began to tell me how he ended up here at Sarpedon. "I never left Seriphos since your last days there, Meduso. Things went on as they normally had for years. The only thing that had changed was me. I was growing stronger and faster. The Seriphos Island Games came around four years later, and King Polydectes noticed that my strength and skills were even greater than they were during the first set of games. He offered me a position as his head bodyguard, but I refused. I had no interest in serving the king for the rest of my life. Later, he became more acquainted with my mother. Eventually, he commanded that she attend some of the dinners and parties he hosted at his fortress. My mother had no choice but to accept his invitations in fear of his power."

"Poor Danaë," I uttered.

"Yes. The king became quite infatuated with her to the point where he offered her his hand in marriage. She reluctantly agreed to the proposal. During their engagement ceremony everyone had brought many riches and gifts for them. However, I did not have much to offer. I knew the king was already disappointed with me for having declined to serve as his guardsman. So, I asked him to name anything he wanted, and I would travel the world to retrieve it for him. It was then that he told me the tale of the gorgons. Two sisters and a brother who were once beautiful and served at Athena's temple. That Poseidon bedded the attractive male brother as an act of revenge against Athena. Because of their disloyalty, Athena turned the brother and the two sisters that defended him into monstrous gorgons. All three of them were cursed with the bodies of snakes. The sisters lost their hair and they were replaced with vile, venomous serpents. The brother's head, however, remained unchanged. He was a beautiful creature that had the ability to charm any male or female mortal."

I shuttered now knowing that this was the tale and rumor that was spread far and wide about me. It hurt to know that no one knew the true side of me. I would be known as the vain and selfish servant who disobeyed Athena and was punished as a result.

Perseus continued. "It was warned that anyone who gazed into the eyes of the gorgons would be petrified and permanently turned to stone, with no way of reversing the curse. That one should not give into the temptation of the male gorgon. Once King Polydectes informed me of this story, he then explained the reasoning behind his narration. The gift he desired before his wedding to my mother was the head of the beguiling mortal gorgon. After I accepted his conditions, I then thought about his story and began to connect the dots like a dazzling constellation. I feared that the male gorgon the king was referring to was you, Meduso. A servant of Athena's with two sisters, who had phenomenal looks that even drew the attention of the god of the sea. I had to know if this gorgon was you. Therefore, I would set off on my journey."

Panic began to stir within me. Perseus may have come to find me, but at the same time, he was also sent here on a mission. A mission to decapitate me and offer my head up on a silver platter to King Polydectes. I knew Perseus well, and I knew he had no intention of killing me. But even so, the thought of him having to murder me with his own hands dug deep in me. I cringed at the very idea of it.

"To be honest, I was unsure of where to begin," Perseus admitted. "The night before I was supposed to sail out to Greece, I was preparing my boat Dictys had given me. I was then greeted by three gods on the beach by my fire. It was Pallas Athena, Hermes, and Hephaestus. They were watching over me and knew of my upcoming journey in search of you. The gods offered their guidance and support. Athena told me of the curse Poseidon had placed on the seas surrounding the island. That no ships could survive the massive waves and storms that he called forth. So, in order to circumvent the sea, they had another plan to get me safely here. Hermes provided me with his winged sandals. I would be able to fly over the sea and avoid Poseidon's damage. Athena then gave me her bronze shield, telling me to be strategic in how I use it. To always look into the shield when I came in contact with the gorgon, so that I would not turn to stone. And lastly, Hephaestus forged a sword of obsidian, the sharpest and most valuable stone known to the gods. He offered it to me."

I then glanced over to the side of the boulder, where the bronze shield, obsidian sword, and winged sandals sat. All were hand-gifted to Perseus, directly from the gods, with their resolution being my death. It stung me to know of this.

"However, Athena explained that there was one more weapon I would need. It was Hades's invisibility cap. I would need to travel to seek out the Hyperboreans beyond the North Wind to acquire it."

"The Hyperboreans? What are they? Nymphs?" I questioned.

"No. They are a race of friendly giants, in the lands far to the north," he corrected. "However, the exact road to get to the Hyperboreans was a mystery, even to the gods. They informed me that the all-knowing Graeae would be able to tell me of the passage to get there. It was then that I recalled the Graeae, or what Hermes referred to as the *grey women*. They were your elder mentors. I remember the humorous stories you told me about how you and Euryale would tease them by stealing their one eye to temporarily blind them. Then you both would play catch with it and sometimes hide it around your oceanic palace." Perseus then snickered as he recited the story.

"So, Hermes led me to your palace to meet them. At first, the Graeae refused to spill any details about how to get to the Hyperboreans. It soon became apparent that I would be getting nowhere with them. Therefore, I stole their eye and told them I would only return it once they told me how to get beyond the North Wind. Once they shared this information, I kept my word and gave them their eye and then departed. Hermes and I headed straight to the back of the North Wind with the aid of his winged sandals. At first, I was timid in knowing I would need to meet these gargantuan creatures and request to have Hades's invisibility cap. But, much to my surprise, these giants were beyond generous and showed me nothing but kindness. I joined them in a lively feast and shared with them the reason as to why I needed to have access to the cap of Hades. These gentle giants freely allowed me to have it without any reservations. Not only did they give me it, but they also offered me an additional gift. It was a magical bag."

Perseus pointed to the small tote right next to his god-given weapons. "That bag has the power to alter itself to become the right size to fit whatever should go into it."

"Like my head?" I accused.

"Meduso, of course not. How could you even think that I would be capable of doing such a thing to you? Yes, if the male gorgon was anyone but you, I would likely do it."

"But what of King Polydectes and your mother? What about Athena, Hermes, and Hephaestus? All of them are expecting you to return having killed me. How do you answer to that?"

"I simply won't. Meduso, I have missed you dearly."

He reached to hold my hands as he declared this. "I have no plans to go anywhere. I want to remain here on this island with you for the rest of my days."

"But in doing that, you are defying the gods, Perseus. I am living proof of what happens when one goes against the gods."

"I'm not necessarily defying them. For all they know, I could be camping on this island waiting for the right time to strike you. And so what if they decide to punish me? What is the worst they could do? Turn me into a gorgon, like you? It would not make much of a difference to me. Plus, I am the son of Zeus. I highly doubt they would cause harm to me, a demi-god."

I had to commend Perseus's bravery in his defiance of the gods. But more so, I admired that it was all because of his love for me. And that is something I would cherish for my entire life.

"But back to my story," Perseus interrupted his own thoughts, returning the conversation back to his tale. "Once I had all of the weapons the gods recommended me having, there was nothing left for me to do but to come here. Hermes guided me and once again, I used his winged-sandals to carry me here, avoiding the potential rough waters and storms Poseidon would throw my way. It was then that I came across you on the beach. The fire you created was the only source of light I was able to see on the island from floating high above during the night. It led me directly to you, and now here we are."

I still could not believe that Perseus had been through

all that he just told me. The most numbing portion of his story was that he was sent here to the island with the backing of the gods in order to kill me. Here he was, before me, with every opportunity to strike, but he refused to do so. I had to believe him. There would be no possible way he would deceive me, right? If he did intend on killing me, he would have done so last night, as I slept. The fact that I was standing here alive gave me hope and negated those thoughts of distrust against him.

"I still cannot believe you found me, Perseus. And you truly wish to stay?" I asked.

"Yes. I waited so long to come back to you. And now that I have, I never wish to leave you." He moved forward to hold me in his arms as he said this.

"Likewise. Now that I have you, I cannot imagine parting ways with you ever again," I added. Once we released our grips from each other, I had an idea. "I do want to show you something."

"Sure. What is it?" he inquired.

"It's a surprise. I don't want to spoil it. I want to see the reaction on your face when you witness it."

"Well, go ahead and show me," Perseus directed.

"Okay. Follow me." I led Perseus beyond Euryale's garden. I was pleased to see that Euryale and Stheno were nowhere to be found. I was not quite prepared to share with them knowledge of Perseus's presence just yet. We ventured beyond the garden and passed a small wooded area leading to the spring. As we arrived, I saw him dipping his head down into the water to drink. It was

Pegasus, looking glorious as ever.

"What? A horse with feathers!?" Perseus gasped. "I've never seen anything like it."

"His name is Pegasus," I shared. "He was a gift to me from Poseidon."

I walked Perseus over to the white, magical horse. I slowly brushed his mane. At first, he was startled when I disturbed him from quenching his thirst. But once he recognized me, he was put at ease once again and resumed drinking.

"Come," I commanded to Perseus. "Don't be shy."

Perseus moved closer and rubbed Pegasus with me. "He is spectacular! How did he come into Poseidon's possession?"

"I'm not entirely sure. Poseidon was not forthcoming with those details. He just told me that Pegasus was a gift for me, and he wished for the winged horse to remain in my care. He further explained that I should use Pegasus in a time of peril. That there could be an emergency where I may need to escape this island, and that I should use him to aid me in that escape," I shared.

Perseus rubbed his chin, deep in thought. "Hmmm. I wonder what sort of urgency Poseidon could think of where he thinks Pegasus will be of that particular use to you."

I shrugged. "I'm not sure of that either. Perhaps if a group of warriors were to ambush me on this island, I would need a means of fleeing, but that wouldn't make sense since Poseidon is preventing that from even occurring. There could also be a natural phenomenon, like a wildfire or even disastrous weather, in which I would need to get away. But at the same time, what about my sisters? How would they get away from here with me? I doubt the three of us could manage to ride Pegasus all at once."

"I'm not sure. But speaking of your sisters, where are they?"

"Most likely in their own caves. Are you ready to officially greet them?" I asked.

Perseus had a worried look on his face. "I really don't have a choice, do I? I can't just stay in hiding forever."

I shook my head. "Nope. You can't. I think it's time they finally meet you." I was surprised at Perseus's trepidation. He had no problem nor fear in defying Athena, Hermes, and Hephaestus, yet when it came to meeting his lover's gorgon sisters for the first time, that was what shook him in his sandals.

Chapter 16

We stood just outside Stheno's cave. I could hear my sisters chatting inside. Perseus was sweating. I was surprised to see this display of nervousness from him. It was refreshing to know that he did have a vulnerable side. The Perseus I knew was fearless, bold, and daring. I had never seen him squirm the way he was doing so now.

"Are you sure we have to tell them? What if they try to attack me or refuse for me to live here on the island with you?" he anxiously asked.

"They wouldn't do that. Just be honest and be yourself. If I love you, they will also love you," I shared.

He let out a heavy sigh and I grabbed his hand, leading him into the cave. Euryale and Stheno were laughing, having been riled up about something they were discussing.

I coughed loudly, announcing myself to them. "Euryale... Stheno... I want you to meet Perseus."

My sisters' expressions instantly changed. Their laughter was put on pause, and they had stern looks written on their faces.

Stheno raised a brow at me. "Perseus? The demi-god from Seriphos?"

I nodded. "Yes. He traveled far and wide to come find me here."

Euryale spoke with confusion. "But how? How did he get here?"

Perseus then piped up. "I was aided by Hermes, Hephaestus and…" He then gulped as a fearful reflex, knowing the last goddess he was about to mention would displease them. "…And Athena."

Stheno's eyes widened and she lunged forward towards him, but I stood in her way, blocking her. She screeched. "He's come to kill you, Meduso! Get rid of him!"

I held her back from getting any closer to him. The vile snakes from her hair bit me in my neck and shoulder, but I continued to fight through the pain. Perseus was startled by this reaction but quickly explained himself. "No. I have no intention of harming any of you. I sincerely came here to live with Meduso. I swear it."

"Liar!" Stheno yelled. I continued to use my strength to hold her back. Her aggression lessened, coming to the conclusion that she would not be able to get by me.

"No, Stheno! He is telling the truth. He slept with me last night. If he wanted to kill me, he would have done so already," I informed her.

"Meduso! You have trusted far too many people in your lifetime. Look where it has landed you," Stheno reminded me.

"That may be true, but I am telling you, Perseus is the only other person I trust my entire life with, besides you and Euryale," I revealed.

"Stheno, you have my word. I will protect Meduso

236

with my life," Perseus added.

Euryale then came forward, placing her hand on our sister's shoulder, attempting to pacify her. "Let's at least hear him out, Stheno."

Stheno grunted. "I have nothing to hear! But mark my word, you are making a terrible mistake, Meduso. And once you are dead, you will not have Euryale or me here to pick up the pieces this time. It will be too late by then." She then glided out of the cave, with her snakes hissing the entire way.

Euryale began to chase her before turning her head back to us. "Just give her some time. I will talk some sense into her."

"Thank you, Euryale," I gratefully said.

She simply nodded and went on, trailing behind Stheno.

"Well, that did not go as you had hoped, did it?" Perseus teased.

I nudged him in his side. "That is not funny. You do not know my sisters as I do. Stheno is obstinate and always holds on to grudges. It could take a long time for her to come around. I did not anticipate for her to be so against this."

Perseus then wrapped his arm around me in comfort. "Even if she despises me, I will not falter nor leave. I will learn to live with that dark, looming presence she may have over me, if I must. So be it. I will never leave you, Meduso."

I could not help but smile at his endearing nature.

"And I never want you to. But I promise, Euryale and I will get through to her, some way or another. Just please, be patient with me."

"Of course, I will be patient with you, Meduso. If eight years of separation from you is not patience, then I do not know what is."

For a few weeks, Stheno kept herself away from us. Whenever Perseus and I did see her heading towards us from a distance, she would purposefully turn to avoid any sort of contact with us and walk in the opposite direction.

I grew to be more vexed with each passing day. How could Stheno not see that me being alive was proof enough that Perseus had no ulterior motive for coming here to Sarpedon? He was not here to harm me, but somehow, she did not want to see this. She had no desire to accept the truth.

The following morning, I woke up early and snuck out of bed. I slowly glided out of the cave as to not disturb Perseus. I knew Stheno would still be asleep at this early of an hour in her own cave. Although my sisters and I agreed to never step foot in one another's personal caves without permission, I felt the need to make a special exception. After all, Stheno was purposefully doing everything she could to avoid us. So, my only way to get her one-on-one with me would be to bombard her with this surprise ambush. She would have no option but to handle the confrontation with me head on.

Just as I had suspected, she was sound asleep in her bed. I spoke loud enough to wake her from her slumber. "Stheno, we need to talk."

She did not bother to roll over to look me in the eyes. "I have nothing to discuss with you, Meduso."

"But why, Stheno? Why can't you just accept Perseus?" I pleaded.

"Enough, Meduso. Please..."

"No. I'm not leaving until you give me an answer. What do you have against Perseus?" I refused to give in to her stubbornness, which I never did as a child. I was now the stubborn one, determined to get answers.

She finally spun around in her bed, rising to face me. "It has nothing to do with Perseus, Meduso. It's you! Have you no sympathy for me and Euryale? Look at where your *love* has brought us, brother. Yet you parade Perseus around on our island and expect us to welcome him so easily, all because you love him? Well, I am sorry, Meduso, but I am allowed to have my reservations."

I lowered my head in shame. I never did consider her feelings. Of course, she was hesitant in being willing to approve of Perseus. After all, my love for Poseidon was what resulted in her monstrosity. She had every right to question my judgment when it came to *love*. "I'm sorry, sister. I should have been more receptive to how you feel," I sadly admitted. "But I love Perseus. I always have. I've shared our stories with you. So, you must know I am not lying or jumping headfirst into this without reason."

She slowly slithered closer to me. "I know you do. And I am sure he loves you just as equally. I just… don't want to see you hurt, dear brother. My anger comes from a place of love. Our love as brother and sister supersedes any other form of love out there," she shared.

I smiled, impressed that she was finally beginning to open up to me. "I appreciate that. And I also understand that you may need time to come around to Perseus staying with us."

"But Meduso, what of Athena? Surely, if she aided that man in travelling to this island, she must expect him to slaughter you."

I shook my head. "Yes. Perseus and I discussed this. He vowed to defy her and the other gods who supported him. He plans to live out the remainder of his life here, protecting me. Protecting *us*."

Stheno breathed deeply before placing her hands on my shoulders. "Are you certain you *love* him? You are sure you are making the right decision?"

"I am certain." I replied. "I would have no other…"

My sister then simply nodded. "That is all I need to know, then. I promise I will make an effort to get to know and accept him. I just ask that you continue to give it some time for him to grow on me. I'm not saying it will take months or years, but just give it a little while."

I leaned forward to hug her. "That's fine. That is all I can hope to ask for."

"But there is one thing that you said that is untrue," Stheno mentioned.

I released from our hug and had an odd expression on my face. "What did I say that was false?"

"That you *would have no other*. You cannot tell me you would have refused to live in Poseidon's glorious palace along his side if given the chance. Who are you to refuse a god?" Stheno retorted. She then laughed.

I could only snicker with her at her rather dry humor. I did not dare to try and correct her. After all, it was a miracle that she was finally starting to take a few steps forward, and I had no desire to push her several steps back.

It was a few weeks later that Stheno would eventually come around. Euryale caught up to Perseus and me, who were strolling along the beach, deep in conversation. She was panting to regain her breath once she caught up to us. "There you both are! I've been looking everywhere for you. Listen, I talked to Stheno and she agreed that it would be a good idea for all of us to have dinner together in the dining cave this evening, and I mean *all* four of us. What do you say?"

I smiled and was finally beginning to be put at ease, knowing that my sister was taking the initiative to invite Perseus and me to dinner. "I think we can arrange that.

What do you think, Perseus?"

He nodded. "That sounds good to me."

"Great! Well, I will get all of the fruits, vegetables, and the wine together," Euryale shared.

Perseus then interrupted. "Well, why don't I catch some fish and get a few birds or eggs for us as well?"

"That would be wonderful! I hope it's not such a short notice for you?" Euryale then inquired, not wanting to cause any sort of imposition.

"Believe me, Euryale, Perseus only needs one hour. You would be surprised at what he is able to catch and hunt down in just that brief amount of time," I replied.

She raised a brow. "Oh? Well, I will leave you both to it then. I will see you later." Euryale hummed as she hurried back towards the forest in the direction of her garden.

Perseus waited until Euryale was at a far enough distance before he continued to speak, not wanting her to overhear what he was about to say. "Your younger sister and Stheno are absolutely nothing alike."

"Believe me, I am quite aware. Yes, Euryale and I were much closer growing up. We played together, laughed together, and on the rare occasion we even cried together. She is just more open and friendlier than our older sister. Stheno has always been independent and stubborn to a fault. She hated the jokes Euryale and I told, and the pranks we would play. It was as if she felt that she was too mature to associate herself with us. However, it was not until we all became gorgons that our relationship took a much different turn, for the better."

"Sometimes, it takes a tragic event or even a near-death experience to bring people closer together," Perseus shared. "The thought of losing someone really forces you to prioritize your values in this world." I noticed Perseus's demeanor change as he stated this. He became suddenly dispirited and I had a suspicion as to the reason behind it.

"Is that how you felt in regard to me, when you first heard the rumor of me being cursed by Athena?"

"Yes. I was more so angry with myself. I failed to protect you. I waited a whole eight years to even try to venture out to find you. When King Polydectes filled me in on the rumor that it was potentially you who faced the wrath of Athena and was being hunted down by the fiercest of warriors, I knew I could not just idly stand by and let that happen." After explaining himself, Perseus stopped in his tracks and wrapped his thick arms around me. "But I am now atoning for that mistake. I will protect you from now until forever."

I too curled my arms around his lower back. "And I will protect you, too." I then separated from his grip and winked at him. "Don't discredit my abilities. I am more than capable of defending you as well. You have yet to see my growing swordsmanship and combat skills."

"Well, you will have to show me some time," he stated with eagerness.

"It's a deal."

Our conversation continued, but my attention was

then caught by the halcyon glow of the sun, that was slowly disappearing behind the ends of the sea. "Oh! I failed to realize it was already getting this late. We better collect the food we promised Euryale," I suggested.

"Let us return to your cave. I will need to borrow more of that fishing line you have. Why don't you go ahead and gather some quail's eggs? I saw a few nests in the trees by the spring," Perseus recommended.

And so, I gathered the materials he required for fishing and then we went our separate ways. He went out to sea and I had to slither up the trees to snatch the unhatched eggs from the nests. Both of us returned just an hour later. I was shocked to see that he had a full line of nearly twenty fish caught. Meanwhile, I was only able to acquire eight eggs in the short time I was given.

"I questioned whether or not the number of eggs I found would be enough, but your fish will surely fulfill our appetites," I shared.

"Well, I alone can eat ten of these," he explained.

How quickly I always forget that he is a demi-god with the stomach of three humans. "That will be fine. I'm pretty sure my sisters and I can eat no more than three at a time, anyway." We both laughed at the exaggerated difference between our food habits.

Not wanting the fish to rot, we decided it was time for us to go to the dining cave to start the fire. Upon our arrival, I was stunned to see Stheno here so early. The wood was already burning in the pit. I motioned forward while Perseus followed only a few steps behind me. Based on the last interaction he had with Stheno, this was a logical position for him to be in.

I was not sure which Stheno I was going to get today. Would it be an irate gorgon, a solemn one, or perhaps a rare, friendly version? It must have been a miracle, because she approached and hugged me, showing nothing but warmth. "Welcome, Meduso. I did miss our daily dinners together." She then passed gaze over my shoulder to Perseus. "I must apologize to you, Perseus. Surely, you must understand the cautions I must take for Meduso's sake."

He scratched the back of his head, seeming slightly on edge. "No. I understand. We both have the same goal in mind, to protect your brother at all costs. We all have his best interest at heart."

I was shocked to see Stheno's lips curl into what I briefly saw as a smile. "Anyway, Euryale has some potatoes and a nice stack of fruits and vegetables for us for tonight. She is currently out in the grove getting the large cups of wine."

"Wine!?" Perseus interrupted so suddenly. "You have managed to create wine here on this island? I thought your sister was joking when she mentioned it earlier."

"No. She was serious. Do not ask me how, but she managed to figure out on her own how to tend to and maintain a grove of grapes and form them into wine. Surely, it was a blessing from Dionysus. You will have to try it!" I clapped as I became excited, remembering that Perseus rarely drank wine when he was in Seriphos.

"Yes. I would be glad to try it," he said, which made me content.

"But, more importantly, if I do not get these fish over the fire, we will be forced to drink on an empty stomach." Perseus then tied the fishing line around the stakes in the ground that surrounded the fire. He neatly tightened the string so that each fish had an equal amount of access to the flames.

"Oh my, Perseus!" Stheno placed her hand over her chest. "Did you catch all of those fish yourself?"

"Of course. It took me an hour, but..."

My sister spoke over him. "An hour!? You caught that many in just one *hour*!?"

He nodded.

"Well, you must teach me your ways, demi-god. I would love to see what techniques you use." And just like that, Stheno and Perseus were carried off into their own discussion together. I did not dare to interrupt. I simply watched them intently, listening from the side. I was beyond overjoyed to see how much they had in common and how invested they were in their conversation with each other.

"...And who came up with this contraption over your eyes? Is that simply just glass stone and a fishing line?" Stheno inquired, with great interest.

"Yes. Meduso and I came up with it," he revealed.

"Ingenious!" Stheno exclaimed.

Eventually, Euryale returned with her hands full, holding the many large cups of wine in her arms. She was slightly spilling the overflowing libations, but not too much was wasted. She was just as astonished as I was to see Stheno and Perseus deep in conversation.

I did my due diligence to carry some of the cups from her hands to sit them down, not wanting her to distract my sister and lover. "Shhh. I'm scared to interject. I don't want this moment to end," I whispered to her.

Euryale replied softly in my ear. "Yes. The longer we can keep this going, the better it will be, for all our sakes."

Unfortunately, no matter how quiet Euryale and I could have been, their one-on-one chatter was put on hold now that the fish were completely cooked. Stheno turned away to gather our hand-crafted plates and utensils, while Euryale cut up the vegetables. We each filled our plates generously with the massive amount of food we had prepared for this feast before moving to sit around the fire.

Stheno was the last to return, kindly handing each of us our cups of wine as we sat and ate. She then raised her cup into the air, motioning for the rest of us to follow her actions. "I would like to toast, to Perseus. Welcome to the Island of the Gorgons. And we hope you enjoy it here as your permanent residence with our brother. And again, I would like to apologize to you for my behavior early on. I should have realized that one additional person here to help protect Meduso is something I should not take for granted."

"Apology accepted." Perseus glowed as he said this.

We all drank from our cups and continued to eat and

have light-hearted discussions throughout the night. After some peer pressure, Euryale had managed to convince Perseus to have well over four heaping cups of wine along with the rest of us.

As everyone laughed and was giddy, all I could do was smile. Despite me being a cursed gorgon, this scene, right here, was all I ever wanted. Sitting around the fire with family and loved ones, just lost and engaged in our own bliss. And lucky for me, these nights would continue on for months to come.

Chapter 17

Since the night of dinner with everyone in the dining cave together for the first time, things progressed very smoothly. Perseus and Stheno would often be on their own during the day, teaching each other new skills and traits they both were accustomed to. This left me unaccompanied, which I often enjoyed. As much as I loved Perseus, it was healthy for me to get some alone time to myself to think and for clarity purposes.

I usually kept myself on the opposite end of the island from where Stheno and Perseus were in order to allow them and me to avoid any sort of distractions. Today, I decided to scavenge the beach close to the cliffs to see if there were any shelled fish I could gather for food. Lately, I found myself experimenting with different types of cooking. I would often gather various types of fish, vegetables and plants with unique flavors. They were all mixed in a pot together over the fire. Some of the mixtures I made were beyond delicious, which I kept in the back of my mind for potential future meals, while others were just sour and off-putting to the taste. I also made a mental note of those terrible things that I mixed together to make sure that I would never do so again.

As I dug into the deep crevices of the cliff to grab some of these organisms, I felt a dark shadow hovering over me. I immediately dropped everything I had in my hands, completely thrown off by the figure right behind me. That glowing auburn hair and those unearthly blue eyes scanned me, almost menacingly.

I gasped. "Poseidon! What are you doing here!?"

"I have come to warn you, Meduso," he shared. "I will no longer curse those who come in close proximity to this island."

I had a sneaking suspicion as to the reasoning behind this, but needed confirmation. "But why?"

"I protected you because you were mine and I wanted no other to have you. But I can see you have captured the heart of another. A heart who also belongs to the gods, I might add. If he weren't a demi-god, I would have disposed of him long ago. But now, my hands are currently tied."

"Yes. I do love Perseus," I confessed.

"Well, be that as it may, I can no longer linger here and watch as another man makes love to you. I look like a fool protecting someone while he lives happily ever after loving another," he shared.

"Please, Poseidon. I beg of you to see past all of that. Your disturbance of the seas has brought peace to my life. I no longer have to be anxious over intruders coming to this island to murder me."

"Enough! I will not stand for this. The others will view me as weak if I give in to you."

"You must reconsider…"

The sea god then cut me off. "I will not. That is final."

His voice became much deeper and stern as I imagined how a typical god would speak. "Once again, you have defied the gods! Your one simple task was to live on this island peacefully, without falling in love with another. But here you stand, completely disobeying all that I demanded of you. Yet you expect me to give you, *my property*, up to some mortal without consequence!?"

It was troubling to see this effect I had on the ruler of the sea. The fact that I had the power to cause grievance to a god was mind-boggling.

"I see there is no use of persuading you otherwise." I must have been feeling rather valiant compared to before, because I felt the need to speak up for myself to Poseidon, despite knowing my place beneath him as a mortal. "You should not feel the need to protect me out of possession and jealousy. You should want to protect me because it was you who took part in what led me to being here and sought out as a target. If I die, it will be because of you. I hope you are able to live with that guilt."

"You are truly stupid and foolish, Meduso! You will be sorry for your actions. I will release this curse and allow any and all of my niece's warriors to come to this island. They will be the ones to kill your new lover and I will stand by and watch until that day comes!"

And just like that, Poseidon was out of sight, gone into the depths of the sea with a flash. For some reason, I had an inkling that Poseidon would still be watching over me, spying to check in on me every now and then. He was a god, after all, with such capabilities.

251

After my unplanned meeting with Poseidon, I felt that I had no choice but to immediately find Perseus and my sisters to tell them all that happened. They had every right to know. Plus, it was imperative for them to learn that Poseidon's curse was lifted, and this meant that there was potential for more danger on the horizon.

I could make out Perseus and Stheno swinging their blades at one another from a distance away. It was Perseus and his hawk-like vision that withdrew his sword once he saw me approaching them.

"Ah, Meduso. What brings you over here?" Perseus asked me.

"Yes. I'm surprised to see you so soon. Is everything alright?" Stheno added.

"Well, about that..." I began. "When I was collecting shelled fish along the cliff side, Poseidon snuck up behind me." I caught a glimpse of Perseus's hand now clenched into a fist at his side.

"What did he have to say?" Stheno inquired. She made a passing glance from Perseus to me, wondering how Perseus would react to learning about my former lover greeting me again.

I crossed my arms over my chest and lowered my head. It was difficult to break this news to them. "He was rather upset at seeing Perseus and me together. Because of this, he is no longer going to protect me. All of the tidal waves and vicious storms are no more. Warriors will be able to easily come and go as they please."

"What a coward!" Stheno yelled.

"Yes. I tried to reason with him. I begged him to reconsider his decision, but he was not willing to budge. So, we must all be prepared for hunters to start making their way back to the island," I explained.

Perseus unsheathed his sword and held it high in the air. "Let the fiercest of warriors come. They will wish they had perished so easily from a storm at sea when I am through with them." I appreciated his optimism and his commitment to defend me given this unfortunate scenario.

His brief speech riled Stheno up as well. "Yes. We will destroy any man who dares to step foot on the Island of the Gorgons. I hope the Athenians bring forth their strongest warriors. I want to send them a clear message that even their best will not be good enough to overcome us."

"Come, Stheno. We must amp up our battle skills more if we want to be ready," Perseus added.

Stheno nodded and they both returned to practicing fighting each other.

"Meduso, why don't you find Euryale and inform her of what has happened? She will need to be prepared, as well," Perseus suggested. He may not have meant to, but he sounded more of a leader whenever danger was eminent. Usually, it was Stheno who took charge in perilous situations, but now that Perseus was present, she stepped to the side to allow him to take the lead.

"I will run ahead and let her know now," I informed them, before turning away to head back to the opposite end of the island.

As I travelled through the forest, I began to wonder what this meant for all of us, moving forward. Things would once again return to the way they were. I would have to fend for myself and we would need to petrify these men and toss their bodies into the wide, vast lake. However, I came to the realization that the near future would pose a few new challenges for me.

I was no longer the only person that could be killed. Although Perseus was a demi-god, he still had the life span of a normal mortal and could also be killed at any given moment. It was only Euryale and Stheno who were the immortals. Now, I would need to not only guard my life, but Perseus's as well.

I was able to spot Euryale on the ground digging in the soil, when I entered her garden. She seemed so at peace. I hated to be the bearer of terrible news and disturb her jubilance. She glanced over her shoulder to see that I was approaching. "What brings you over here today, brother?" She rose on her serpent body so that she was at eye-level with me.

"Well, there has been a recent development that affects all of us."

"Really? What kind of development?" Euryale curiously asked.

"Poseidon's curse on the warriors at sea... is no more." I did nothing to beat around the bush with this news. Best to just come forthright with this information to her.

"What? How do you know this?"

"He approached me this morning when I was scavenging for food by the cliffside. It was not the most pleasant of conversations. The gist of it is that he is jealous of my relationship with Perseus and no longer feels the need to protect me. He believes that he has been made a fool of," I revealed.

"Men can be such babies!" Euryale exclaimed. "So, does this mean..."

My sister did not even have to finish that sentence for me to know where she was going with it. I nodded in affirmation.

"Yes. It is very likely that we will see warriors make their way to this island in the near future. Make sure you are prepared at any given moment," I warned.

"I will make sure I am. But look on the bright side, at least we have a demi-god on our team this go around," Euryale replied.

I smirked at her assurance and positive view about this situation. "You're right. Any extra number on our side is a good thing."

"Well, I wouldn't consider Perseus as just a *number*," Euryale corrected me. "He's the entire sum!"

Just as predicted, the warriors became more numerous on the island. We became an unstoppable duo, Perseus and I. We were a force to be reckoned with. The number of warriors that descended upon our island were very few at first, but then they continued to come around more frequently with each passing week. Our strategies worked for the most part. I would draw the intruders in, while Perseus would sneak from behind them with a single blow for the kill. On the rare occasion, a hunter would have acute senses and detect Perseus's presence. When this happened, I would be swift in making sure that I moved behind Perseus, and I was there at all times. When we were in this precise formation, the attacker was forced to have to close their eyes when going against Perseus in fear of glancing over his shoulder and into my eyes. However, most of the warriors failed to do this, and within a matter of seconds, they were cast into stone.

Even when Perseus slayed the men and killed them with his sword, I came upon their lifeless bodies and opened their eyelids, gazing into their pupils. We made sure everybody was turned to limestone before we disposed of them into the lake. Having them completely solidified was less messy and avoided the spilling of blood. I'd rather have to lug a heavy statue through the forest rather than carry a body that had liquids and guts pouring out of it. The heavy load to carry was more tolerable than having my heavy stomach to carry the smell of rotting flesh.

Eventually, months had since passed and the warriors were becoming more creative with their weapons and their defenses. Some men brought various angled shields with them. They used these to catch me in their vision before fighting. Sometimes, up to five men joined forces in a single ambush against us. Others thought as Perseus and I had, and had transparent glass devices over their eyes, that were held up by rope tied behind their head. Not once did they ever have to swing a sword in pitch blackness.

One day, a large ship arrived, bringing with it at least twenty soldiers. Except they weren't soldiers. As Perseus and I scoped them out, we noticed their shredded garbs. There were no breastplates, nor shields. They seemed disheveled and not very organized. Must have been a common band of thieves, I assumed. Some of these men had long-swords while others had smaller daggers in their hands.

"Run ahead and get your sisters," Perseus commanded. "We will need their help for this one. I will keep an eye on them."

"Okay. Just don't do anything reckless," I requested.

"I won't," Perseus replied. It relieved me to hear him say that. He planted a parting kiss on my lips that lingered as I left his side and glided through the forest to find Euryale and Stheno near our caves.

"We have trouble and could use your assistance," I

shared.

"How many?" Stheno asked.

"At least twenty," I revealed.

"My goodness! We've never had that many at once before," a shocked Euryale stated.

"I will grab our swords," Stheno announced. "Euryale, go along with Meduso and I will catch up with you two."

We both nodded to her and made haste as we moved through the forest, returning to Perseus, who remained in the same exact spot where he was when I left him. My heart rose out of my stomach when I saw that he was unharmed and untouched.

Euryale and I crouched down with him. These men were extremely rowdy, running around on the beach yelling and shouting obscene comments. I could not tell whether or not they were angry with one another or joking around. It was a bizarre scene to witness. We continued to study their moods when Stheno had joined us.

"Tell me what I need to know," my oldest sister demanded.

"There's not much to tell," Perseus explained. "I am unsure of their battle skills. They seem a little clumsy to me based on first impressions. Right now, they are unloading items from their ship. It looks like they plan to camp out here."

"Do they intend on attacking us at night?" I asked.

"They could be. But that would be extremely foolish of

them," Perseus replied.

"Yes. That would put them at a disadvantage. Their sight will be limited and they do not know the island as we do. It would be a poor decision on their part if they did," Stheno explained.

"Well, no matter what the case, we will need to keep an eye out on them," I recommended. "It would be wise of us to make the first move when they will least expect it."

"What are you thinking?" Perseus asked me.

I was honored that he valued my opinion, even when it came to war and battle strategies, which were his specialty. "I say we attack at sunset if they do not make any moves until then."

Everyone remained silent and no one disagreed with my idea.

Stheno then spoke up. "Then it is decided. We strike at dusk."

A few hours had passed, and there was still no sudden movement by the motley herd that was now camped out on the beach. The sun was beginning to set, so we knew it would be any moment before we made our presence known to these men.

We resumed mapping out our plan of attack as we patiently waited.

"Euryale, you will ambush them from the west side, Stheno from the east, and Meduso, you will move in head on," Perseus explained. "I will stand guard and stay just behind Meduso."

Everyone knew that Perseus would have to stay by my side. After all, my sisters could not die, so it only made sense that I had Perseus there to aide me in battle. Of us gorgons, I needed it the most as the only mortal. That part was obvious.

"Hopefully, these men will be so ill-prepared that they will forget to shut their eyes. We should have most of them finished off before the battle even begins. As for the rest, we will just have to fight each of them, one by one, until none are left standing," Perseus told us.

And so, the sun's apex was eliciting its last glimmer of light. Everyone took their assigned places in the forest. Once the last shed of light was no longer visible, we made our charge, each of us coming at them from all angles, backing them into the water. They had no place to run. The school of fish had nowhere to move, but directly into the net of us fishermen.

Many of the men weren't even facing us. It was not until the shouting of some of their comrades that they turned to see what all the ruckus was about. But by then, it was too late. We made quick work of them. The first round of men could not even take a step forward before being transformed to stone. Even many in the second group of men behind them also became petrified. This battle was becoming much easier than I had anticipated.

As for the few men that remained, they were forced to have to close their eyes and lunge forward to strike at the closest gorgon to them, although their swings were aimless. They hit air with every swing, nowhere near their desired targets. Euryale snuck around behind two of the men near her and stabbed them in their backs. Stheno only had one attacker in her line of vision and she feared nothing about him. She simply moved forward and slashed the man's throat with her sword.

The last man standing came forward, with his dagger pointed in my direction. I was ready for him. But in the blink of an eye, he was gone. He had disappeared. Actually, he was not the only one gone. Everyone was missing. The dead bodies, Euryale, Stheno, everyone. And I was no longer on the beach. I was back in my bed cave with the fire lit. I then realized, after all these years of absence, and assuming they went away, I was having another vision from the Fates.

I stood in the cave facing the wall. Perseus jogged forward with a perplexed look on his face. "Meduso! Stop! You cannot do this!" he shouted. "Please, do not do this for me! You mustn't!"

"I'm sorry, Perseus! I have to. I can no longer put you through this. I will always love you…" I then watched my dream-self raise a sword and cleanly sweep it across my neck. My head rolled to the floor of the cave, with my blood, as black as obsidian, dripping and spreading all over the ground. Perseus fell to his knees, holding his head in his hands. He wept.

The barbaric scene ended, and the beach with the many men lying across the sand was now a blur, slowly coming into focus.

"Meduso! Look out!" One of my sisters screamed. I was unsure which of their voices the yell was coming from. Once my view became clear, I saw the man with the dagger just feet away from me, sprinting forward. All I could feel was my body being aggressively pushed to the side. Perseus had shoved me out of the way. I fell down into the sand.

Quickly attempting to recover from the blow, I turned around and horror struck my face. I could see the man's dagger plunged deep into Perseus's side. I screamed at the sight of it and rose to my feet, slithering towards the man. Everything that happened next felt like it occurred in slow motion. As the man pulled his dagger out of Perseus's gut, I could see the crimson liquid drip from its tip and more blood pouring out of the laceration carved into my lover's skin. My hands clawed at the man's face, nails digging into his forehead and cheeks. I pried his eyelids open, despite all of his resistance. Once I saw those cold, brown irises of his, it was all over for him. His statuesque body fell into the sand. I wrapped my head around to see Perseus now stumbling backwards until he could no longer maintain his balance. His legs gave out and his eyes closed. He fell to the ground, unconscious.

Chapter 18

I could not lose him again. This was not an option. I would not know how to go on without Perseus. His knife wound was severe. My sisters assisted me with carrying him back to my cave. For the next week, I tended to him on hand and foot at every second of the day. He was coming out of his comatose state more and more as the days progressed.

I treated his deep cut with all of the medicinal herbs and plants I could possibly find on the island. Peonies, Hellebore, Yarrow Plant, just to name a few. I knew my mother's teachings of herbal remedies would come in handy one day. Now, I would be eternally grateful to Ceto for having had to put up with my constant annoyance at learning about all kinds of plants and flowers.

"I don't see why I need to memorize all of these. It's not like there are any flowers here in the ocean," I once told my mother with vexation.

"Believe me, son. There may come a time when you are on the surface where you or someone close to you is injured. These lessons will have been meaningful then."

"But what is the likelihood that I will end up hurt or injured? I'll be in a temple," I reminded her. "I doubt anything drastic can happen there."

"That may be the case, Meduso. But I want you to be fully prepared for anything life may throw your way. It could happen when you least expect it to. And perhaps you may never have to apply this knowledge throughout your life, but by the off chance that you do, you will be thankful that I taught you about these medicinal properties of plants on the surface." And my mother's philosophy would prove to be helpful. If she did not teach me how to use these plants as a panacea, then who knows if Perseus would be breathing right now.

Although my spirits were rising, knowing that Perseus was healing well, I still had remorse for what happened to him. I was the one culpable for him being stabbed. I blacked out during our fight with the island intruders. Had that not happened, Perseus would not have had to push me out of the way and save me, thereby taking the blow that was intended for me.

This led me to recalling the vision I had that very moment. Every day since, that premonition has haunted my mind. Were the Fates accurate with this? Would I end up killing and beheading myself in front of Perseus? It couldn't be true. How could it be? I would never attempt to cut my own throat. Why would I ever even think to consider that? On the other hand, every prophecy the Fates have conjured up through my visions has happened in real life, thus far. Why should I think this one could be any different?

As these lingering questions continued to consume my thoughts, I noticed Perseus attempting to sit up in the bed. He let out a heavy grunt, tolerating the pain he had to endure with every sudden movement he made.

I reprimanded him. "You should not be getting up like that. Your wound is still healing, and this could exacerbate the bleeding."

"I have to move around, Meduso. Otherwise, I will become too stiff to fight."

"Fighting is the very last thing you should be worrying about," I clarified.

"No. The longer I have to lay here, the greater the chance that warriors will sneak onto the island. I need to get better quickly."

"But right now, you are in no condition to even hold a sword, Perseus. Stheno and Euryale are keeping an eye out on things while I care for you. They have already dealt with a few warriors who have arrived at the island since your fall, and they are doing just fine," I reassured him.

"I'll give it three more days," he announced. "No matter if the wound is not fully healed, I will rise to my feet and continue to practice and prepare for battle."

I let out a sigh, knowing there would be no use in arguing against his stubbornness. Perseus sensed my reluctance in agreeing to these terms he presented to me. "Come here," he said. He reached for the back of my neck. I leaned forward to give him easier access to it. He then pulled me down to him for a passionate kiss. Our lips separated and I felt him trace his slippery tongue down my neck. I let out a light whimper at the pleasurable, yet ticklish, wet touch.

My chest pressed into his, as I now laid on top of him in bed. He let out a painful moan once I did this. I was so caught up in the moment I had completely forgotten about his injury and that any slight contact with it caused him to ache.

"I'm sorry," I immediately apologized.

"No. It's fine. I just... nevermind. Don't worry about it," Perseus replied. He then gripped my cheeks with his hands, wanting my lips to return to their rightful place against his. The interval that they had been separated from one another for was far longer than he wanted, even if it was just for a few seconds. We then made love, although I was slightly distracted the entire time. Even as I found myself locked in the passion, I had to be weary of his laceration.

An hour later, we rested on each other, my head leaning against his chest. "Promise me something, Perseus."

"Sure. What is it?" he inquired.

"Promise me that you will not put yourself in harm's way in order to save me ever again. It's one thing for you to fight alongside me, but it's another to sacrifice your life for mine. I know we have never had this sort of conversation before, but it's important for us to talk about."

"But Meduso, you must understand. I do not want to live without you. I would rather die than go on in life without having you by my side," Perseus declared.

I had a feeling Perseus would announce something along those lines. But I had the same exact thoughts as him. I would rather die than go on living without him, too. "I feel the same way, Perseus. But please just accept that if it is my time to leave this world, then let it be. Do not substitute yours for mine. When it comes down to it, think about what you still have left to fight for. You have a mother back home, friends, and family. There is still so much you have to hold on to and care for beyond me. As for myself, I only have you and my sisters. And don't forget, my sisters are immortal. They can fully care for themselves, of course."

He shook his head. I could see his eyes begin to water. "Don't say such things, Meduso. It's like you are determined to die."

"No. I'm not wishing that at all. How could you say that? I just want us to be prepared, if by chance another scenario arises where my life is in crisis. You should not jeopardize your own life, for mine. Does that make sense?" I clarified.

Perseus sighed and pressed his forehead into me. "I understand. It's just hard to talk and even think about these sorts of things."

"I know. So, as long as you promise me you will not take a dagger for me like you did last week, then my mind will be put at ease. Can you promise me that?"

He remained silent. I could feel his tears transfer from his cheek to my skin as he pressed his face against mine. "I can't, Meduso. I can't make that promise. I'm sorry."

Chapter 19

Three days later, Perseus was still not fully recovered. However, he was able to rise to his feet and walk around. Despite my constant pleading with him to rest and to still remain lied down, his hard-headedness triumphed. He refused to listen to my advice.

"I said three days, Meduso. No more and no less. I cannot stay in that bed for another minute," Perseus said. "And where is my sword? Where have you hidden it?"

"If you want to defy me and walk around, by all means go ahead, but don't think for one second I am going to condone you lifting a sword when you are just coming out of recovery for the first time."

"Grrrr. Fine. Have it your way," he replied, seeming defeated. "Just allow me to take a stroll around the island. I need some fresh air."

I nodded. "That, you can do."

Perseus went on his way. As much as I wanted to follow him to make sure he was okay, I knew he would prefer to be alone. After all, I'm a very independent person and value the time I have to myself. With Perseus constantly having me at his side for the past ten days, I am sure he appreciated the opportunity to be able to walk the beach on his own.

I sat in my cave alone for several minutes. Once I saw

a shadow appear on the cave walls, I assumed it was Perseus who had returned. Except it wasn't him, nor my sisters. It was a complete stranger. I reached for my sword and held my eyes wide open, gazing at the man. However, this person was able to stare directly at me with no harm done. He did not turn to stone and continued to walk towards me. He could not have been a mortal. Was he a god?

"Do you ever get tired of drawing a sword every time you meet a new person? Perhaps a welcoming greeting or a simple hello would be nice." He had a coy smirk on his face as he said this. I studied him closely. Fairly handsome, with some boyish features about him. He was not overly muscular, but had an athletic and fit build to him.

I was still on high alert. I refused to sheath my sword, unsure of who this person was who managed to get by my sisters and navigate the island to find me in this cave. "Who are you? Why have you come here?" I asked him with a slight aggression in my voice.

"Really? Did your sea monster parents not teach you about the gods of Mount Olympus?" He pointed to the brilliant white wings on his helmet and a matching set of wings that accentuated from the back of his gladiator sandals.

Once he made these features obvious to me, I recalled the Graeae and their descriptions about each of the gods and goddesses they told me about, including this one.

"That one is known as a trickster," Deino would say.

"You both would actually get along well with the cruel pranks you love to pull," Pemphredo would add.

"Yes. He is a darling to the gods. He can smooth talk his way out of anything," Enyo claimed.

Now, this same god was before me, gracing me with his presence in my own bed cave.

"Hermes..." I stated.

"Correct! And to think I was starting to lose faith in your intellect there for a moment." He chuckled as he stated this. "So, can you now put down that sword? Is that so much to ask?"

I slowly dropped the weapon to the ground.

"Smart boy! I knew you weren't so dumb. But speaking of dumb, I see my half-brother is walking the beach with a severe wound. Is that so?" Hermes inquired, although I was not sure why he was asking me this when he obviously knew the answer. Did he just want confirmation for his own self-esteem?

"Yes. Perseus stepped out for a while," I replied.

"Perfect. That leaves us some alone time to have a little discussion. But first and foremost, do you happen to have my second pair of winged sandals I lent Perseus?"

I nodded and pointed over to them in the corner of the cave.

He walked over and picked them up. "Great. Seeing as how he will no longer be needing these, I will be taking them off his hands."

I stood dumb-founded. Hermes still did not answer my question. "I asked why you are here..." I reminded him.

"Ah. Is that how a polite host should be addressing his guest? With that dreadful tone?" he questioned.

He was now starting to irritate me. Hermes may have been the messenger of the gods and also known as the god of roads, flocks, travelers, and thieves. But really, he should also add the *god of annoyance* to his many titles. I am quite surprised no one has thought to bequeath him with that honor.

"I can see you are not amused," he observed. "Very well. Let me just cut to the chase. You, Meduso, are becoming quite the nuisance to us gods."

My eyes widened in shock at what he had just informed me of. I was also bitterly confused. "How so!?"

"First, you seduce Poseidon. Then, you defy Athena. No matter how many warriors are sent to this island, you refuse to die. Somehow, you managed to seduce Poseidon once again, to the point where he cursed all of the seas around here in your honor. As a result, Zeus gave permission for me, Athena, Hephaestus, and even Hades to pick a strong warrior to expedite your death. But not just any warrior. Zeus insisted on his demi-god son, Perseus of Seriphos, to be that warrior. Unbeknownst to Athena, Hephaestus, and I, *you* had an affair with Perseus when you were younger. Of course, we had to spy on you both and your interactions here on this island to figure that out. We were all quite astonished to learn this information."

I was taken aback. To think that the gods and goddesses had such conversations about me and even watched over me as much as Hermes had insinuated. I had no idea I was discussed and often viewed in such a manner by them.

Hermes then continued. "And when we went to Zeus to report this, he claimed he already knew all of it. That he was testing his son, Perseus, to see if he could give up love for his honor and vainglory. But clearly, we know the result of that test. A complete and utter failure! You have somehow bewitched him. He is wrapped around your fingers, just like all of the men you have managed to attract and seduce in your lifetime."

"I am not a tempter, nor as vile as you make me out to be," I defended.

"Maybe not. But still, it cannot be denied that you have caused great turmoil among the gods. Athena and Poseidon are at greater odds because of your actions. Athena, Hephaestus, and myself have wasted a significant amount of time supporting and aiding Perseus, all for nothing. And surely, once Zeus learns that Perseus has chosen love over his legacy, which we have not informed the King of the Gods of this yet, he will be vengeful and likely kill you both. And to think one single mortal could cause all this trouble. I must honestly say I am quite impressed, Meduso."

"But I did not mean for any of this to happen," I explained.

"Oh, gorgon boy! Intent does not necessarily correlate to consequence. That is why we often use the phrase *live and learn*. But I have come to warn you of the predicament you are putting yourself and Perseus in. Right now, Perseus's mother, Danaë, has fled King Polydectes' fortress," Hermes shared.

"What!? Does Perseus know about this?"

"No. Of course not. How could he possibly know? Anyway, she had second thoughts on her engagement to the King once she realized how much of a tyrant he really was. Therefore, she refused to take the King's hand in marriage and has sought refuge at a temple on an adjacent island near Seriphos. She will likely be found by the King's men in the near future and there is no doubt of the actions the King will take when he does, in fact, find her." Hermes swiped his index finger across his throat to provide a dramatic effect to his story.

"No. We cannot allow Danaë to be killed by Polydectes. Perseus must return to Seriphos to protect her," I replied.

"Good! I am glad to see we share the same opinion. Yes. Perseus must return to his home land. It is his destiny to be a hero among mortals and recognized by the gods as one, too. But we are still in quite the dilemma here. We both know Perseus will never return to Seriphos with *you* in the picture," Hermes pointed directly at me as he stated this.

The herald of the gods was right. Even I knew this to be true. As long as I was alive and well here on this island, Perseus would never dare to leave me. "Well, what can I do to persuade him to return to Seriphos?"

"Now, that is the real question you need to discover

for yourself, dear gorgon. I already know the answer, but it would be too easy for me to reveal it to you. Zeus had already tested Perseus, to which he failed. Now it is my turn to test you, Meduso. Let us see if you can pass this test and find a way to make Perseus leave this island and return to Seriphos. Somehow, deep down, I think you already know the answer, but are afraid to admit it to yourself. It will not take much creativity to figure it out. But alas, my time with you has expired. I will be taking my winged-sandals with me. I wish you luck, Meduso."

Hermes then turned and sprinted out of the cave. Less than a minute later, Perseus had returned to me. I tried to change the expression on my face, so I did not look as bothered as I felt from my meeting with Hermes. But Perseus knew better. He could see past my looks to know when I was disturbed. "Is everything okay, Meduso?"

"Of course, everything is fine. I was just worried about you. That's all. But now that you're here in one piece, I am relieved."

But this was a complete lie. I had such a great burden on my shoulders now. And based on everything that had transpired, I knew I had a difficult decision to make. I continued to mull it over in my mind. There was only one way he would leave this island.

I then remembered what Perseus had mentioned to me on one of the first days he arrived here.

"I waited so long to come back to you. And now that I have, I never wish to leave you. I have no plans to go anywhere. I want to remain on this island with you for the rest of my days..."

I knew what I had to do. The vision of the Fates led me to believe this day was bound to come. Hermes also confirmed it in his own baffling way. The next few days, I spent as much time with my sisters as I could, just smiling and retelling some of the most memorable stories from our childhood. They found my behavior quite odd, but I did not have the heart to tell them of my plan. However, I wanted to make sure that my last days spent with them were nothing but joyful and pleasant. I loved them both dearly. They had sacrificed so much for me and I will forever admire them for putting family first before anything else.

After my last conversation with them, I returned to my personal cave to meet Perseus. As I entered it, the space around me completely transformed.

I was now floating in the sky from the looks of it. Nothing but white clouds and endless blue was before me. Beneath me, I could see a figure also flying in the air. It was Perseus. He was sitting on a glorious pearl animal. Was he riding a white falcon? No. As the image became clearer, I recognized those majestic wings. He was riding Pegasus. Perseus turned behind him. I followed his line of vision to see that they were heading south from our island. He and Pegasus soon descended towards the surface, heading for a rocky ledge against the sea. The waves crashed against the cliffside without mercy. Examining the precipice more closely, I saw a beautiful young woman chained to the cliff. I also took notice of a giant scaled creature emerging from the sea, heading straight towards the woman. Its jade, slippery tentacles flapping in unison, helping to propel the monster closer to the cliff. Pegasus swept forward, closer to the sea monster. Its hideous mouth opened as it snarled, revealing its blade-like fangs ready to prey on the victim chained to the cliff. But Pegasus and Perseus flew down to the ledge and swept right between the sea monster and the trapped woman. Perseus raised my severed head out of a bag and made sure the creature stared right into my eyes, turning it to stone. The sea monster fell back into the ocean depths, leaving a crash of waves hitting the sides of the cliffs from the impact of its fall.

My vision finally returned to normal, and I was finally back on my island at the entrance to my cave. I did not even have to think about the vision I just saw. There was nothing more to debate about. The Fates had spoken, and I knew what they had in store for me. I was fully aware that the decision I would soon make was for Perseus's survival. If I allowed us to remain on this island together in each other's arms for any longer, it would only cause wrath from the gods. They were likely to find a way to kill us both. Not only this, but his mother's life was also at risk. If Perseus did not leave this island, he would be unable to save her.

My destiny was revealed to me. It was as clear as a bright sunny day. I could not shun it. As I stepped forward, I could not just end myself right then and there. I needed to feel Perseus, to feel the touch of my lover, one last time. I fell right into his arms and tilted my head, so it rested against his chest. His hands caressed my back as I leaned into him.

"Is everything okay, Meduso?" he asked this so innocently, with such naivety. He had no idea what pain and grievance I would be causing him, and that killed me on the inside.

I could not respond to him. How could I lie to him and tell him everything was fine, when only minutes later I would end my life right in front of him? I kissed him one last time. I tasted and felt those soft lips of his. I wished for that touch to be the last lingering feeling on my body, before I would depart from this world.

Once our passionate embrace was put to a close, I glided past him towards the wall at the back end of the cave. I reached for his own sword that was hand-crafted by Hephaestus himself. This would be my final speech to my lover. My epitaph.

"Perseus... There is no easy way for me to tell you this," I began with.

He lifted his head and watched me intently. "Tell me what?" The passion in his eyes that he always had killed me in this very moment.

"I had two visions, Perseus. The first showed myself slitting my throat, beheading my own self. The second, was you using my head to kill a giant sea monster, saving a woman chained to a cliff," I revealed.

Now I felt awful. I bombarded him with this so instantly. I barely gave him any time to process what I had just told him.

"Meduso... no! It cannot be! Please do not tell me you actually believe this vision!" he exclaimed.

"I do, Perseus. I believe all of it. I also know that your mother is in danger. And if you do not return to Seriphos, she will die," I said boldly, then moving the blade in my hand at an angle towards myself.

"No!!! Meduso! Stop!" he screamed this, louder than I ever heard him scream before. The tears started pouring down his face. "I cannot live without you, Meduso! Please don't do this. I am begging you. Don't..."

Seeing the agony burn within him pained me to no end. I could not bear to see him hurt so badly. Ending my own life would be less painful than watching Perseus suffer like this right before my eyes. "Perseus, you must live without me. You have others to live for. You must take my head. Use my gaze in battle. Take Pegasus and fly south of here. That is your destiny. As for *my* destiny... my destiny is meant to help and save you. Use me to save yourself, Perseus. Don't let Athena's curse on me actually be a curse. Let it be a means of salvation for yourself."

He moved forward, but I raised the sword closer to my head, prompting him to not take any further steps towards me.

"Please don't, Meduso!" he begged.

"I'm sorry, Perseus! I have to. I can no longer put you through this. I will always love you..." I swung the blade with all my might across my throat. My last vision in this world was of my loved one, leaping forward to me as he wept. In a way, he was such a captivating creature coming forth to me. I would rather have no other picture as my last in this very world.

Throughout my whole life, I was bitter and worried about being stuck in my oceanic palace with my sisters, my parents, and the Graeae, unable to live the real world. Even in Athena's temple, I felt imprisoned and isolated, not able to experience this crazy, beautiful world and its opportunities. But now that I look back on it, I realize that I lived my life in one eclectic whirlwind of an adventure.

I lived in a gorgeous sea palace among gods and majestic creatures of the ocean. I was able to meet my soulmate on the surface. I tempted and made love to a god, thereby defying another. I experienced another part of my life in a unique manner, as a gorgon monster. I knew what it felt like to have love lost, only to find it again with Perseus's return to me. And I cannot forget the love my sisters had for me on top of that. But most of all, I was a mortal that made the gods worry and even quiver, sometimes second guessing themselves and their actions. And if I was a mortal that was capable of making the gods squirm, then I must have lived... and oh, how I lived!

Act III

Perseus: The Tragic Hero

Chapter 20

Why did he do this to me? How could he? I could not bear to look at Meduso's lifeless body on the ground. I knelt on the cave floor with my hands covering my eyes. All of our hopes and dreams to remain living peacefully on this island just vanished right before me.

I pounded my fist into the ground in anger, screaming out loud, "Why? We could have continued living this life together! But you... you just..." I could no longer even allow any other words to escape from my mouth. My breathing rate had intensified, and I was on the verge of hyperventilating into an unconscious state, but I managed to maintain the little amount of sanity I had in this very moment.

I sat still for a few hours, just staring ahead at the cave walls. I felt absent-minded just glancing ahead in my own bizarre trance, mourning the loss of my beloved Meduso. But at the same time, I also came to realize what needed to be done.

Meduso had assigned me a mission. He wished for me to use him to travel south for some odd reason. Then he wanted me to return to Seriphos to save my mother. I could not let Meduso's death be in vain. I would live out the rest of my life in his honor and his name.

I rose to my feet and retrieved the magical bag that

was given to me by the Hyperboreans. Reluctantly, I grabbed Meduso's head by the hair and placed it in the bag. Right before my eyes, the bag shifted shape so that the head fit perfectly in it.

I continued to sob. All of this was still so difficult to believe and comprehend. I prayed to be able to end this ongoing nightmare I believed I was experiencing, but no pinches could wake me from it. It was my reality that I had to face.

Reaching for Athena's bronze shield, Hades' invisibility cap, and Hephaestus's sword that Meduso used to kill himself, I wiped the cold blood clean from the blade. I began packing a few essential items, knowing I would need to depart this island very soon. I could not muster up the courage to witness Stheno and Euryale's reaction when they came to find out about Meduso. I had to escape before then. The agony would be intolerable for me.

But I would soon have to push through this, because I was able to hear Stheno and Euryale chatting. They were coming into the cave, laughing to themselves. I placed my glass eyewear back on, wrapping the fishing line around my head. As I did this, they stood still just blankly staring at Meduso's headless body on the floor.

Their gazes shifted from Meduso to me, as I held my weapons in both hands.

"You!? You did this!?" Stheno screamed.

"M-Meduso!?" Euryale cried.

"You planned this all along! I should have never

trusted you!" Stheno irately declared.

I heard the rage behind their voices. "I swear it was an accident!" I backed further up, away from them.

"Lies!" Stheno howled as she glided towards me, lunging at me with her claws raised.

I quickly placed Hades's invisibility cap on my head. The second it was on, Stheno sliced at the air, completing missing me. The gorgon moved back, realizing I had disappeared, her eyes darting in all corners of the cave, unsure where I had gone.

"Coward! Show yourself!" Stheno demanded with a heavy screech.

Euryale, on the other hand, was doing her best to cope with all that had happened. She kneeled on the ground with a waterfall of tears flowing from her eyes, howling in pain. "Perseus! How could you do this!?" she wept. "My poor brother!"

I had no time to respond to Euryale. Despite my deepest sympathies for her, I knew that a single syllable from my lips would only reveal my location to Stheno. I had no choice but to remain silent and tiptoe out of the cave with Meduso's head in the tote. I would not dare look back at the disheartened Euryale.

Yet, in thinking about how Stheno and Euryale were also suffering from their brother's death, the empathy ate at my heart, devouring me from limb to limb.

My tears began to fall. I could not tell if they were invisible to the ground they struck or not while I was wearing the invisibility cap. Still, I deeply cried while heading straight for the small spring beyond Euryale's garden, where Pegasus was tied to a tree. Right now, my only destination and means of escape from this situation was just as Meduso had revealed, which was to fly south of here on Pegasus.

This was the moment I finally had a second to breathe, now that I was safe from the clutches of Stheno and Euryale. A moment to think on all that had transpired. And with it came a fury of tears and curses against the gods. I threw my helmet off in despair. "Why!? Why did this have to end this way? Meduso... I'm sorry..." I pleaded with myself. "Meduso was everything, my sun, my moon, my *Katasterismoi*." I pressed my head into Pegasus's side in defeat before falling to my knees. "I did everything I could to protect you. I swear!" I cried to my lover.

Pegasus curled his neck to wrap his head around me, rubbing his snout against my face in a form of comfort. The horse could sense the sorrow overcoming me.

After taking a few minutes to compose myself, I rose to my feet, wiping the tears from my eyes. "We must proceed onward, Pegasus. Meduso wouldn't want us to cry ourselves to death. No. He would want us to live and fight for the greater good."

I stepped towards the tree Pegasus was strapped to and reached for Hephaestus's sword to unsheathe it. With the blade, I cut the rope to release the white stallion. Hopping on the horse's back, I clicked my feet against Pegasus's side, motioning for him to take off. "Come on, boy. We must depart," I whispered to him.

As we took off, I could hear shrieking cries coming from behind me. I recognized the voice it came from. It was Euryale's. Her bellowing wails over her dead brother echoed for miles. It was a noise that I knew would haunt me for the rest of my life.

Pegasus and I were still in flight for a long period of time. Although I had no idea where I needed to head to, I still knew exactly what I was looking for. I recalled Meduso's recent vision from the Fates, and so I scanned the sea beneath me searching for some indication of trepid waters.

As I searched around, something peculiar finally caught my eye. It was a gargantuan fin of a sea monster, synchronously slithering with the undulations of the water. I shifted my gaze upward to pinpoint where it was heading. In the far distance, I could make out a faint structure. Upon flying closer to it, I soon recognized that it was a rocky cliff overlooking the sea. I rubbed the horse's mane, signaling for Pegasus to descend. Everything was now coming into full view. I could see that it was not just a bare cliff the monster was targeting, but a woman chained to it, just as I had anticipated. The very same woman from Meduso's vision. The alluring prey of this vile, odious predator.

I squeezed Pegasus with my knees, leading the majestic stallion to glide directly toward the imprisoned woman. As we narrowed in, the massive tentacles of the sea creature made an appearance. Their billowing scales wafting a rancid smell in the air was enough to make me queasy. However, I kept my mind focused, ignoring the foul stench around me.

"Help! Please!!!" the woman mercifully cried, tugging against the chains with all her might. Her wrists raw and swollen from the sheer number of times she made a desperate effort to escape. An effort that was in vain.

The prodigious creature's head rose out of the water snarling, displaying its countless sharp fangs. The blustering sound from the monster pierced through the ears of everyone within a mile radius from it. The female mortal again cried out in horror, begging for her life.

The massive face of the monster moved closer to her. She twisted her head to the side and clenched her eyes shut to avoid the horrendous sight before her. The woman knew her life would be over in a moment. Her fists tightened, imagining the worst possible pain that would overcome her just before her death.

Above her, I reached my hand into my bag, pulling out Meduso's head. Pegasus swept right in between the woman and the monster. I flashed the head of my lover right in line with the vision of the vicious creature. As the sea monster stared directly into the bright flaxen eyes of the beheaded gorgon, it froze, unable to create any sort of noise or motion. The lower half of its body hardened, and the limestone quickly rose up the length of the monster's torso, eventually reaching its face. The stoned corpse of the foul creature plummeted into the sea, submerging to the bottom of the ocean floor.

The chained woman still held her eyes shut, but slowly opened to peek out of them, shocked that she was still alive and could only hear the crashing of the waves against the cliffs from the sinking of the monster.

I hopped off Pegasus and broke right through the woman's chains with Hephaestus's blade, thereby freeing her. She rubbed her wrists, still aching from the tightness of the metal cuffs that held her captive. "You saved my life, warrior! I cannot thank you enough. Tell me. Who are you?"

"I am Perseus of Seriphos. Son of Zeus."

Her eyes widened at the mention of the King of the Gods. "Well, hero, you have my eternal gratitude. I am Andromeda, Princess of Aethiopia."

I raised my brow. "You are the princess of this land and yet you were barbarically chained to the side of the cliff as a feast for that sea monster?" I asked in complete disbelief.

"Yes. Poseidon cursed our land when my mother, Queen Cassiopeia, claimed that I was the most beautiful woman across the seas. She boasted that I was more captivating than even Poseidon's nymphs. Because of my mother's vanity, Poseidon sent this monster to stalk and wreak havoc across the coast of Aethiopia. The monster ravaged many men and women. No matter the number of sacrifices that were made, the sea creature still lingered. My father and mother sought counsel from an oracle who informed them that we would be freed from the monster only if I was offered up to it. I resisted this, and tried to run away, but was eventually found. They forced and dragged me to the cliffside against my own free will. But you, Perseus, have saved me! And not just me, all of Aethiopia as well."

Andromeda's tale was not only bizarre, but completely cruel. For her to have to suffer and sacrifice her life all because of her prideful mother was startling to me. The two of us glanced around to see an onset of townsfolk and warriors approaching. Quickly, Andromeda lunged forward to wrap her arms around me and whispered in my ear. "Please. Do whatever you must, but take me away from here," she pleaded.

"What? You want to leave your homeland?" As soon as I asked this, even I realized the answer to my own question. Of course, she would want to leave Aethiopia having been completely betrayed by her mother, father, and her people, who left her to die on the side of the cliff.

Before Andromeda could even respond to me, we were bombarded by the loud cheers and chants from those who had just witnessed my bravery. They huddled around me, offering compliments and decencies before escorting me to the king and queen's castle with Andromeda trailing behind.

I was led through a labyrinth of halls before entering a large set of double doors leading into a massive open space. At the end of the room sat two thrones occupied by a middle-aged man and woman.

I stepped towards them, glancing about the room to see everyone was now on the ground kneeling before them, including Andromeda. Out of courtesy and not wanting to disrupt their customs, I too went down, lowering my head.

A maiden beside the thrones spoke up to make the introduction. "Your highnesses, King Cepheus and Queen Cassiopeia of Aethiopia. You may rise," she announced. Everyone rose to their feet.

"Young warrior," Queen Cassiopeia stood up. "Because of your heroic actions not only is my beautiful daughter alive and well, but you have also saved countless other lives that would have been sacrificed to Poseidon's sea monster. For that you have our deepest gratitude."

King Cepheus scrutinized me carefully. "Tell me your name, warrior. Where do you come from?"

"I am Perseus from the island of Seriphos. I am the son of Zeus, himself," I revealed. Gasps fell over the crowd in the throne room. Maidens, warriors, and others who stood by were caught in deep whispers, a major distraction to the king and queen.

"Silence!" the queen yelled. A hush fell over the room at her command. "Well then, young demi-god, clearly that explains how you were able to stop that abhorrent beast from threatening our land and people. Only someone with the blood of a god coursing through their veins could attain such a feat. Nevertheless, we are completely in your debt."

"For your heroic actions, we must honor you with a ceremony. We shall hold a parade and feast in your honor, demi-god," the king declared.

As down as I was feeling, with thoughts about Meduso, I could only nod and accept their gesture of gratitude. "That would be wonderful."

Cheer erupted within the room. Everyone was relieved to no longer have to fear the sea monster from terrorizing Aethiopia ever again. Not a single person was in low-spirits, except for me. As the claps and newfound optimism from the people around me seemed contagious, it did nothing for me; for I lowered my head, only able to think about Meduso. How I wished Meduso could be here with me to experience this upcoming festival in my honor. What I would give to be able to be back on the island with Meduso and his sisters right now. To have one more chance to lie with him. To feel his touch, his lips.

A single tear drifted from the corner of my eye, which I quickly wiped, wanting no one to catch sight of my despondence.

Chapter 21

The parade went on as promised. I was amazed by the grand gestures the king and queen made to honor my courage and bravery. Countless warriors, dancers, bards, and animals made their way by us in organized unison, while we sat in the tallest stand overlooking the parade path, draped with white cloth to serve as a tent for us. I sat in a smaller chair beside King Cepheus while Queen Cassiopeia and Andromeda were on the other side of me, admiring the glorious performance that was going on below us.

As grateful as I was for all the trouble the king and queen went through to put on this show for me, I could not find myself to be as elated as the crowd around me. Thoughts of Meduso and the tragedy that unfolded still lingered in my mind. I still missed my lover and knew that nothing would be able to change that.

I watched as Andromeda was lost in conversation with Queen Cassiopeia, but then saw her turn to catch my gaze over her mother's shoulder. I feared that she became aware of the gloom in my eyes and my sullen demeanor.

That evening, a large feast was held for me. There was enough wine around the room that would even put Dionysus's parties to shame. The food was abundant, and the drinks were flowing. Still, this did nothing to alleviate me. I stepped out of the banquet hall and onto the balcony for some fresh air.

I leaned over the stone railing overlooking the vast plains below me that disappeared into the distance. Above me, the moon was brilliantly lit. The stars shining ever so brightly, serving as a beacon for all who were lost among the darkened Earth. *Katasterismoi*, I thought to myself. I recalled the nights Meduso and I spent out on the beach by the fire, staring up at the intricate patterns in the night sky hovering above us.

My endearing memories were interrupted by soft footsteps behind me. I quickly turned around, startled by what seemed like someone sneaking up on me from behind.

"Don't be frightened. It's just me," Andromeda stated.

I let out a deep sigh. "My apologies. You have no idea of how on edge I have been over the years, fearing the potential of someone sneaking up on me, ready to kill me with a single blow."

Andromeda slowly approached me, softly placing her smooth palm on my shoulder. "You are right. I do not know of all that you have been through. Although, I must say, I know it must have been quite a great deal, given at how depressed you seemed during the earlier ceremonies. I watched you, demi-god. The cords on your heart were being plucked at. I could sense something was amiss. Please tell me, what is it that has caused you such grief?"

I continued to look out into the deep night sky, not daring to look at her as I spoke. "I came here to save you and Aethiopia not of my own free will, but because the gods demanded it."

"Oh?" Andromeda looked down to the ground, moving her arm from my shoulder to placing it on the ledge, glancing out at the dark scene before us over the horizon. "But if the gods demand you to obey them, it must be in good faith," she explained. "It must be a blessing to receive such a message from the gods. They should want nothing but to give you good fortune, no? At least that was what I was always taught."

I turned to my side to look Andromeda in her crystal blue eyes. I could truly understand why her mother bragged about her beauty. "It was both a blessing and a curse," I explained. "Yes. They revealed a wonderous fate that lay before me, but it was at such a great cost. A cost that I was not willing to make."

"And what cost could be so worthwhile to hold you back from being a Greek hero?" she asked.

"The loss of a lover. The love of my life had to be sacrificed for me and the rest of the world."

Andromeda placed her hand over her mouth in disbelief. "I'm so sorry, Perseus. But I am at a loss here. Why did *she* need to be sacrificed in order for you to become a hero of the gods?"

I let out a long and heavy sigh. "It wasn't a *she*. It was a *he*." I tugged on the bag against my hip that contained Meduso's head, a constant reminder of my inner turmoil. "His name was Meduso. He was the love of my life. The only person I ever loved and will ever love."

Andromeda could not help but question me. "…*loved* as a friend, you mean?"

I shook my head. "No, princess. I loved Meduso with every bone in my body. He was the one person I was meant to be with."

Andromeda was taken aback by my response. I'm sure she wondered how a man could love another man in such a way. She was likely not accustomed to such a love affair in these lands. "I see. Well, I am sorry he needed to be sacrificed for your cause. But I hope it was truly for the greater good. Surely, he should not be forgotten," she explained.

Little did I know that Andromeda could not help but think that this was clearly a message from the gods. That I was not allowed to love another *man* in my lifetime. That it was only right for me to love a woman. She was putting her own pieces to the puzzle together in her head. She thought the gods specifically led me to her, to save *her*, to love *her*. Why else would a demi-god arrive on a gallant horse to destroy a sea-monster in order to keep her alive? Deep down, Andromeda believed that I was destined to be hers. That I was to be her man. It had to have been prophesized by the gods. She thought there was no other explanation for it.

I could only lift my head and turn away from her, thinking on her sentiments. "Yes. I will never forget him. But I am unsure of how to proceed," I revealed. "I have no clue of what to do. No idea of where to go from here."

I was in a vulnerable state, willing to relinquish

opinion and power over to her. Any form of direction was something I would be willing to accept at this point, not knowing of what my next steps should be.

"We were destined to meet Perseus. The gods wanted you to come here to find me. And I truly believe you are *my* destiny. You must take me away from Aethiopia, my hero. I fear that yours and my presence here will only be of more danger to the both of us."

"What do you mean?" I asked.

"You must know, Perseus, there have been many suitors after me. Many men who have requested my hand in marriage. When they realize you are the man that was destined for me, as foretold by the gods before us, surely they will want you dead."

I began to feel sorry for Andromeda. She was a woman without power and control. To only be told what to do, and even serve as a sacrificial lamb by her very own parents was something that completely disgusted me. And in this very moment, I knew it was imperative for me to take Andromeda away from this land and with me on the journey that lied ahead.

"Then, we must leave here at once," I resolved. "Let us depart later this evening. We must make out like thieves in the night, unheard and unseen."

Andromeda nodded. "Yes. Let me gather my immediate belongings. Meet me at my bed chamber in a few hours when the rest of the castle is asleep. We can make our escape then."

I placed a kiss upon her forehead. Although it was

meant to be a kiss of friendliness and out of concern, I would later learn that Andromeda took it as a whole different sort of meaning, one that tugged at her very heart.

I laid awake in the guest chamber the king and queen offered me. King Cepheus was thoughtful enough to send me three of his most beautiful maidens to attend to my every need and desire. But I was not having any of it. I refused their kisses and advances at me, tossing full goblets of wine in their direction, hoping they would get drunk enough, quick enough, to pass out and leave me alone.

Once the maidens were sound asleep scattered unflatteringly across the chaises and my bed, I realized it was the perfect time for me to leave this place. I wrapped my tunic around me and grabbed the bag with Meduso's head and Hephaestus's sword. They were the only two imperative items I assumed I needed for my trek away from here. I snuck my way down the corridors of the castle towards Andromeda's room just as she had described its whereabouts to me among the vast halls. Three light knocks on her bed chamber door was the signal she instructed me to perform in order to know it was me that was there, ready to lead her out of this castle.

We avoided all the guards and warriors in the palace,

sneaking by each and every one of them, until we arrived at the castle entryway, which consisted of several men that now surrounded us in our escape.

"And where exactly do you think you're going?" A bald, hefty man, stood directly in front of us, blocking our path of escape. He was rather tall and large, compared to the other warriors around him.

"Phineus," Andromeda spoke. "You must let us pass. I have now refused your offer of proposal three times now. What more is there to discuss? Please, leave me be!"

Phineus was King Cepheus's brother, which meant that he was Andromeda's uncle. Earlier, Andromeda had informed me that he had been promised her hand in marriage, despite the princess's constant refusal. Now that I was in the picture, the king's brother knew that his plans to marry her were in jeopardy. "No. Not until I get what is rightfully mine. It is my duty, my destiny, to have you, Andromeda. You will not leave here without accepting me as your husband."

Phineus and his henchmen approached, closing in on me. "I'm warning you. Do not come further," I yelled.

But the king's brother and his men continued to stand their ground. "You will not threaten me, demi-god. I am not scared of you. If you dare to take what is mine, then you must suffer the consequences." Phineus pressed onward and raised his sword towards me.

I leaned into Andromeda's ear. "Close your eyes."

"What?" she questioned my motives.

"Just close your eyes, for your own safety," I

demanded.

Andromeda did as she was instructed, and the second she did, I withdrew the head of Meduso out of the tote attached to my hip. I held the eyes of the gorgon open and closed my own, spinning it around in a circle to make sure that it faced all of the warriors around me who were impeding our escape. Hearing no further movement, I opened my own eyes and returned the head to its place in my bag. Feeling safe, Andromeda too opened her own eyes, astonished by what she was witnessing. Eight statues around us, all of the purest limestone.

"But how!?" Andromeda asked.

"We must go! I will reveal it to you later!" I explained.

She took my hand and we sprinted out of the castle. I could no longer stand the thought of Andromeda staying here on this land, having been completely betrayed by her mother, father, and her people. I needed to bring her with me, as far away from this toxic nation as possible. I brought her to the cliff side where Pegasus was tied up and then broke him free with my sword. I took Andromeda's hand and we climbed aboard the horse's back, flying off into the lit-up night sky. I vowed that we would never return to Aethiopia again.

Chapter 22

I held on tightly to Pegasus as we continued to fly towards the only place left for me to go, which was home at Seriphos. Andromeda clung to me from behind, wrapping her hands around my waist to hold on. "So, are you going to tell me how you miraculously turned eight men and a sea monster into stone?" she asked.

I let out a deep sigh, afraid to have this conversation with anyone. However, I felt a kindred spirit with Andromeda. I assumed I could trust her. After all, how could we not trust each other? I saved her life and took her away from her homeland at her request. If anything, Andromeda owed me so much, including her undying loyalty.

"It wasn't me that turned those men into stone." I then reached with one hand to hold up the sac that contained Meduso's head. "It was this. The head of the mortal gorgon is in here. Surely, you've heard of the tale of the gorgons?"

Andromeda nodded. "Yes. A handsome brother and his two sisters who defied Athena and were thus cursed with the body of snakes and forever turning mortals into stone for whomever gazed into their eyes."

To hear this version of my lover's legacy spoken of gave me a sinking feeling within my gut. I hated the idea of Meduso being painted in such a terrible light. As if everything that had happened to him was ill-fated and deserving for his actions. I knew this was not the case at all.

"But the brother and his two sisters did not defy Athena like you think. They were truly innocent in all that had happened. There was a complete misunderstanding," I shared.

"So, you actually managed to hunt the gorgons down and behead the mortal gorgon? You really are a hero," Andromeda seductively whispered into my ear. Her admiration for me continued to grow with each new story she learned about me.

"I wouldn't call myself a hero."

"Now you're just being modest. Of course, you're a hero. Not only did you save me and all of Aethiopia, but you managed to slay the monstrous gorgon to avenge Athena. If you're not a *hero*, then what are you?"

I dwelled on this for a moment, trying to find the right words to say before responding. "I'm just lost, is all. I lost the love of my life and I'm not sure what else there is to live for," I admitted.

Andromeda pressed the side of her face into my back, an attempt to soothe and comfort me. "You mentioned earlier that your lover, Meduso, had been sacrificed. That it was the will of the gods. What did you mean by that?"

"I'm not sure how else to say it, so I'll just be completely up front with you. The male gorgon, I beheaded, his name was Meduso…"

Andromeda lifted her head, placing one of her hands over her mouth in disbelief. "You mean to tell me that Meduso, your lover, was in fact that gorgon that you beheaded?"

I gave a very long and slow nod, not wanting to elaborate much else on the subject. It was too hard of a discussion to now have with her. I was not capable of divulging my true feelings and sentiments with her.

"I see…" Andromeda pondered for a moment. I could tell something was not quite right to her. Perhaps she was confused over how I could possibly love a gorgon. How a man could love such a foul creature. That I must have been misguided, or better yet, maybe even cursed. Could I have been beguiled by the creature? Did I fall under the gorgon's spell, and was forced to love the monster? Little did I know that these were her very exact thoughts.

She assumed that the gods did not want me to be with Meduso. So, they must have known I was not truly in love with the gorgon. Having Meduso sacrificed was the only way to free me from the emotional clutches Meduso must have held over me. That the gods led me away from the gorgon and into Andromeda's arms. She thought I was meant to be hers and only hers.

After several hours of flying into the night, Pegasus eventually landed on the beach of Seriphos. I led the horse and Andromeda into the nearby forest, tying Pegasus to a tree in the clearing.

"Is this your homeland?" she asked.

"Yes. This is Seriphos. Come. We have no time to waste."

I escorted her into the village. I first checked my mother's stone home, only to discover no one was there. I then searched around the village for her whereabouts. As I entered Dictys's home at the northern-most end of the village, I was relieved to find that no one was there, either. The place was completely empty. My last thought was to make sure they weren't in my own home. I returned back down the village path and peeked into my house only to see that it too was vacant. Once I stepped into my bedroom to verify no one was there, I immediately regretted it. It was a huge mistake on my part. The very moment I laid eyes on my bed, memories of Meduso and me curled up next to one another, wrapped in each other's arms, flashed across my mind. I shook my head in a desperate attempt to dismantle these thoughts.

As I strode back down the path of the village with Andromeda, I heard soft footsteps approach from behind me. I turned to see that it was a young boy chasing after us. "Perseus! You've returned!"

"Anatolius!" I shouted as the boy sprinted towards me. We embraced in a hug before I released him from my grips.

"I knew it was you! I watched you from my window,

but wasn't sure if I was imagining it or not. I cannot believe you've returned," Anatolius stated, before glancing over at Andromeda. "And is this a friend?"

I smiled at the boy. "Yes. This is my friend, Andromeda."

Andromeda extended her hand to the boy, in the most amicable way possible. "Nice to meet you, child."

Anatolius accepted her offer and shook her hand back. "You too!"

I was still anxious over everyone's absence, wondering where most of the others were. I felt the need to cut the introductions short and get right to the point of my return. "Anatolius, where are my mother and Dictys?"

The boy's face immediately shifted into a frown. "You don't know?"

"Know what?" Perseus asked.

"Your mother, Dictys, and a few others left the island a few days ago. They are all safe."

"Thank the gods!" I exclaimed.

"Your mother refused to take the king's hand in marriage," Anatonius revealed. "King Polydectes then threatened her to reconsider and so she and all those who defended her fled, seeking refuge at one of Apollo's temples on the adjacent island of Sifnos. She will likely be found by the king's men in the near future and there is no doubt of the actions the king will take when he does find her. But you have returned Perseus! You can put a stop to all of this!"

I kneeled on the ground so that I was at eye level with

Anatonius. I placed my hands on the boy's shoulders. "Thank you for your loyalty, Anatonius. But I must ask a favor of you. I need Andromeda to stay with you for the time being." I then glanced over to her. "Andromeda. I need you to remain here in the village."

Andromeda stepped forward, shaking her head in protest. "But..." she began.

"No. It is for your own safety," I interrupted. "I must go to Polydectes's fortress to end this once and for all. There will likely be many guards on duty, and I need to be swift in making my way towards the king. You would only hold me back," I coolly said to her, as a matter of fact. It may have been condescending, but it was the only quick way for me to get my point across to her.

Andromeda had no choice but to give in. "Very well. I will remain here. But promise you'll return back to me." She lunged forward, throwing her full weight into my body, holding onto me for dear life. Her face was just inches from mine. She stared directly at me, but I refrained from giving in to her desired intimacy and turned my head to the side.

"I'll come back. I promise," was all I uttered. I simply kissed her on the forehead before running away from the village.

I trekked through the forest and snuck into the heavily guarded fortress from the rear entrance. It was surprisingly not difficult to get through. Apparently, the king was busy hosting a banquet that was occurring in the Great Hall. I overheard a few of the townsfolk chatting as

I snuck around the corners inside.

I peered around a large column to see all of Polydectes's men gathered at the tables around the room, eating and drinking with merriment. The king was sitting on his throne at the very center table of the hall. I knew it was now or never. I reached into the bag attached to my hip, grabbing Meduso's head by the hair, yanking it out. I counted softly to myself. *One... two... three.*

I emerged from the column, exposing myself to everyone at the entrance to the hall.

Screaming and yelling like an enraged mad man with my eyes closed, I drew the attention of everyone there. Not a single eye was blind to the head of the beautiful man that I held in my hand. Meduso's eyes glimmered like topaz and every man and woman in that hall perished. King Polydectes could not even say a word, for he too was turned to stone.

I placed the head back into the tote, before opening my own eyes. I had no sympathy for anyone that was also petrified, even some of the village folk. The fact that these people could celebrate and be merry with such a tyrannical king and support him, meant that they allowed Polydectes to threaten my mother, and were okay with it. And therefore, I felt no remorse for perishing them.

I then stepped forward. It was still hard to believe what I had just done. I moved towards the throne in the center of the room, where the king sat still, now frozen forever. The King of Seriphos was no more.

Not long after the incident, news of King Polydectes's death travelled far and wide. My mother, Dictys, and some of the other villagers returned to Seriphos by boat just a few days later. My mother's hands were spread out, arms wide open, as she stepped onto the shore. I grabbed her in a tight hug.

"My Perseus! You have returned and saved us all!" she cried out.

I smiled. "I had no choice, mother. I could not sit idle and allow King Polydectes to commit the atrocities he was able to get away with. His time had come."

Andromeda also came forth, escorting Pegasus towards us.

"And who is this lovely creature?" Danaë asked.

"His name is Pegasus. Is he not magnificent?" I asked.

My mother could not help but shake her head and smile with amusement. "I was not referring to the horse, although it is marvelous. I was talking about *her*," she raised her hand in the air towards Andromeda, who presented everyone with a pleasant smirk.

"Oh. This is Andromeda, princess of Aethiopia." I reached for Andromeda's hand and lifted it towards my mother to hold. "Andromeda, meet my mother, Danaë."

The women exchanged introductions and became lost in pleasantries while I became distracted by something else coming from the sea. Dictys dragged his boat onto the shore before stepping towards me, wrapping his hand around my shoulder, patting me on the back. "I knew you had it in you, boy. All of Seriphos owes you gratitude. This place can once again be the tranquil island it was always meant to be."

"Yes. But the island is in need of a new king. A humble one," I explained. "And that king should be you, Dictys. I trust that you will serve our people well."

The old fisherman nodded. "It would be my honor. Except I refuse to live in that barren fortress. I will still remain in my house in the village, among my people."

My mother stepped from behind, disrupting our short reunion. "Come. Let us all return home. I will cook us a splendid meal and you can share all about your adventures and travels with me. I want to hear every last detail."

That evening, everyone drank wine as I shared everything that had happened once I left Seriphos, including how I was supported by Hermes, Hephaestus, and Athena themselves on my journey to slaying the mortal gorgon.

"And tell me about this gorgon. Was he a hideous, fearsome creature?" Danaë asked.

No. He was the most beautiful creature I ever laid eyes on. He was the love of my life and his sacrifice is what led to all of you being able to live and breathe at this very moment. This was what I wanted to say out loud to my mother and everyone, but the words never came out, for some reason. Instead, I would keep this information to myself.

I would go on to live a peaceful life, becoming a king myself. Just as the Oracle at Delphi had prophesized, I would eventually kill my grandfather, the King of Argos. It was a fluke accident in a stadium where I competed in various games. The discus throw, which was my worst event, would lead to King Acrisius's demise. I threw the heavy discus off course, striking the king in the head, as he sat in the crowd, watching the competition. Acrisius would have no time to dodge the flying object. Upon impact, he was instantly dead.

Andromeda and I would be married and grow old together, admiring the accomplishments of our nine children: seven sons and two daughters. Even in my progressive age, not a day went by where I did not think about Meduso. Every night, I would make it a habit to go outside and gaze up at the glorious mosaic of stars in the night sky. Over the years, I was able to recognize that Artemis had rearranged these glimmers of light.

I recalled my and Meduso's first night on the beach together in Seriphos when we were younger, sitting by the fire, staring up at these patterns in the obsidian sky.

Katasterismoi, I remembered Meduso telling me. *These lights are organized by Artemis and are shaped to tell heroic stories of the past.*

I believed in my heart that one of these stars told the story of Meduso. A story of love and heroism. Although I knew I would go down in history as a tragic Greek hero, it was Meduso who was the true hero.

Epilogue

Andromeda: The Torn

I sat in my bedchamber, staring at my reflection in the mirror. I could not understand where the time had gone. I lived a long and blissful life as queen, watching my nine children grow up. Now, my husband, Perseus, lied in his bed, sick.

Perseus and I knew it was only a short amount of time he had left in this world. I returned to sit beside him in bed, holding his hand firmly.

"My dear Andromeda. I know I do not have much longer to live. I can feel it in my bones," Perseus revealed.

"Do not say such things, my king." I rubbed the top of his wrinkly hand with my thumb.

Perseus placed his free hand on top of mine. "You must listen to me. I've been thinking a lot over these past several days and what I will be leaving behind in this world."

"And you are leaving so many great things," I confirmed to him. "You have nine beautiful and healthy children who are coming into their own. You are such a glorious king who the world and gods have come to respect. Let us not forget of the many tales of your heroism that will go down in history."

"But there is one story that I've kept to myself. That *we've* kept to ourselves," he recorrected.

Deep down, I knew exactly what my husband was

referring to. I knew all along that I could never hold a candle to his former lover. Despite the two of us growing close and old together over the many years, I could always see a downcast look in Perseus's eyes at least once a day. I knew it was then that he was thinking of Meduso.

"And I think you know it too," Perseus continued with. "I want you to share my story with the rest of the world when I pass. I do not want his name to be spoken so poorly of. It's important that Meduso gets his true story told. You must be the one to do it, Andromeda. It is a dying man's wish."

A tear fell out of the corner of my eye, hearing my husband speak of such things. But I could only respect his request. "Very well, my king. I will make sure everyone knows of yours and Meduso's story."

A smile crept up on Perseus's face. He would go to sleep that night with that smile permanently pressed on his face, knowing that his one and true love in this lifetime would be known to the rest of the world. It would be how he would die overnight, with an endearing smile, knowing he would once again be seeing Meduso soon, in the Underworld.

I woke up the following morning, screaming and crying over the sight of my husband's stiffened body. The guardsman took his body away, setting it up for the proper ceremony to celebrate the king's life. I put on my royal garbs that afternoon, knowing I would have to step onto the balcony of our castle and give a speech to our people, informing them of the details behind the late passing of my husband, their king they were loyally devoted to. It was during this time that I was prepared to share the story of my husband and his love affair with Meduso to the rest of the world.

I watched myself in the mirror, studying my drooping face very closely, before realizing that I possessed the courage to inform the public of all this. As I stood now determined and confident, I made my way out of the bed chamber and down the hall. The guards had all gathered on the terrace, ready for my arrival.

I slowly moved down the corridor, heading towards the balcony. Suddenly, my focus was disrupted. I glanced up at the ceiling, noticing a small white dove take flight. "How did that get in here?" I asked out loud to myself.

The bird flew behind me, and I could not help but turn back around to follow it, wondering where it was headed to. *Could this be some sort of sign?* I thought to myself. The dove turned down the hall and entered an open door that led into the atrium full of greenery and the most colorful of exotic flowers.

I stepped foot into the open space, watching the white bird settle in the grass. "Now what is the meaning…" But before I could even finish that statement, a golden aura surrounded the dove. The animal fully transformed into a glorious woman, in the purest of white tunics. Her hair as golden as the setting sun. "Who are you?" I questioned, alarmed by the woman's sudden appearance.

The goddess revealed her identity. "It is I, Pallas Athena."

I covered my lips with my hands. "I've heard so many stories about you, Goddess, from my husband." I slowly kneeled down, bracing myself, by placing my hand on the stone bench beside me.

"Rise, Andromeda. You do not need to address me with such formalities."

I rose back up to my feet. "Might I ask what has prompted your appearance today, my Goddess? Have you come to bear witness to the passing of my husband?"

Athena shook her head. "No. I actually came to speak with you."

"With me?" I pressed my palm to my chest, feeling the intricate beats of my heart.

"Yes. I am aware that you are determined to speak highly of Perseus to his people. And with that, you plan on telling them about Meduso as well. Is that not true?"

I was taken aback by the goddess's comment. At first, I wondered how Athena could possibly know that that was my intent. But then I regained my better senses and knew that the powers of a goddess could obviously have allowed her to know of mine and Perseus's conversation about sharing Meduso's story with the rest of the world.

"Yes. It was my husband's dying wish, after all," I truthfully told her.

"I see..." Athena then began to pace about the atrium.

"I am not here to force you to do otherwise, but I do want you to reconsider."

"Against my king's request!?" I exclaimed.

"Yes. Think about it, queen. If you were to disclose to the rest of the world that King Perseus had a former *male* lover, what would they say?"

I crossed my arms over my chest, gazing at the ground, deep in thought. "I never really did consider that."

"Not only this, but what about his *legacy*? Everyone already views Perseus as a hero among men. If you told them an alternative story of him beheading the gorgon to one of tragic love, the people would view him differently."

"Would they really?" I asked with skepticism.

"Of course they would. His name would forever be tarnished. King Perseus would no longer go down in history as a hero to gods and to the world. Is that the legacy you want for your late husband?"

I was at a loss for words. I was torn now, unsure of whether or not to listen to these wise words given to me by the goddess or to move forward with fulfilling my husband's final request.

"It is your choice, my queen. But know that your decision here will forever shape the future of what you and your husband leave behind in this world." Athena turned her back towards me and transformed back into a dove, flying off, out of the castle.

I fell onto the bench, needing to have a seat to

comprehend all that had just happened. I placed my hands over my face, crying over the choice I would soon have to make. No matter what, I would be disappointing someone and it hurt me to the very core. After several minutes, I finally wiped the tears from my eyes and made my way back into the halls of the castle and towards the balcony.

I climbed the stairs and stepped outside, overlooking the railing at the thousands of people below me who had come to pay their respects to my late husband.

"Thank you all for coming!" I shouted over the masses. "We all have a great man that we lost today. A man, a father, a king, and above all else a *hero*!"

I paused for moment while the crowd yelled and cheered over my comment. I stared down at the ground mumbling to it as if Perseus were overhearing me. *I'm sorry my king.*

I rose my head back up and continued to speak. "King Perseus may have left for the Underworld, but his heroic tales and legacy will live on in our world. All hail King Perseus, the slayer of the vile and vicious gorgon!"

And thus was the beginning of a long falsehood of narrations that would be passed down from generation to generation. Perseus would still be known as a gorgon slayer. Even the descriptions of the mortal gorgon would be altered from mouth to mouth, eventually being portrayed as once a beautiful woman, instead of a handsome man.

It would only be Perseus who would know the full accurate version of Meduso's story. After all, he loved and lived through it.

B.J. Irons

Excellent LGBT fiction and by unique,
wonderful authors.

Thrillers
Mystery
Romance
Young Adult
& More

Visit us at
www.spectrum-books.com

Or find us on Instagram
www.instagram.com/spectrumbookpublisher

Printed in Dunstable, United Kingdom

75682135R00190